THE FLYING BEAVER BROTHERS
AND THE MUD-SLINGING MOLES

MAXWELL EATON III

ALFRED A. KNOPF
NEW YORK

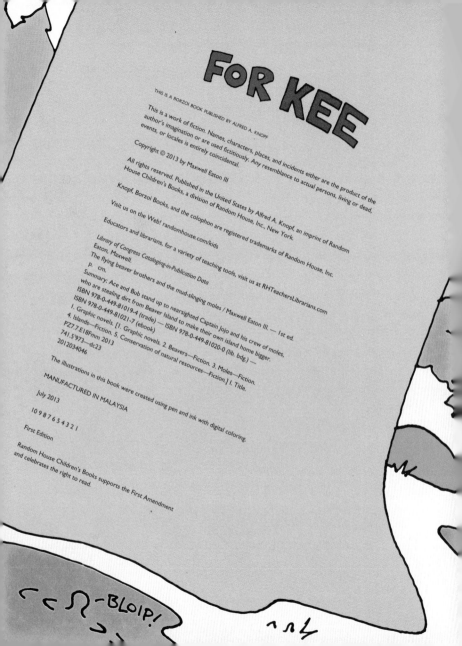

FOR KEE

THIS IS A BORZOI BOOK PUBLISHED BY ALFRED A. KNOPF

Copyright © 2013 by Maxwell Eaton III

All rights reserved. Published in the United States by Alfred A. Knopf, an imprint of Random House Children's Books, a division of Random House, Inc., New York.

Knopf, Borzoi Books, and the colophon are registered trademarks of Random House, Inc.

Visit us on the Web! randomhouse.com/kids

Educators and librarians, for a variety of teaching tools, visit us at RHTeachersLibrarians.com

Library of Congress Cataloging-in-Publication Data
Eaton, Maxwell.
The flying beaver brothers and the mud-slinging moles
p. cm.
Summary: Ace and Bub stand up to nearsighted Captain Jojo and his crew of moles,
who are stealing dirt from Beaver Island to make their own island home bigger.
ISBN 978-0-449-81019-4 (trade) — ISBN 978-0-449-81021-7 (ebook)
ISBN 978-0-449-81020-0 (lib. bdg.) —
1. Graphic novels. [1. Graphic novels. 2. Beavers—Fiction. 3. Moles—Fiction.
4. Islands—Fiction. 5. Conservation of natural resources—Fiction.] I. Title.
PZ7.7.E18Fmm 2013
741.5'973—dc23
2012034046

The illustrations in this book were created using pen and ink with digital coloring.

MANUFACTURED IN MALAYSIA

July 2013

10 9 8 7 6 5 4 3 2 1

First Edition

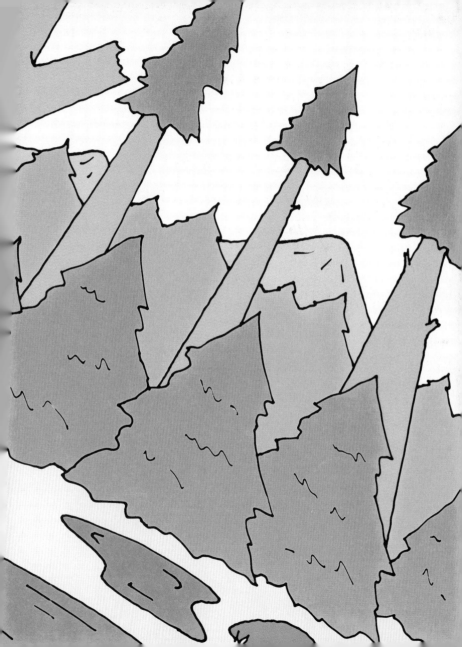

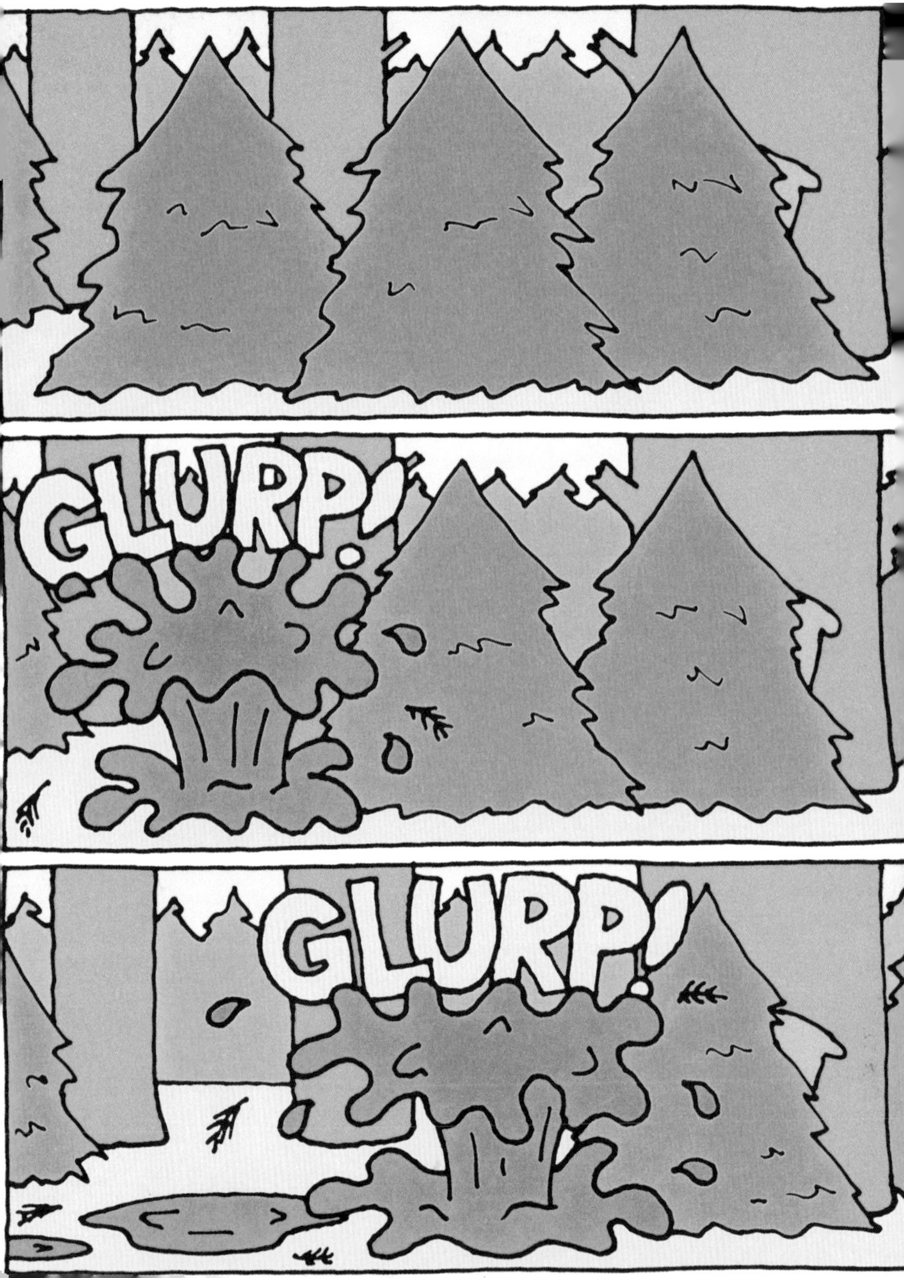
GLURP!
GLURP!

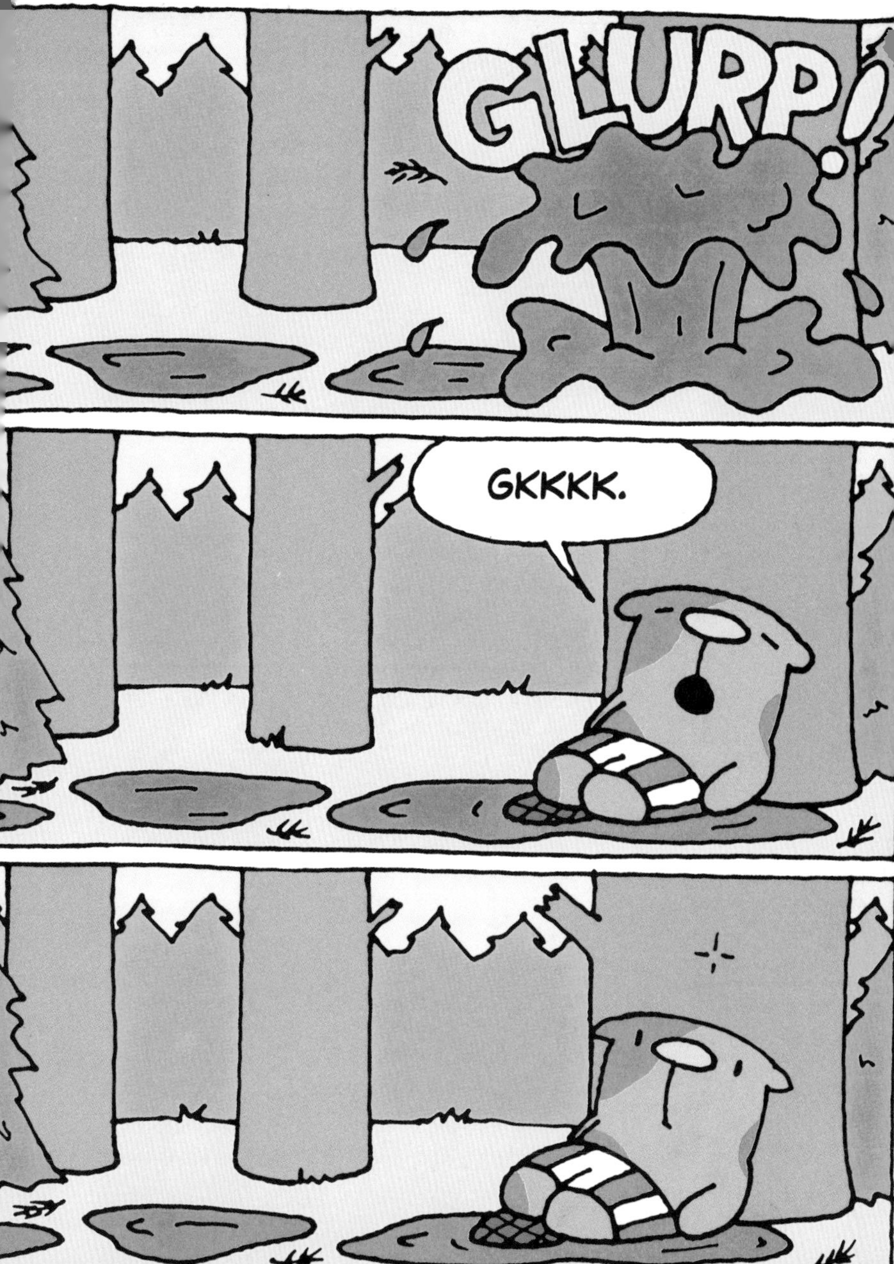
GLURP!
GKKKK.

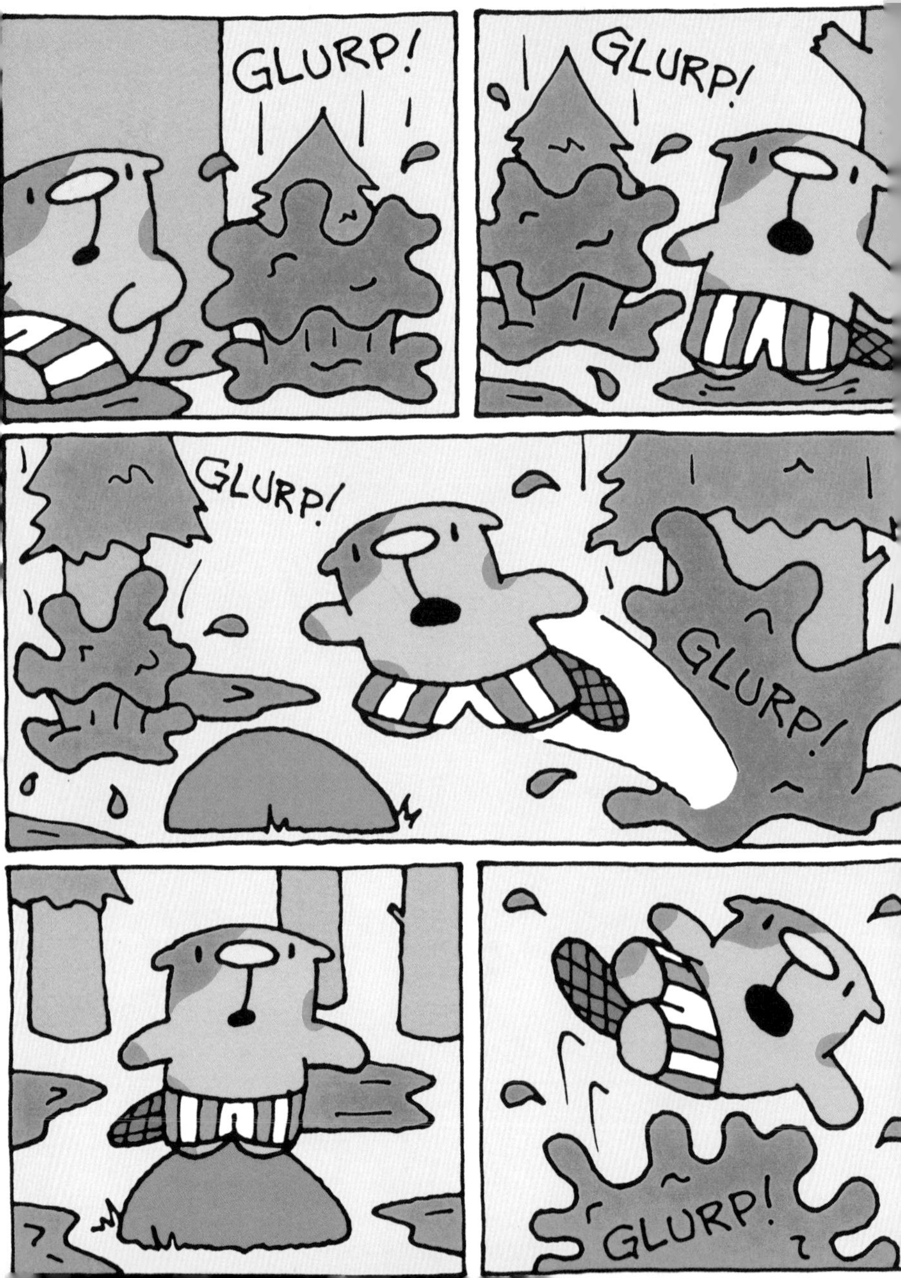
GLURP!
GLURP!
GLURP!
GLURP!
GLURP!

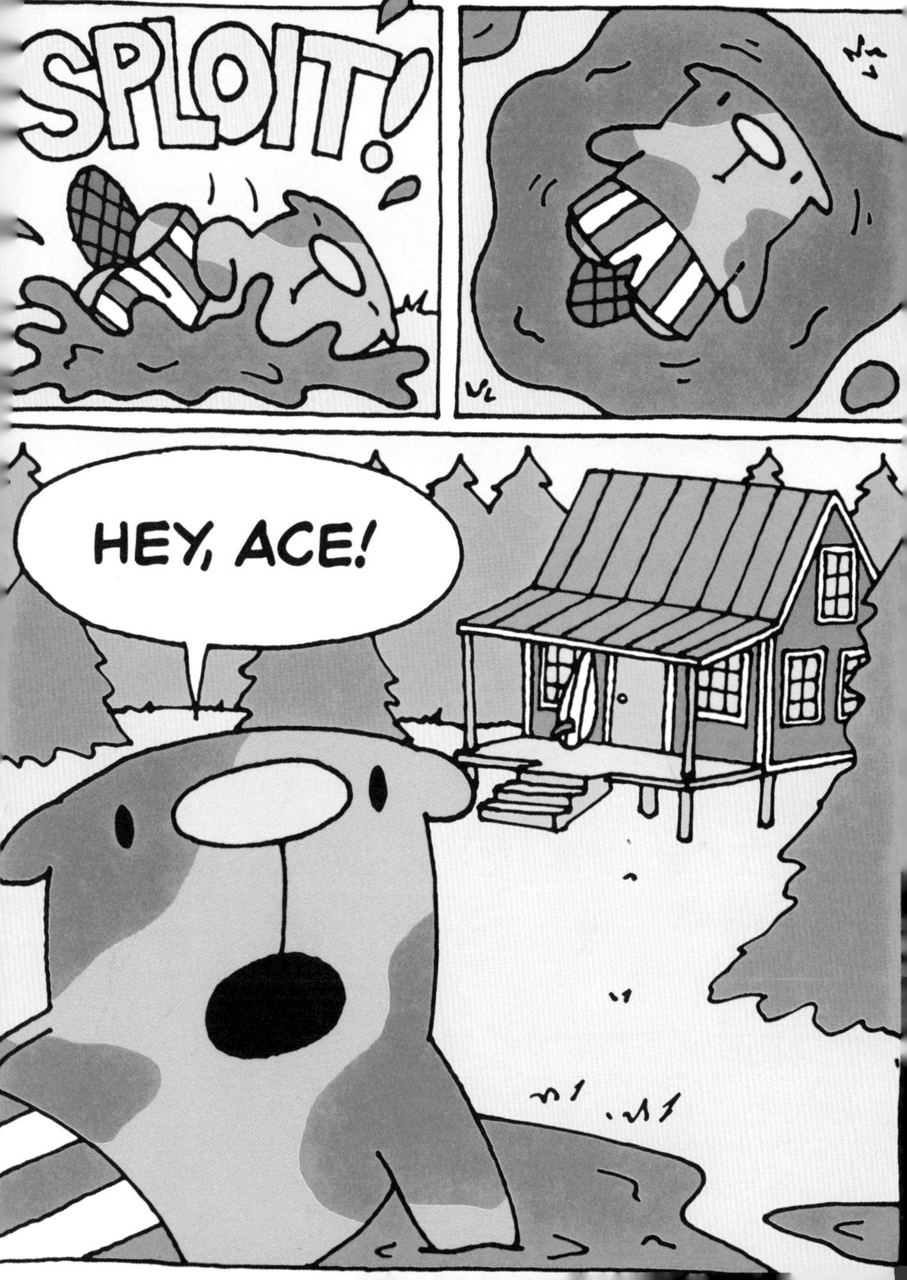
SPLOIT!
HEY, ACE!

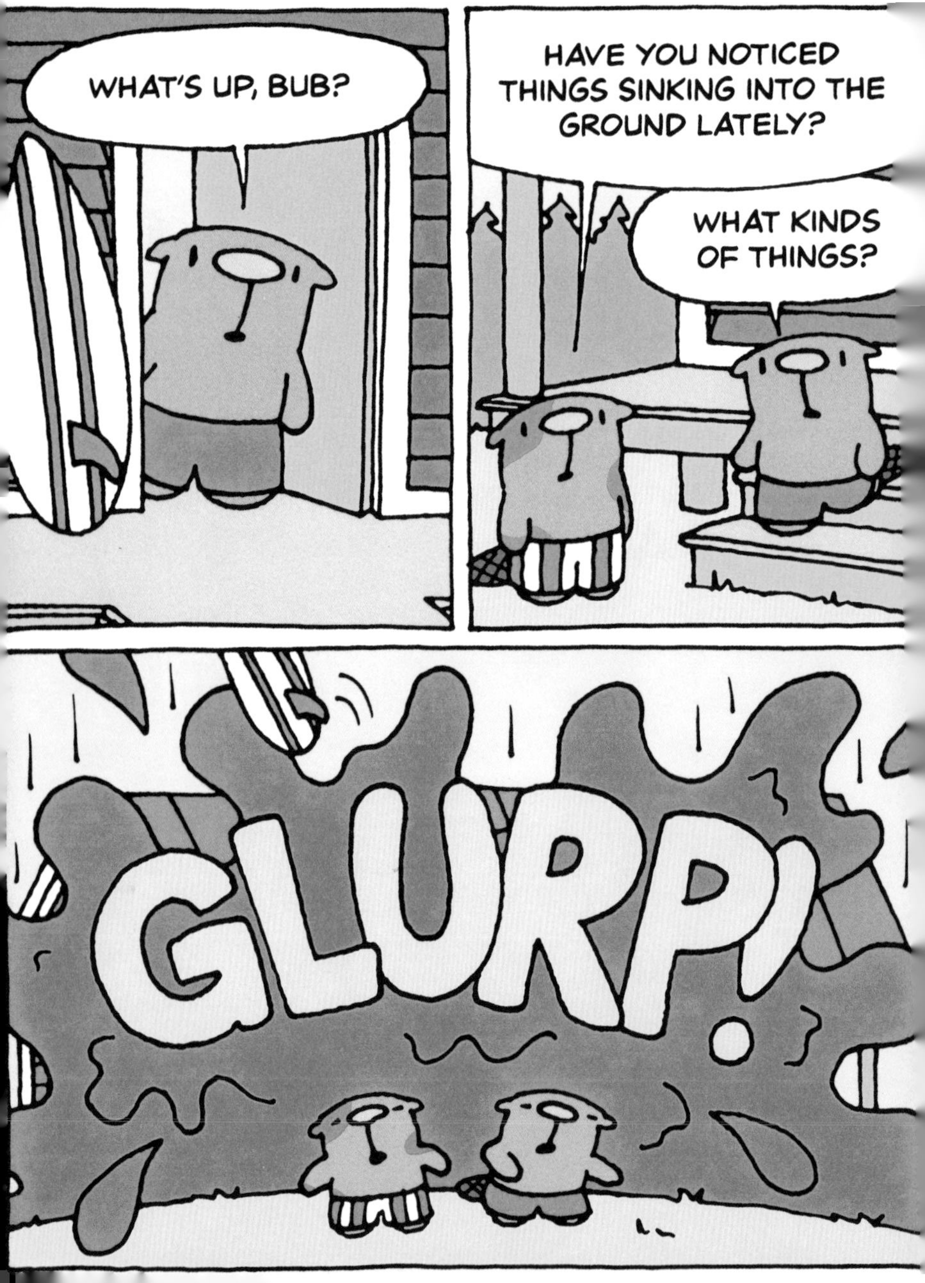
WHAT'S UP, BUB?
HAVE YOU NOTICED THINGS SINKING INTO THE GROUND LATELY?
WHAT KINDS OF THINGS?
GLURP!

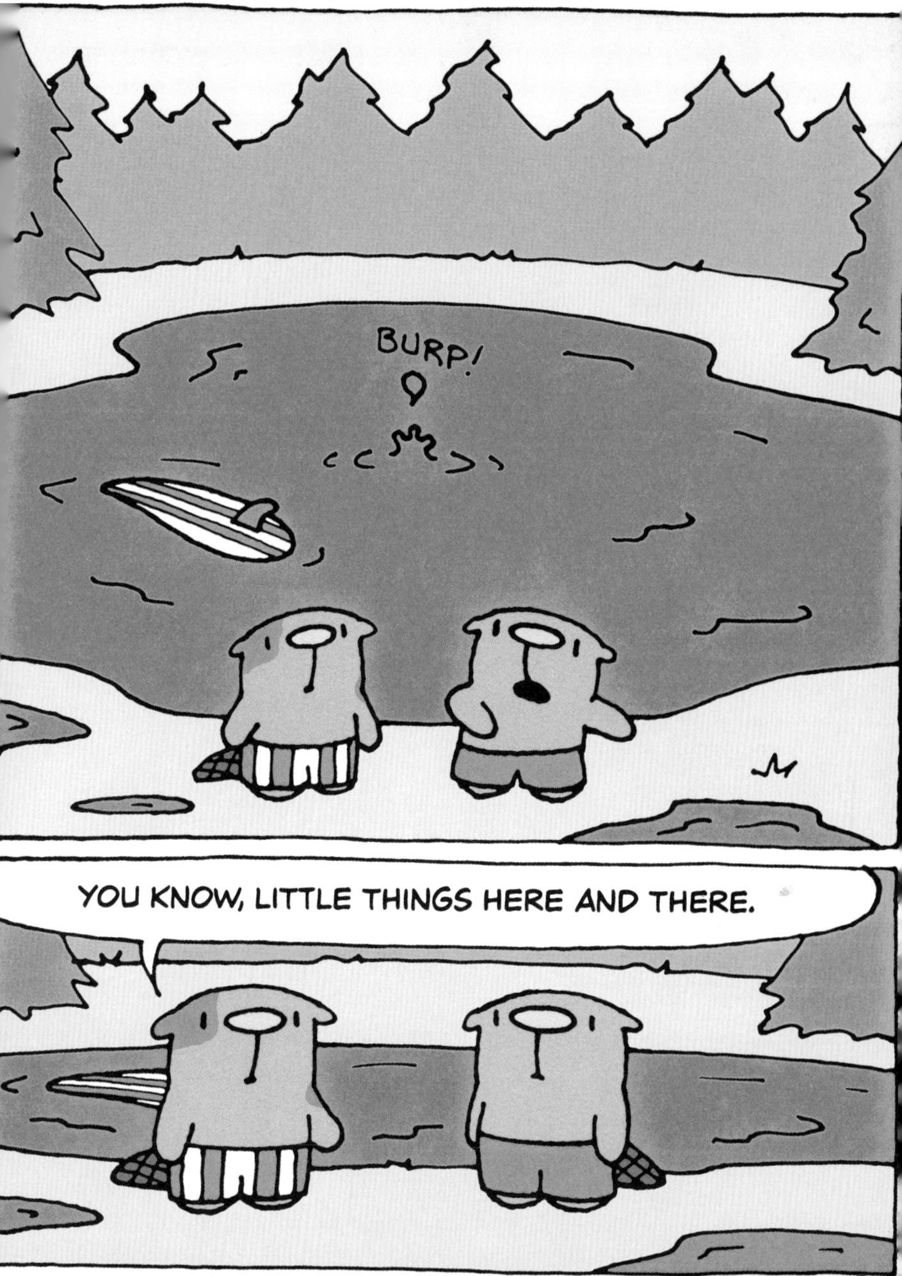
BURP!
YOU KNOW, LITTLE THINGS HERE AND THERE.

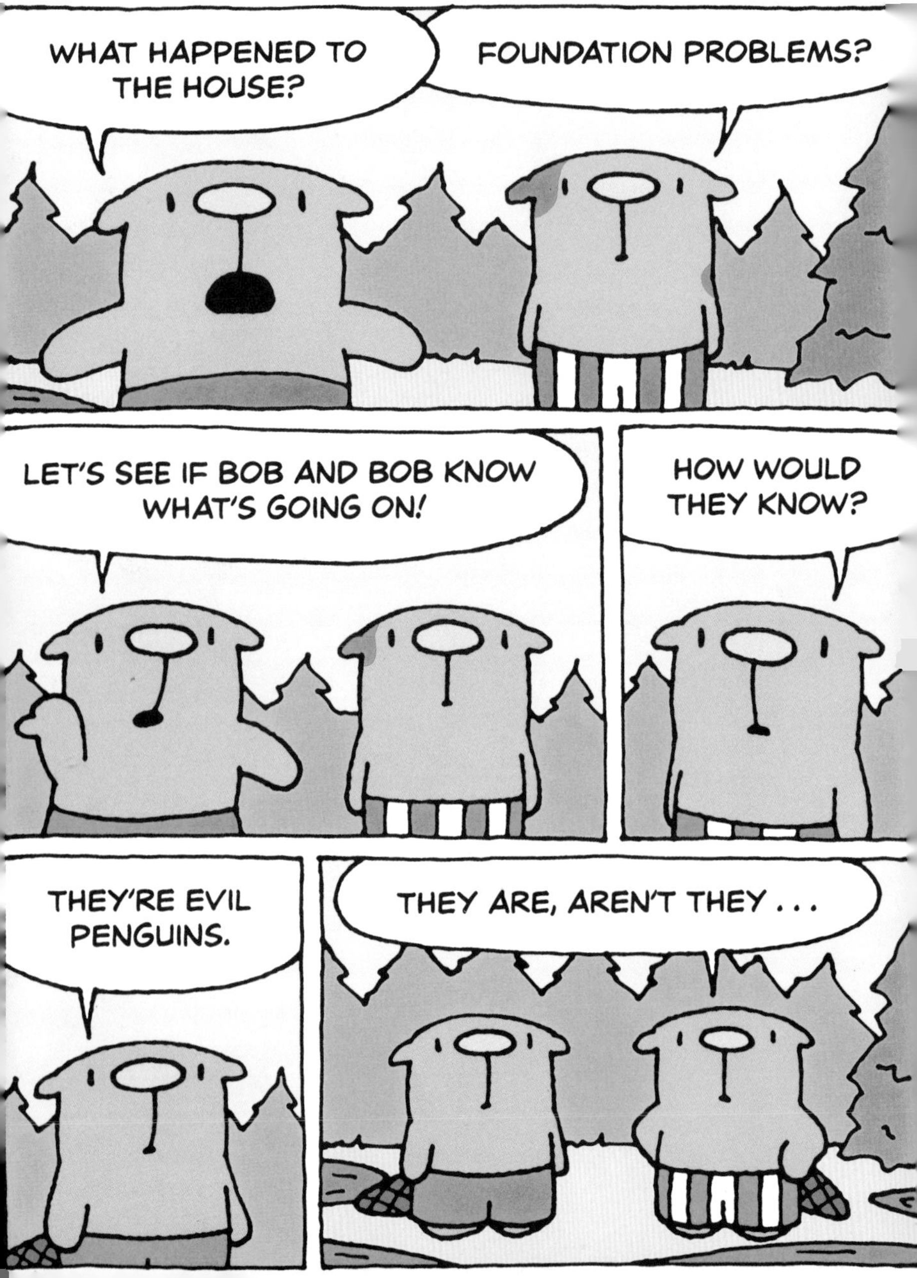
WHAT HAPPENED TO THE HOUSE?
FOUNDATION PROBLEMS?
LET'S SEE IF BOB AND BOB KNOW WHAT'S GOING ON!
HOW WOULD THEY KNOW?
THEY'RE EVIL PENGUINS.
THEY ARE, AREN'T THEY . . .

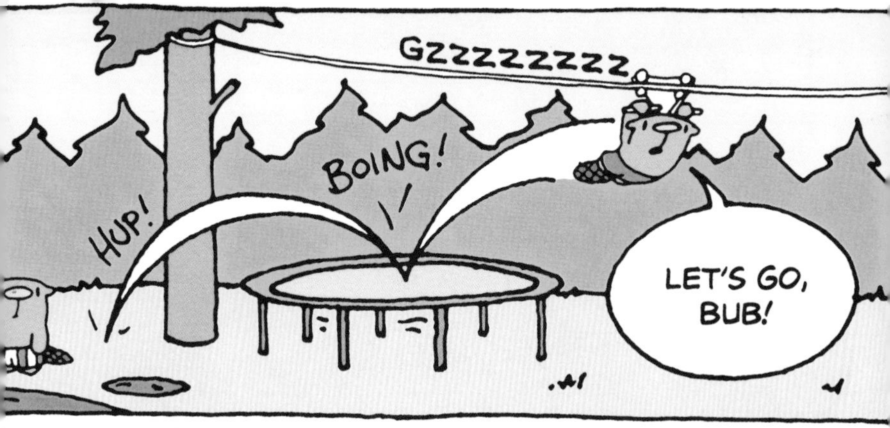
GZZZZZZZZZ
BOING!
HUP!
LET'S GO, BUB!

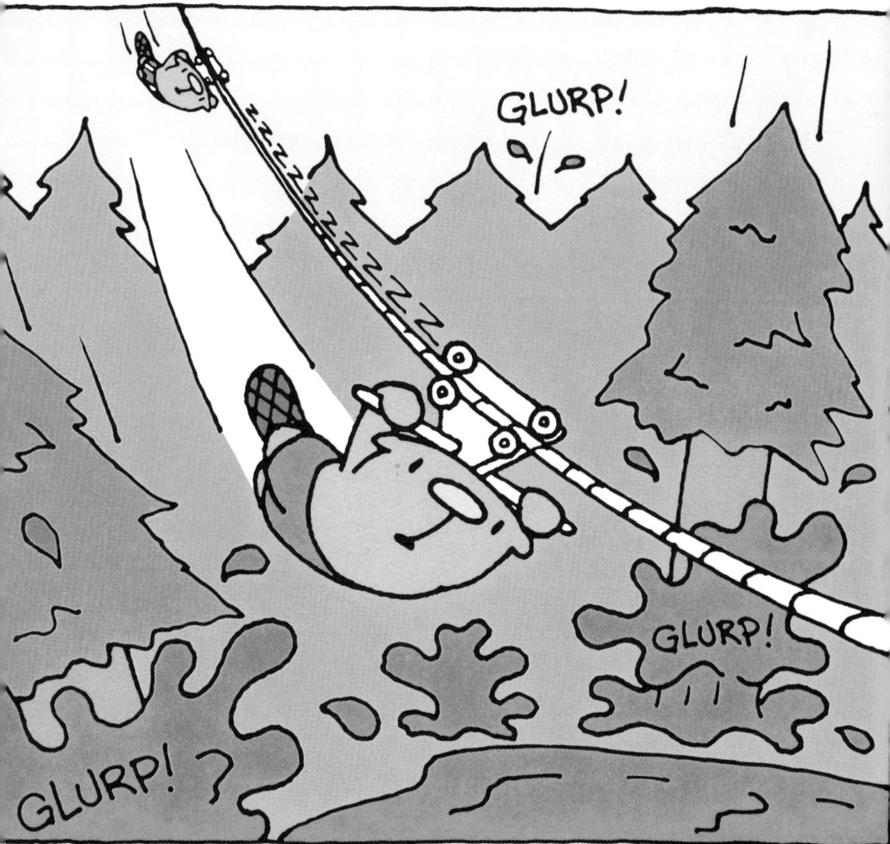
GLURP!
GLURP!
GLURP!?

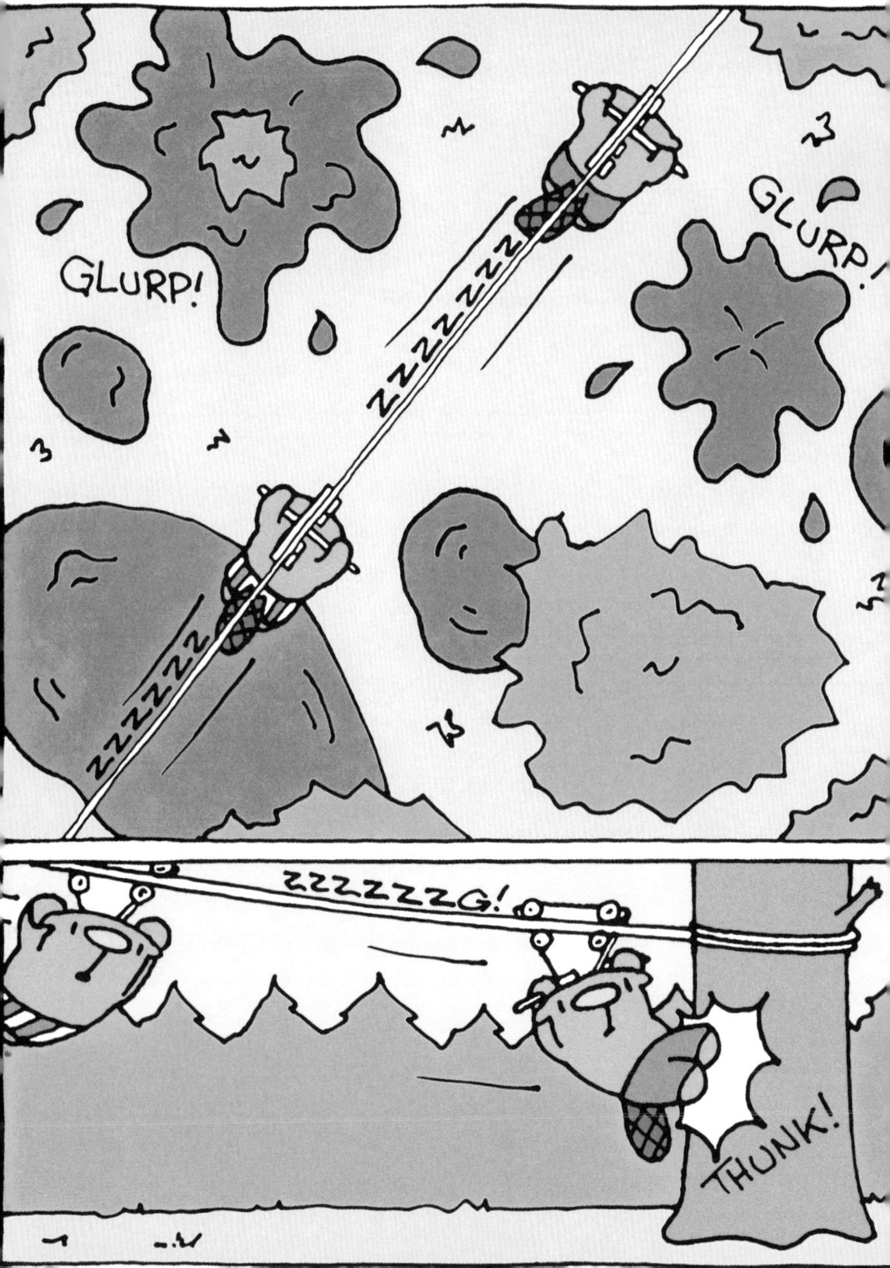
GLURP!
ZZZZZZZZ
GLURP!
ZZZZZZZ
ZZZZZZZG!
THUNK!

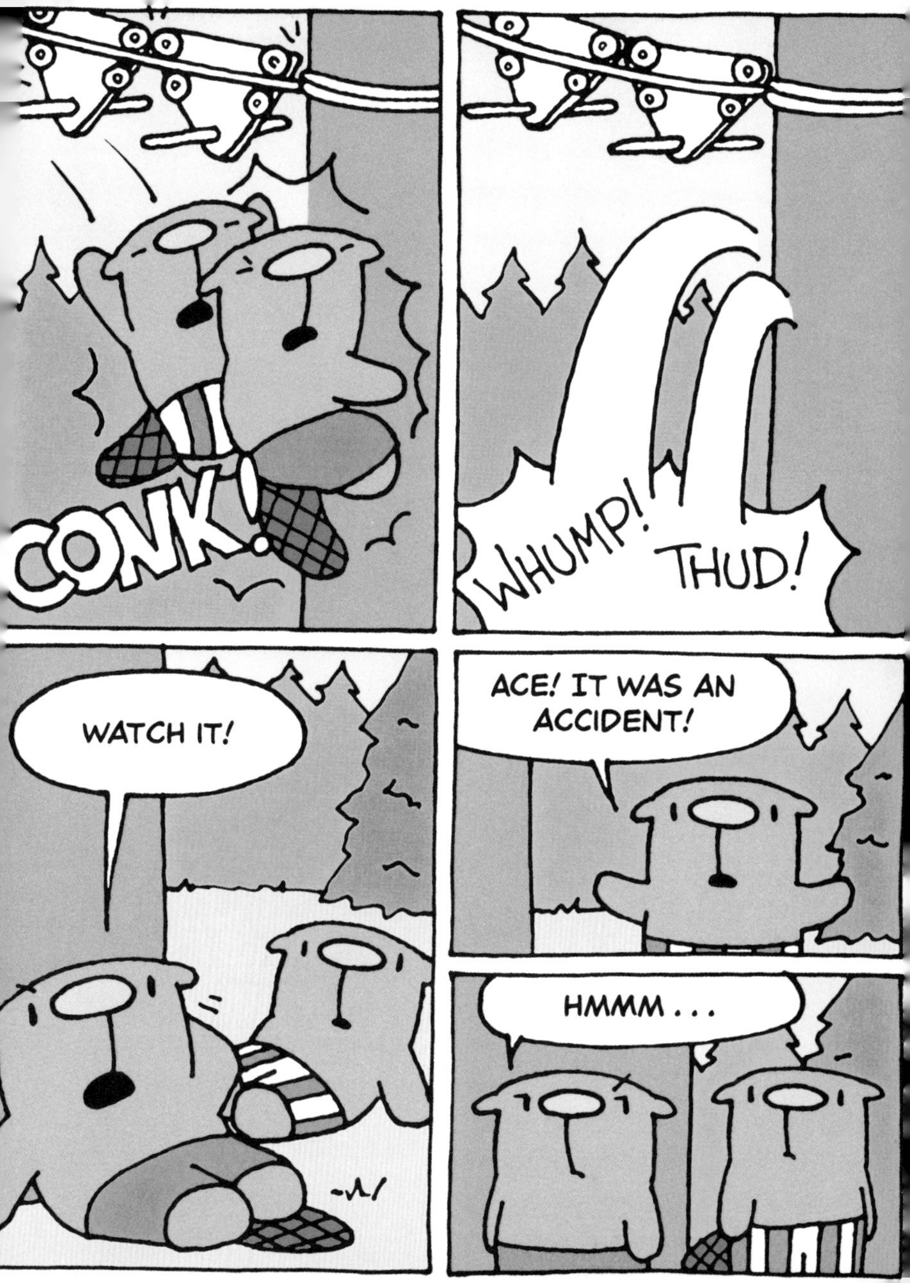
CONK!
WHUMP!
THUD!
WATCH IT!
ACE! IT WAS AN ACCIDENT!
HMMM . . .

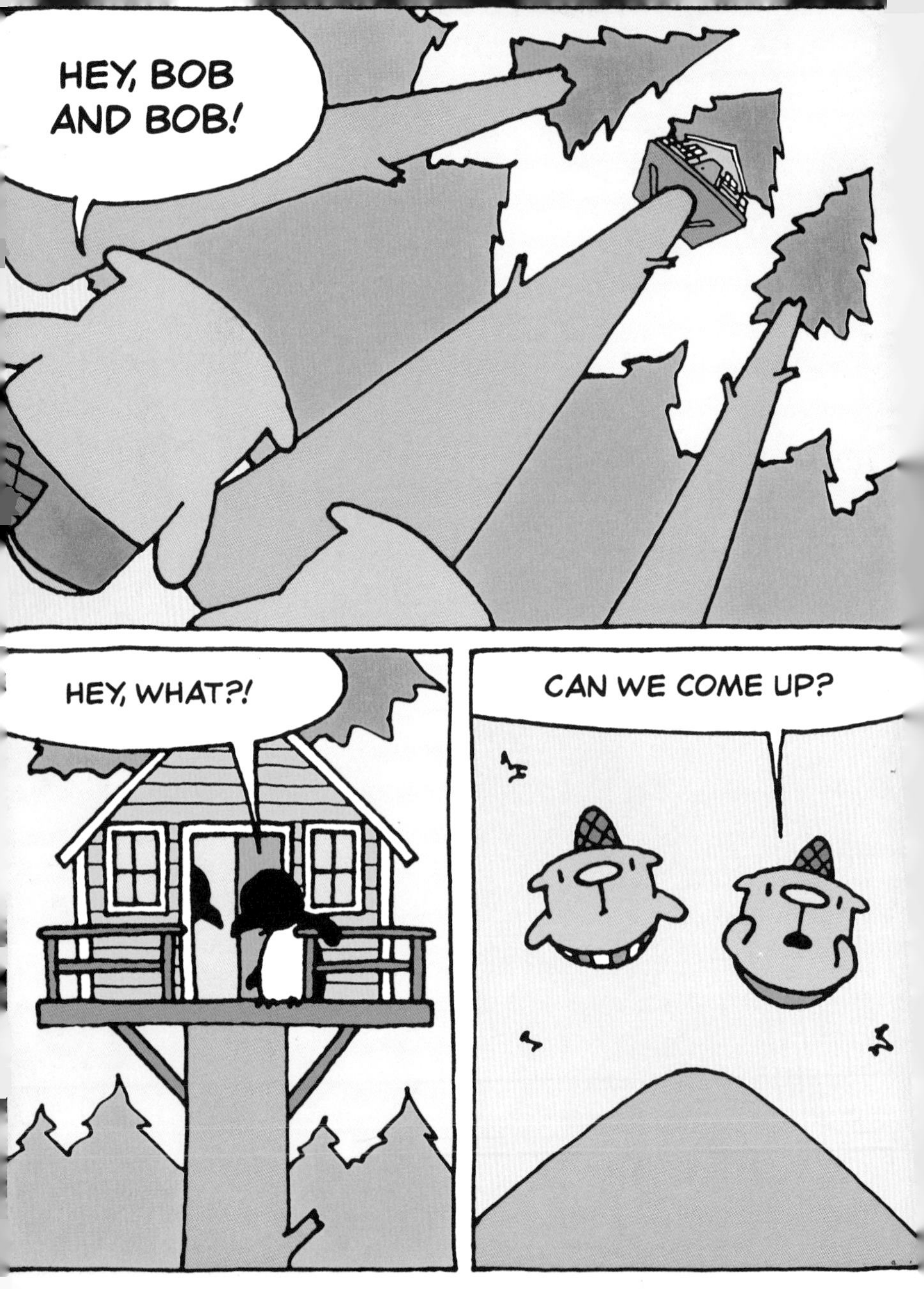
HEY, BOB AND BOB!
HEY, WHAT?!
CAN WE COME UP?

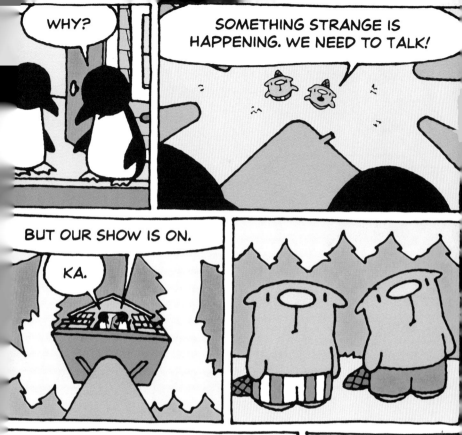

WHY?

SOMETHING STRANGE IS HAPPENING. WE NEED TO TALK!

BUT OUR SHOW IS ON.

KA.

WE NEED TO TALK!

FINE. I'LL THROW DOWN THE LADDER. . . .

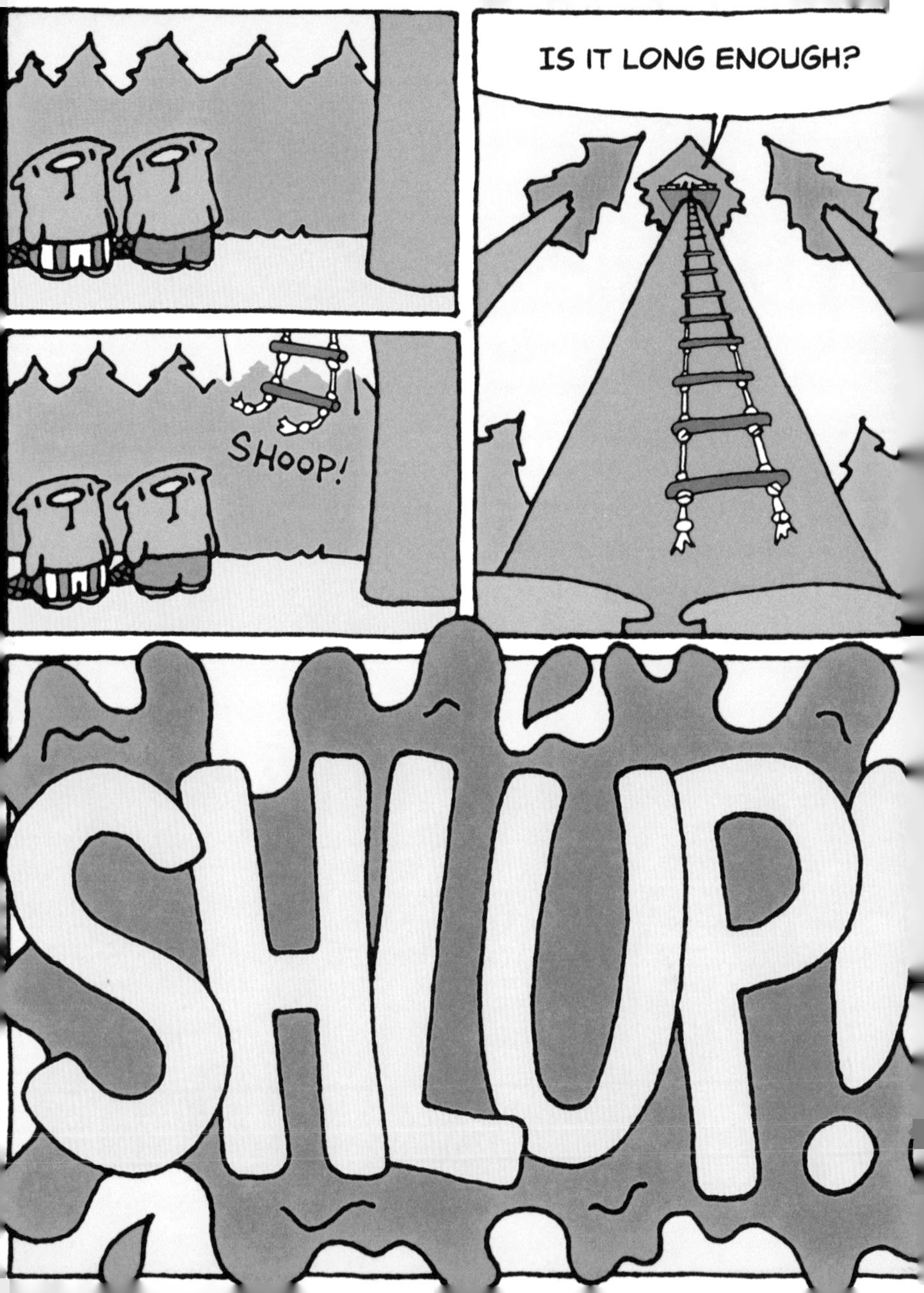
SHOOP!
IS IT LONG ENOUGH?
SHLUP!

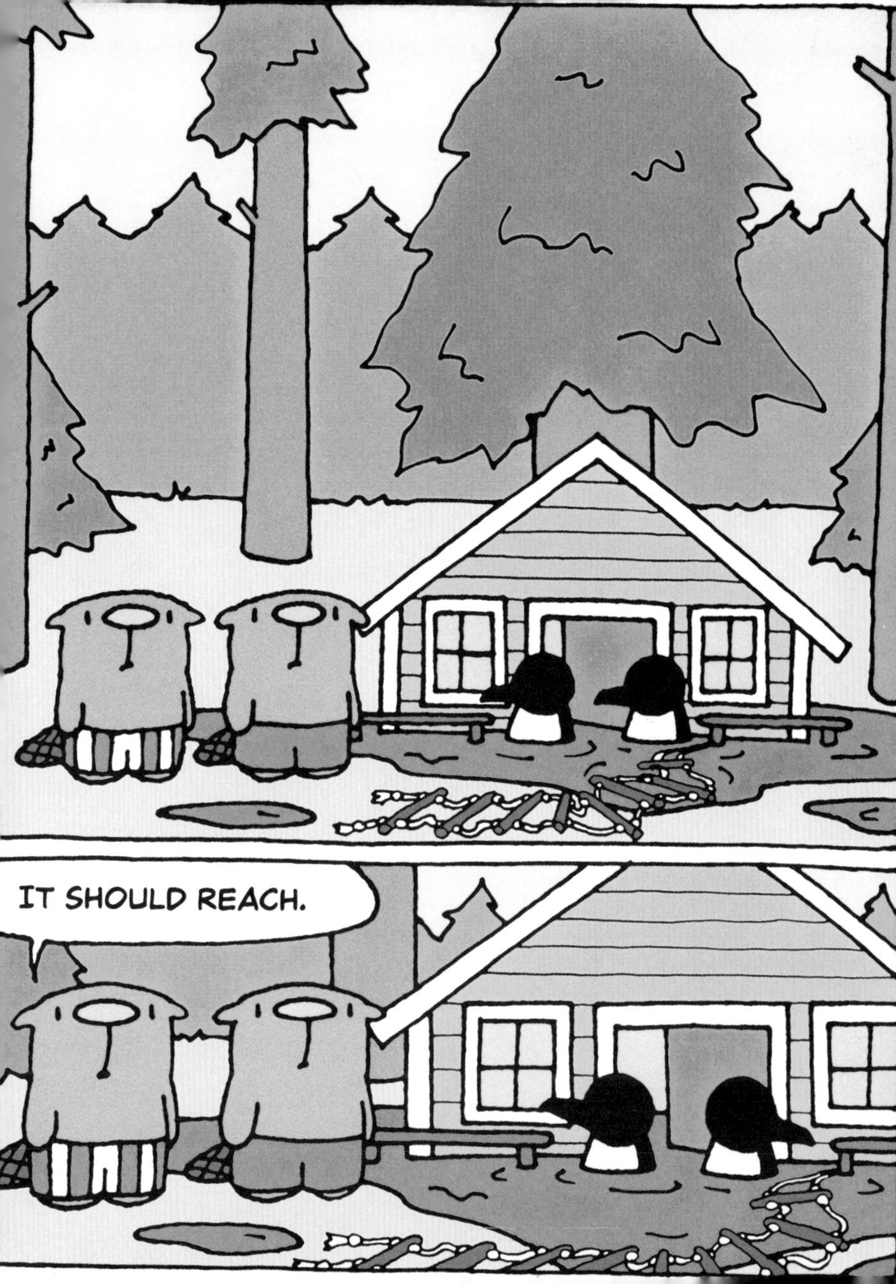
IT SHOULD REACH.

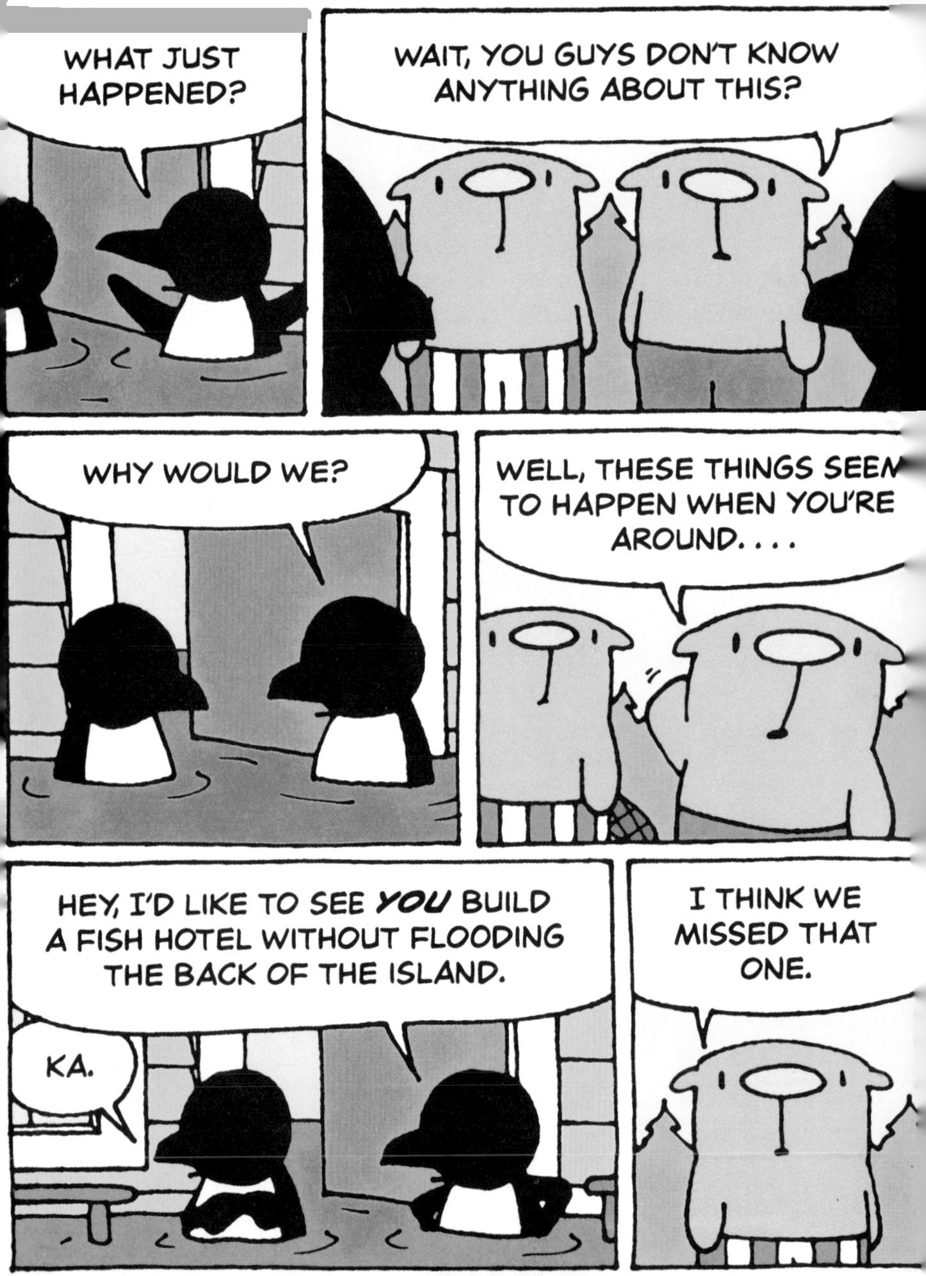
WHAT JUST HAPPENED?
WAIT, YOU GUYS DON'T KNOW ANYTHING ABOUT THIS?
WHY WOULD WE?
WELL, THESE THINGS SEEM TO HAPPEN WHEN YOU'RE AROUND. . . .
HEY, I'D LIKE TO SEE *YOU* BUILD A FISH HOTEL WITHOUT FLOODING THE BACK OF THE ISLAND.
KA.
I THINK WE MISSED THAT ONE.

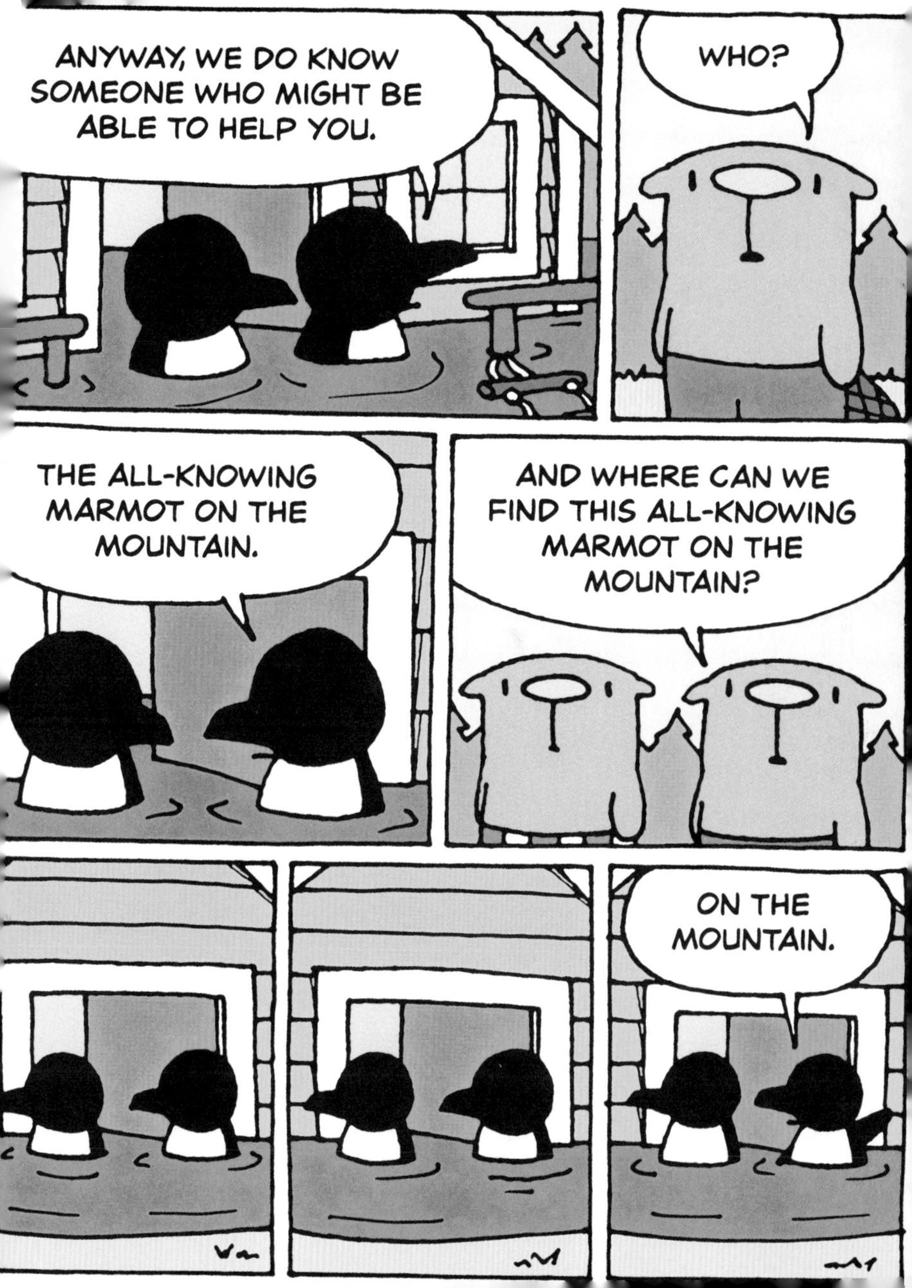
ANYWAY, WE DO KNOW SOMEONE WHO MIGHT BE ABLE TO HELP YOU.
WHO?
THE ALL-KNOWING MARMOT ON THE MOUNTAIN.
AND WHERE CAN WE FIND THIS ALL-KNOWING MARMOT ON THE MOUNTAIN?
ON THE MOUNTAIN.

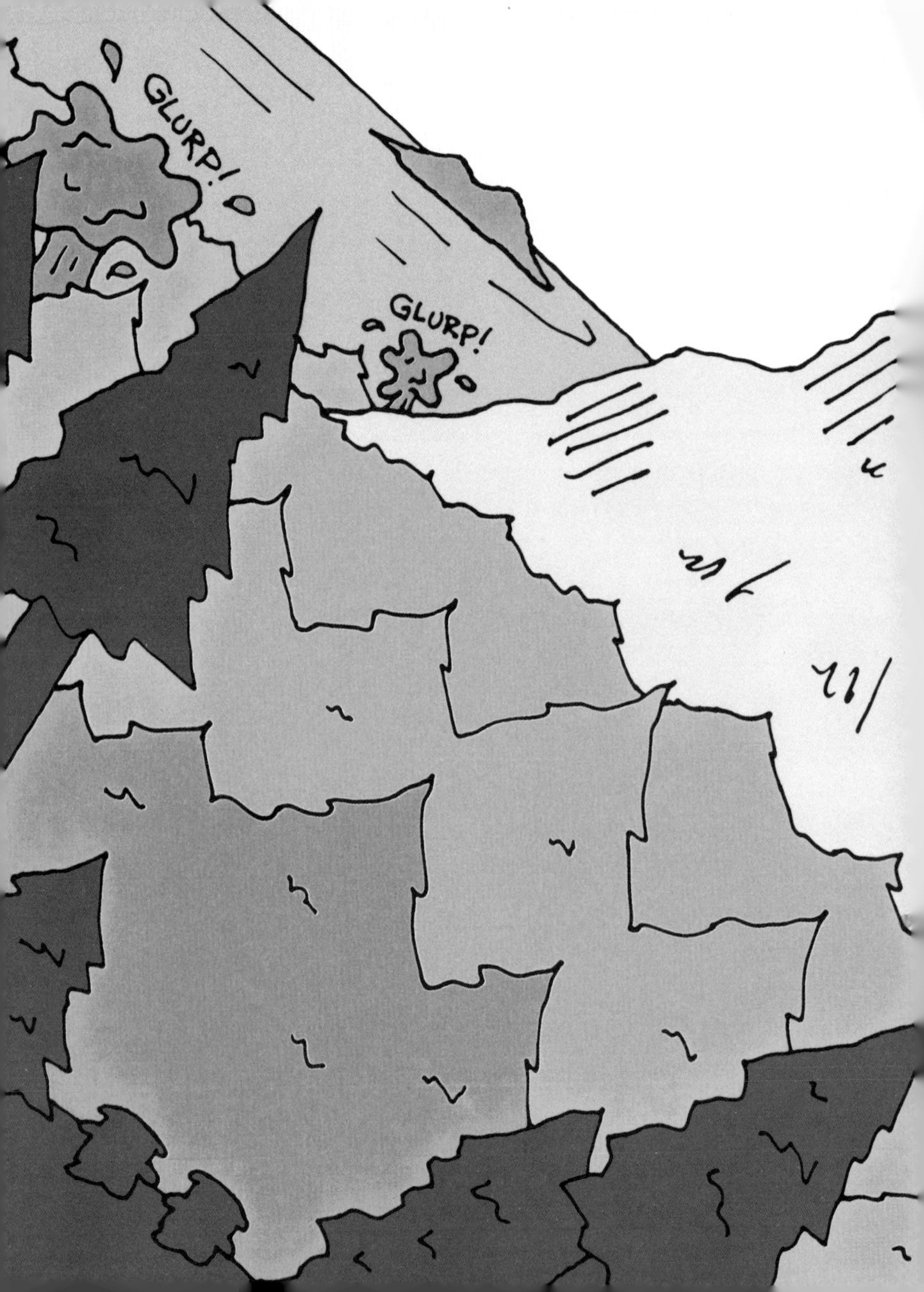
GLURP!
GLURP!

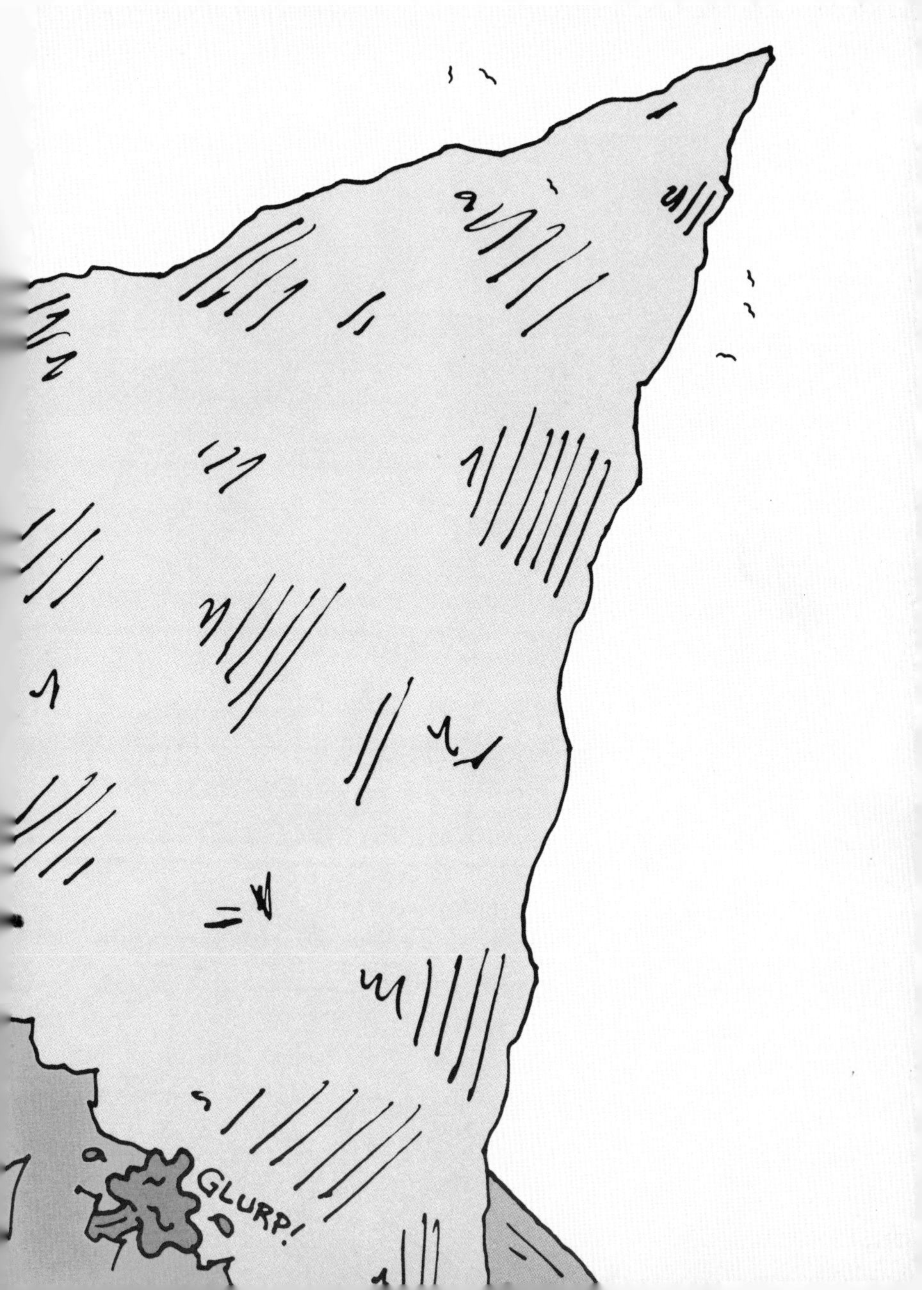
GLURP!

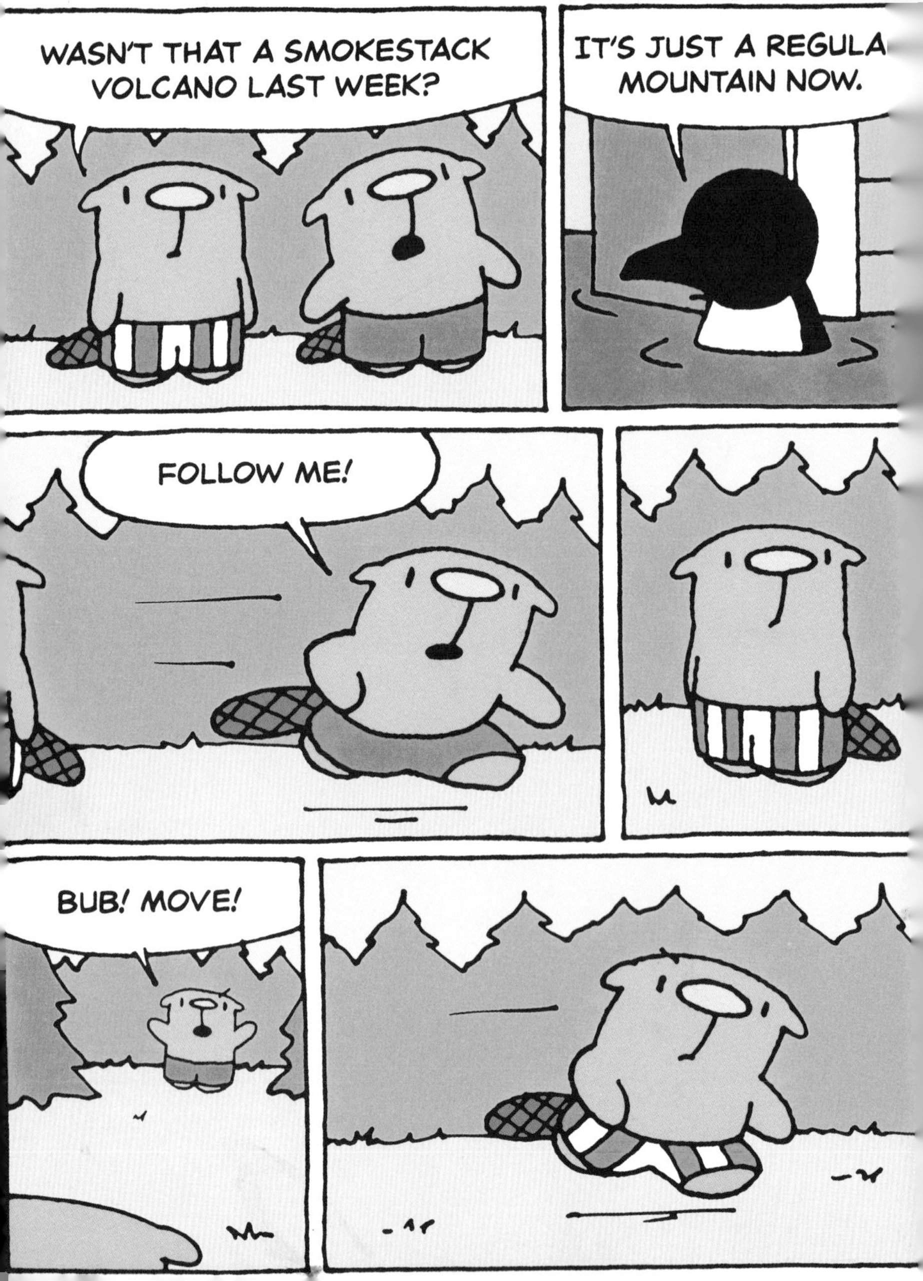
WASN'T THAT A SMOKESTACK VOLCANO LAST WEEK?
IT'S JUST A REGULA MOUNTAIN NOW.
FOLLOW ME!
BUB! MOVE!

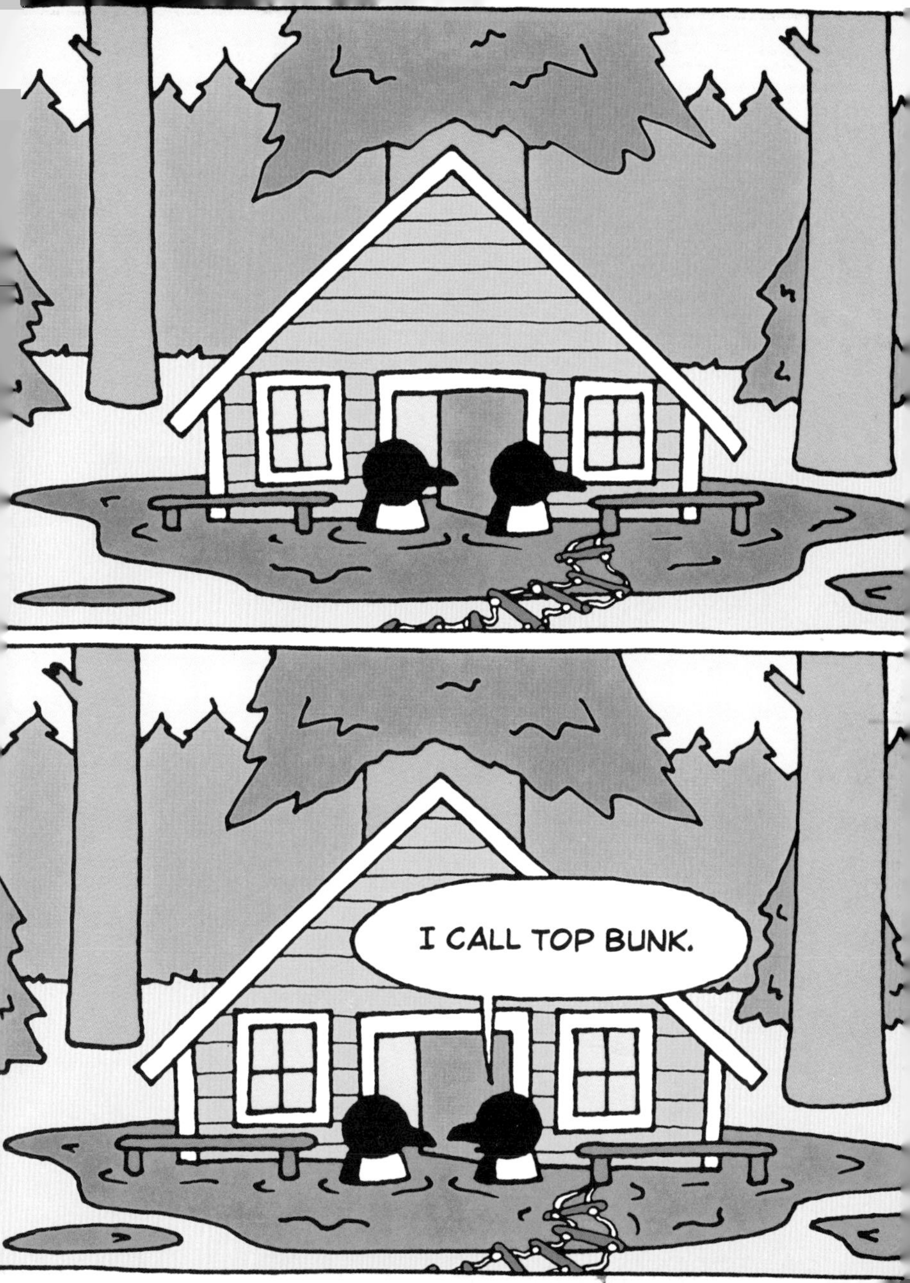
I CALL TOP BUNK.

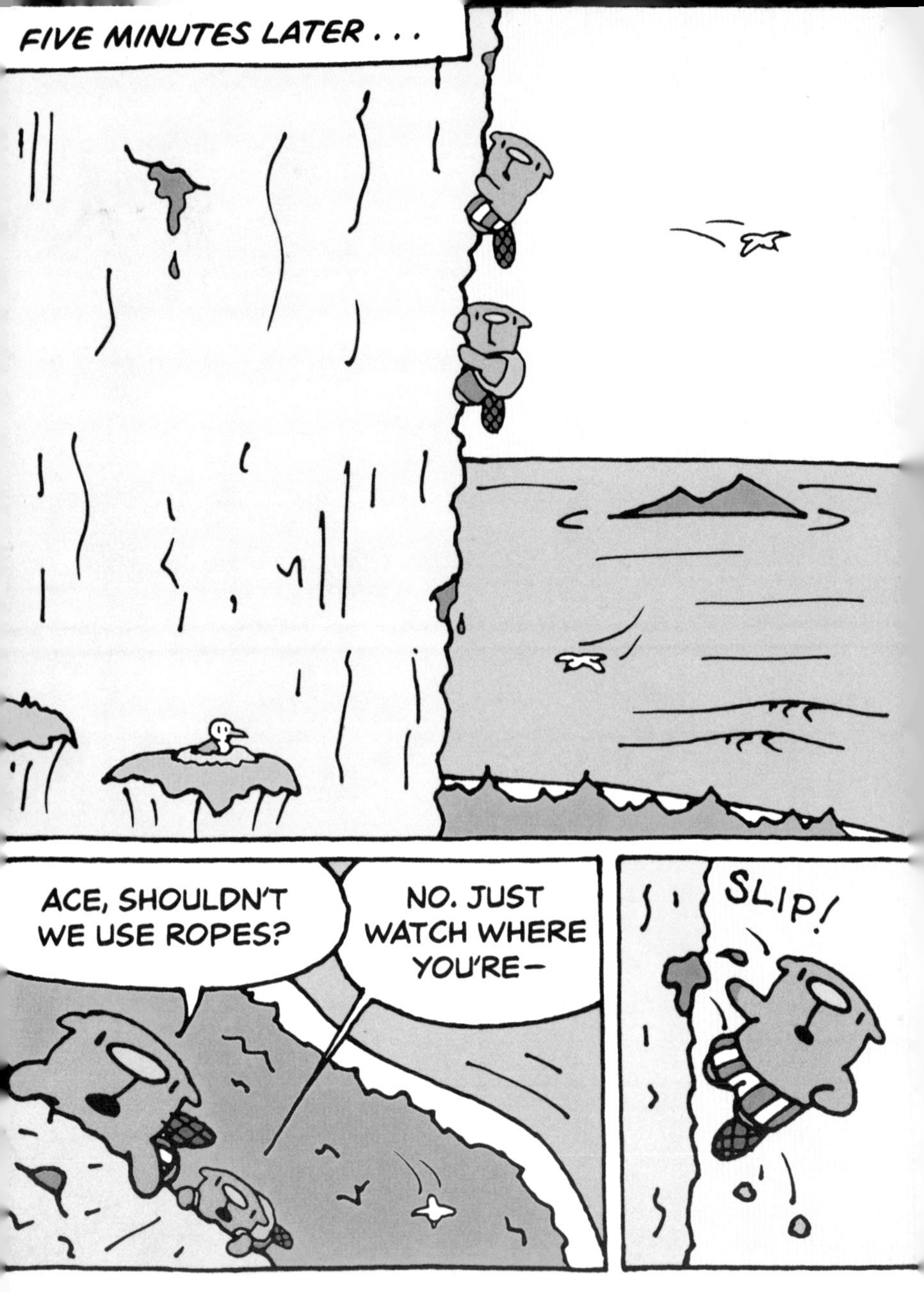
FIVE MINUTES LATER . . .
ACE, SHOULDN'T WE USE ROPES?
NO. JUST WATCH WHERE YOU'RE—
SLIP!

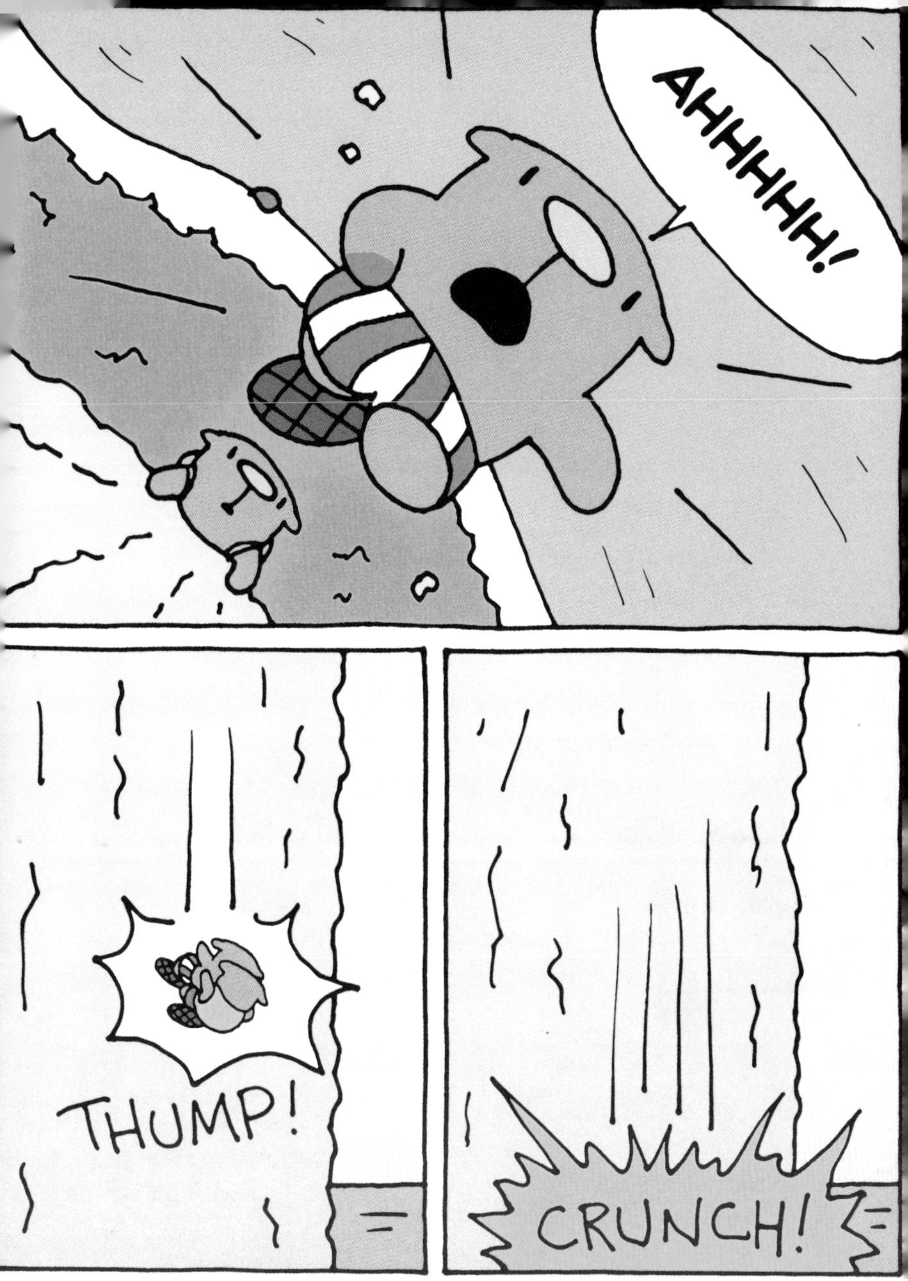
AHHHHH!
THUMP!
CRUNCH!

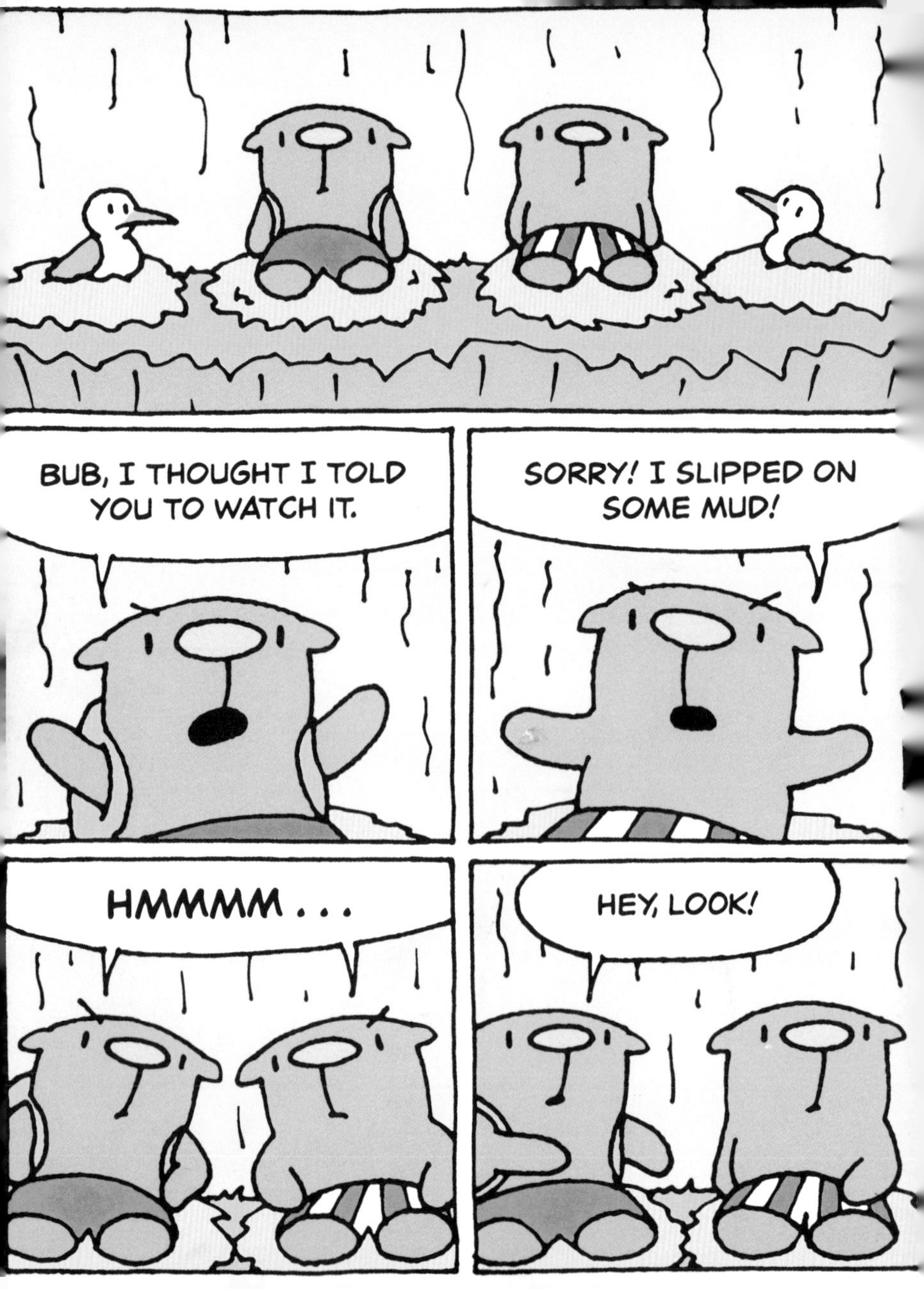
BUB, I THOUGHT I TOLD YOU TO WATCH IT.
SORRY! I SLIPPED ON SOME MUD!
HMMMM . . .
HEY, LOOK!

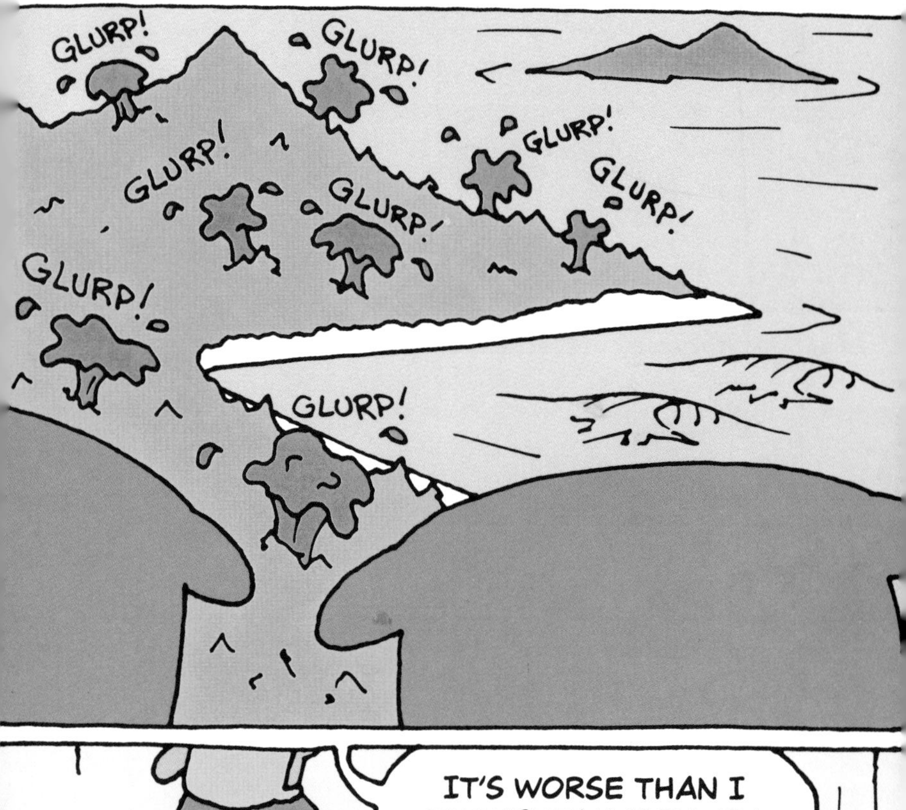
GLURP!
GLURP!
GLURP!
GLURP!
GLURP!
GLURP!
GLURP!
GLURP!

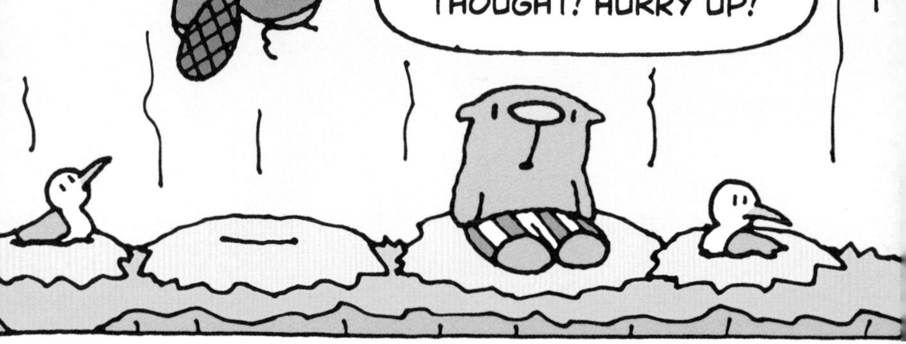
IT'S WORSE THAN I THOUGHT! HURRY UP!

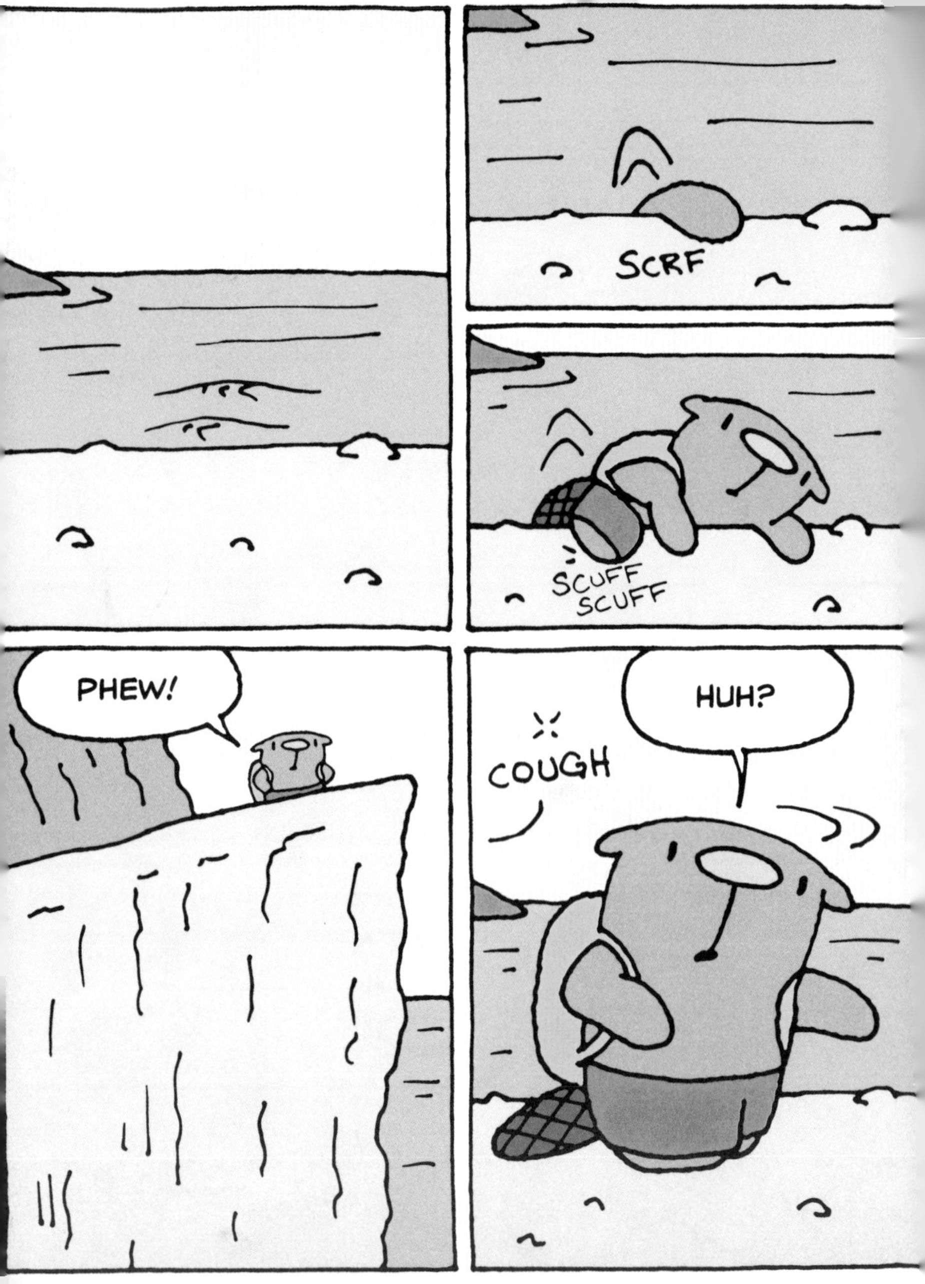
SCRF
SCUFF SCUFF
PHEW!
COUGH
HUH?

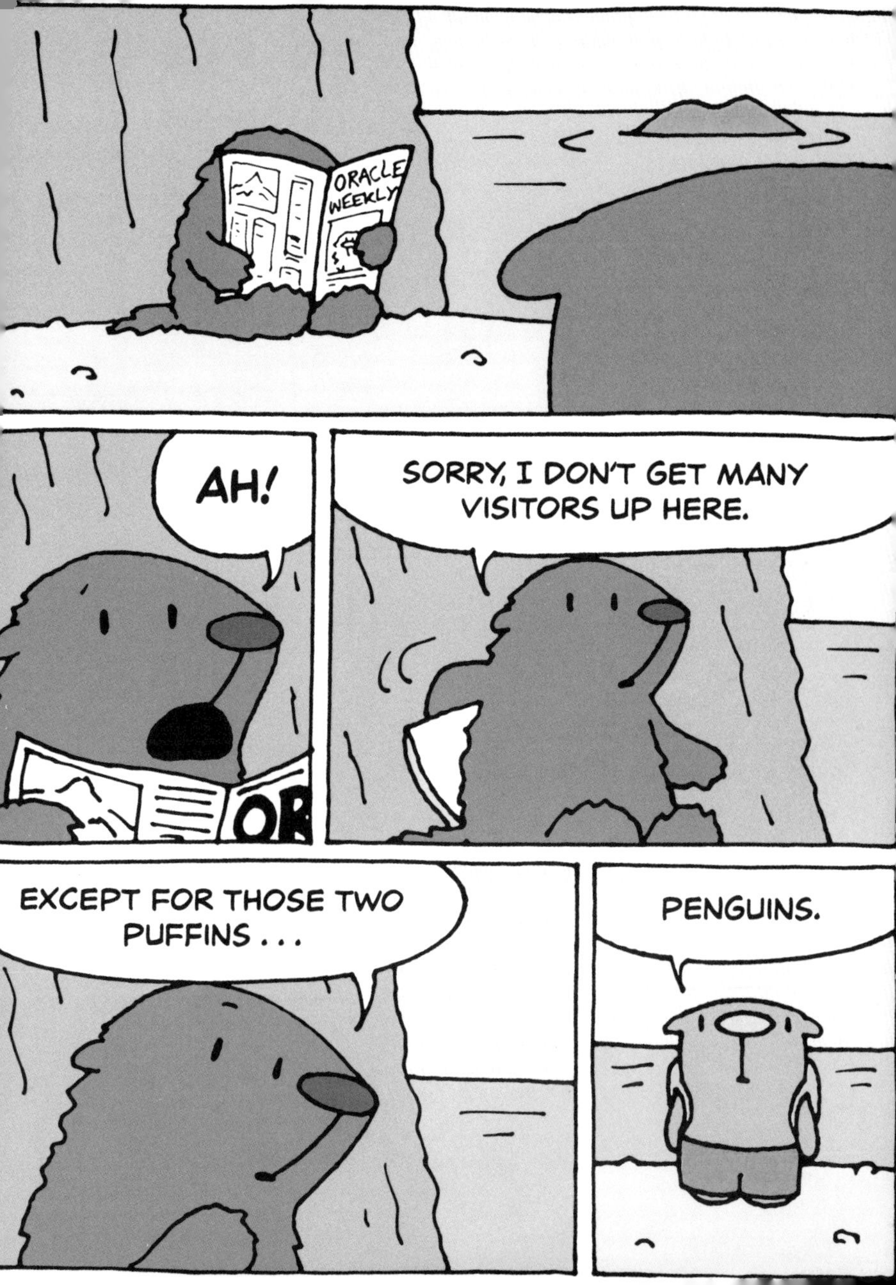
ORACLE WEEKLY
AH!
SORRY, I DON'T GET MANY VISITORS UP HERE.
EXCEPT FOR THOSE TWO PUFFINS . . .
PENGUINS.

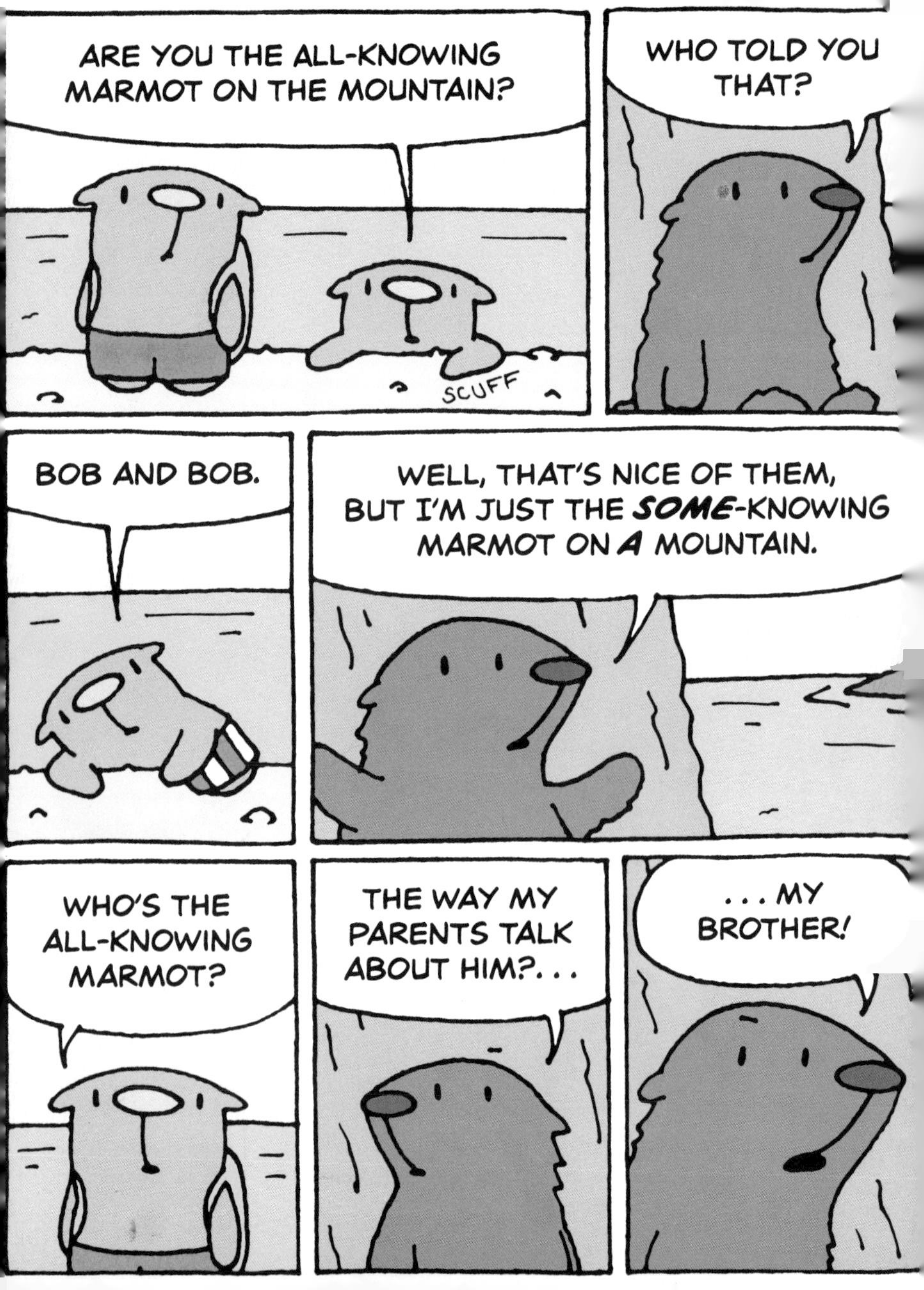
ARE YOU THE ALL-KNOWING MARMOT ON THE MOUNTAIN?
SCUFF
WHO TOLD YOU THAT?
BOB AND BOB.
WELL, THAT'S NICE OF THEM, BUT I'M JUST THE SOME-KNOWING MARMOT ON A MOUNTAIN.
WHO'S THE ALL-KNOWING MARMOT?
THE WAY MY PARENTS TALK ABOUT HIM?...
...MY BROTHER!

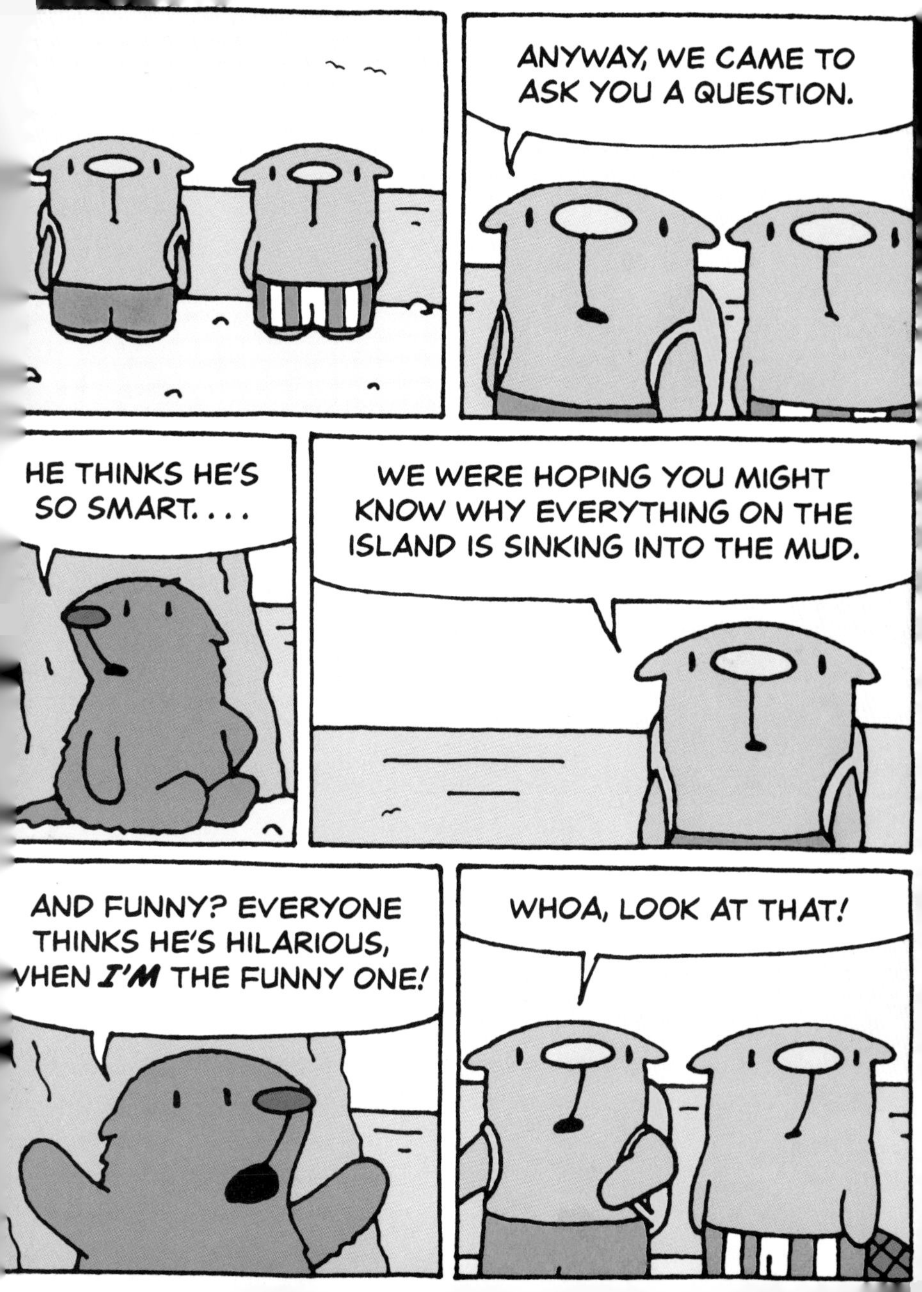
ANYWAY, WE CAME TO ASK YOU A QUESTION.
HE THINKS HE'S SO SMART. . . .
WE WERE HOPING YOU MIGHT KNOW WHY EVERYTHING ON THE ISLAND IS SINKING INTO THE MUD.
AND FUNNY? EVERYONE THINKS HE'S HILARIOUS, WHEN *I'M* THE FUNNY ONE!
WHOA, LOOK AT THAT!

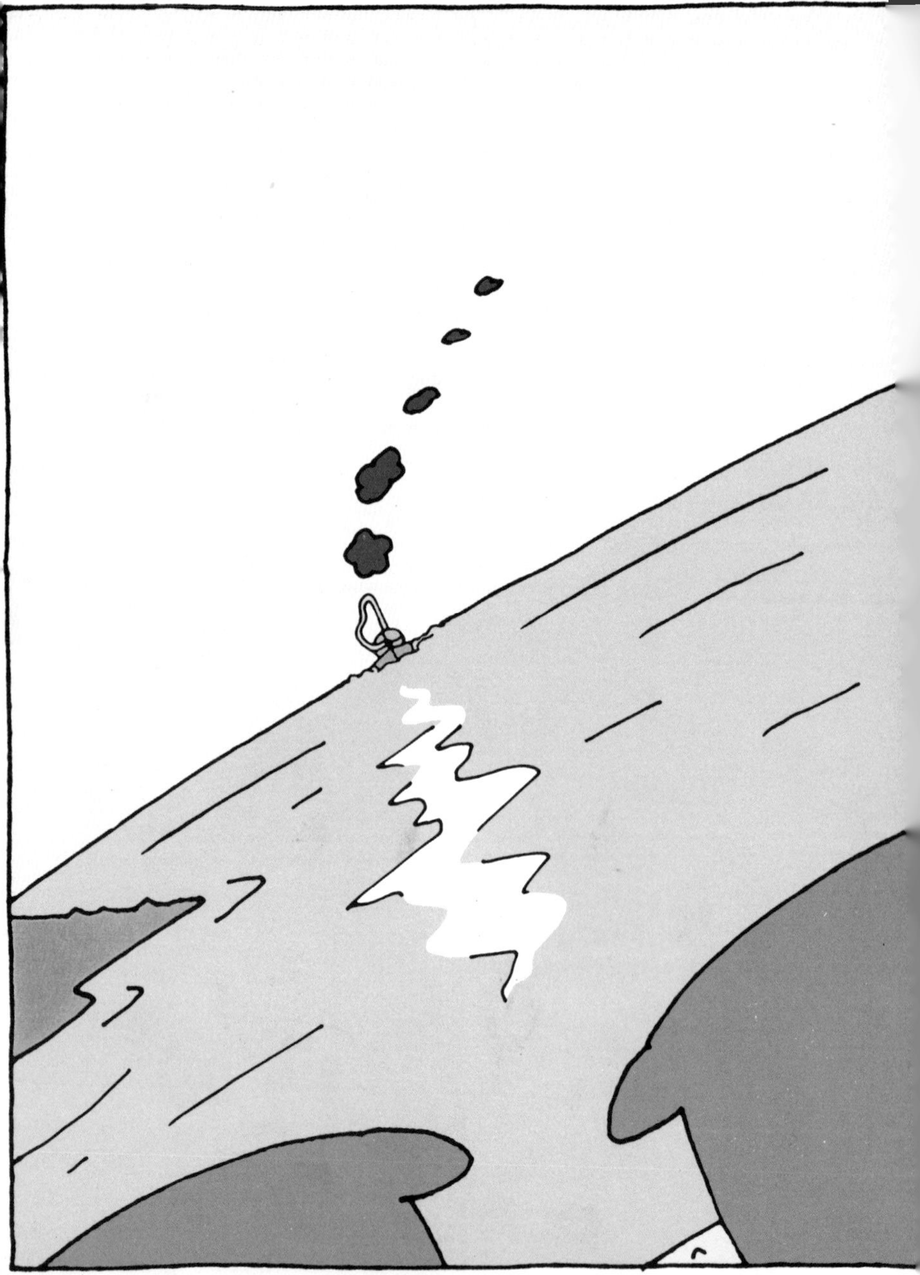

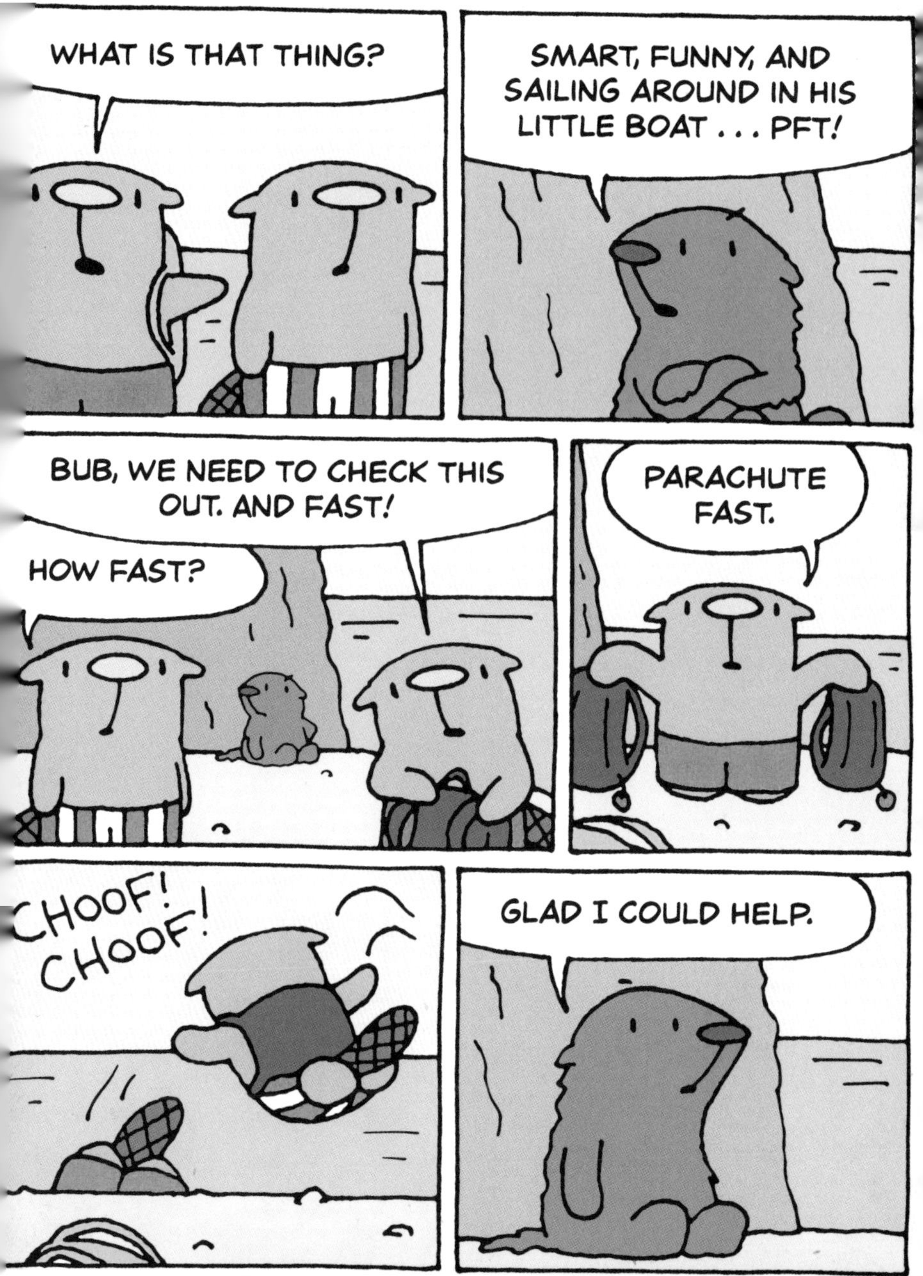
WHAT IS THAT THING?
SMART, FUNNY, AND SAILING AROUND IN HIS LITTLE BOAT . . . PFT!
BUB, WE NEED TO CHECK THIS OUT. AND FAST!
HOW FAST?
PARACHUTE FAST.
CHOOF! CHOOF!
GLAD I COULD HELP.

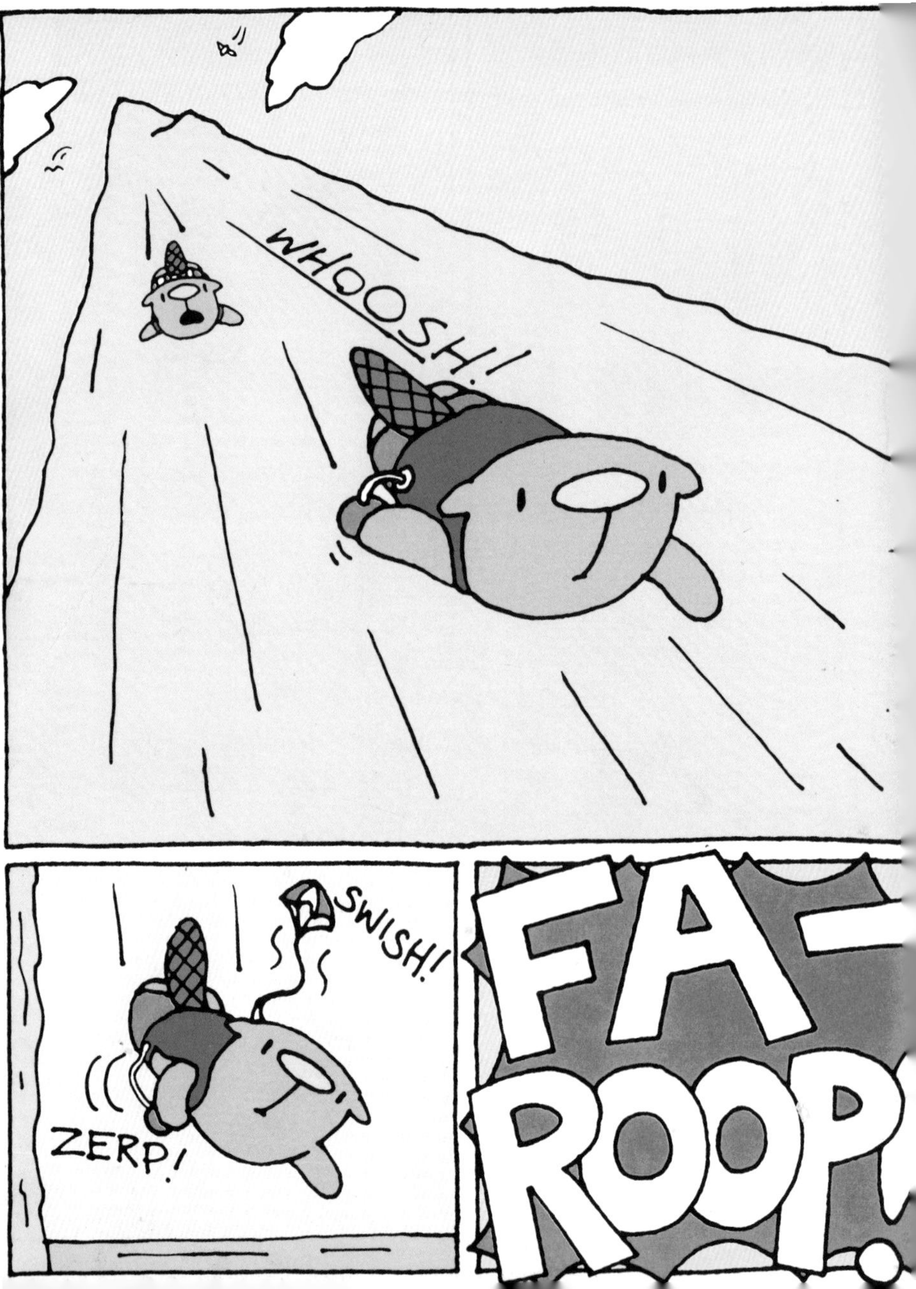
WHOOSH!
SWISH!
ZERP!
FA-ROOP!

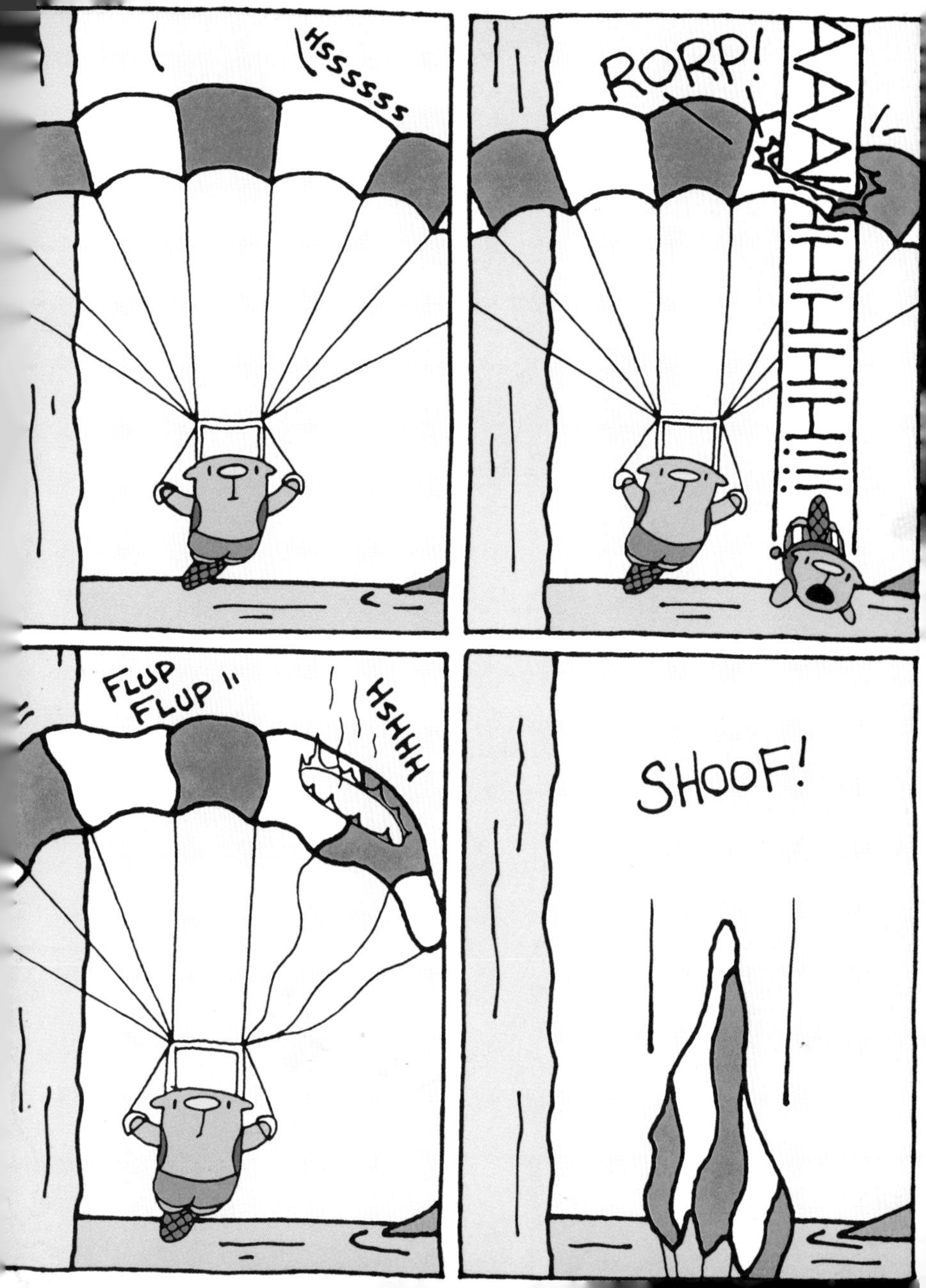
HSSSSSS
RORP!
AAAHHHHH!!!
FLUP
FLUP!!
HSHHH
SHOOF!

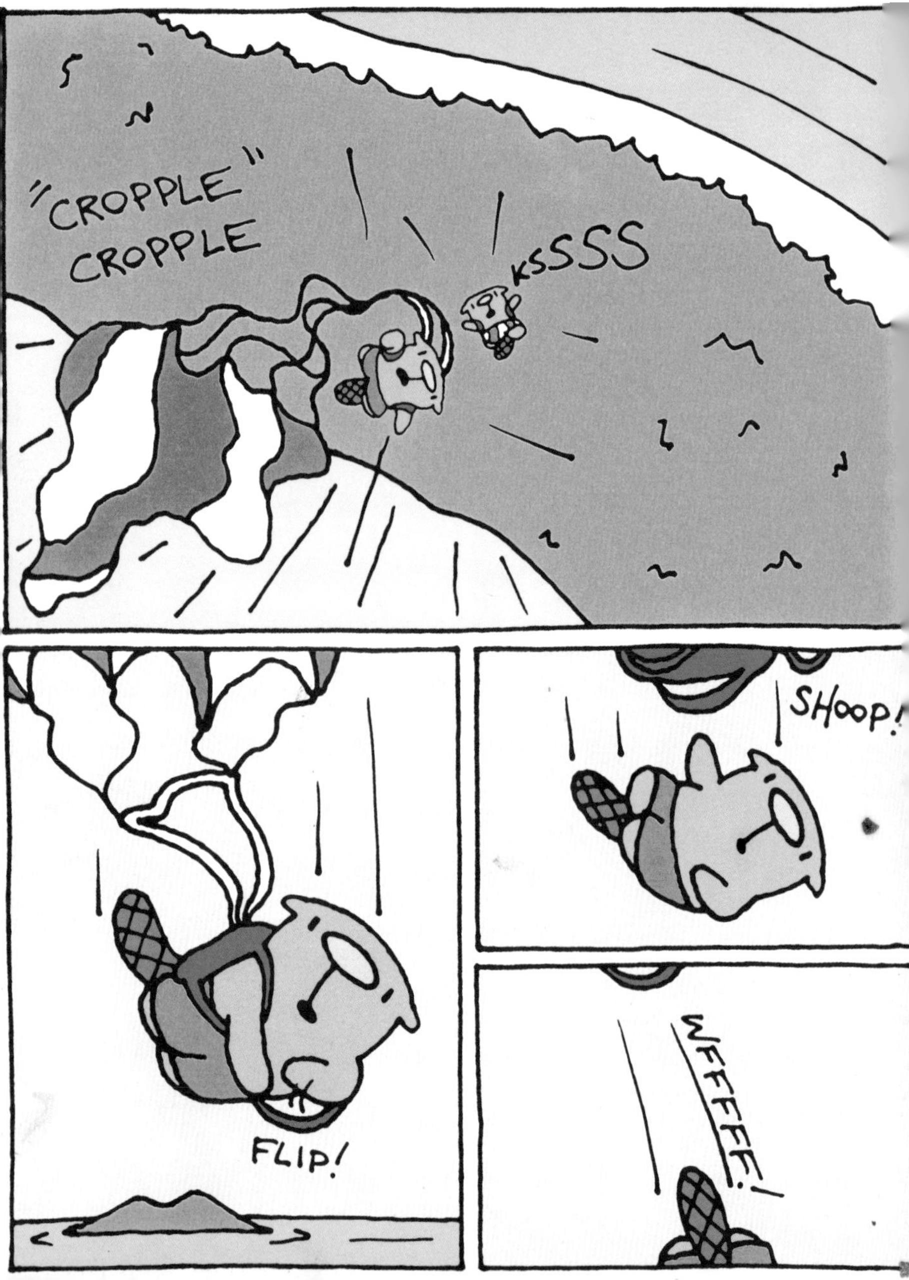
"CROPPLE" CROPPLE CROPPLE
KSSSS
FLIP!
SHOOP!
WFFFFF!

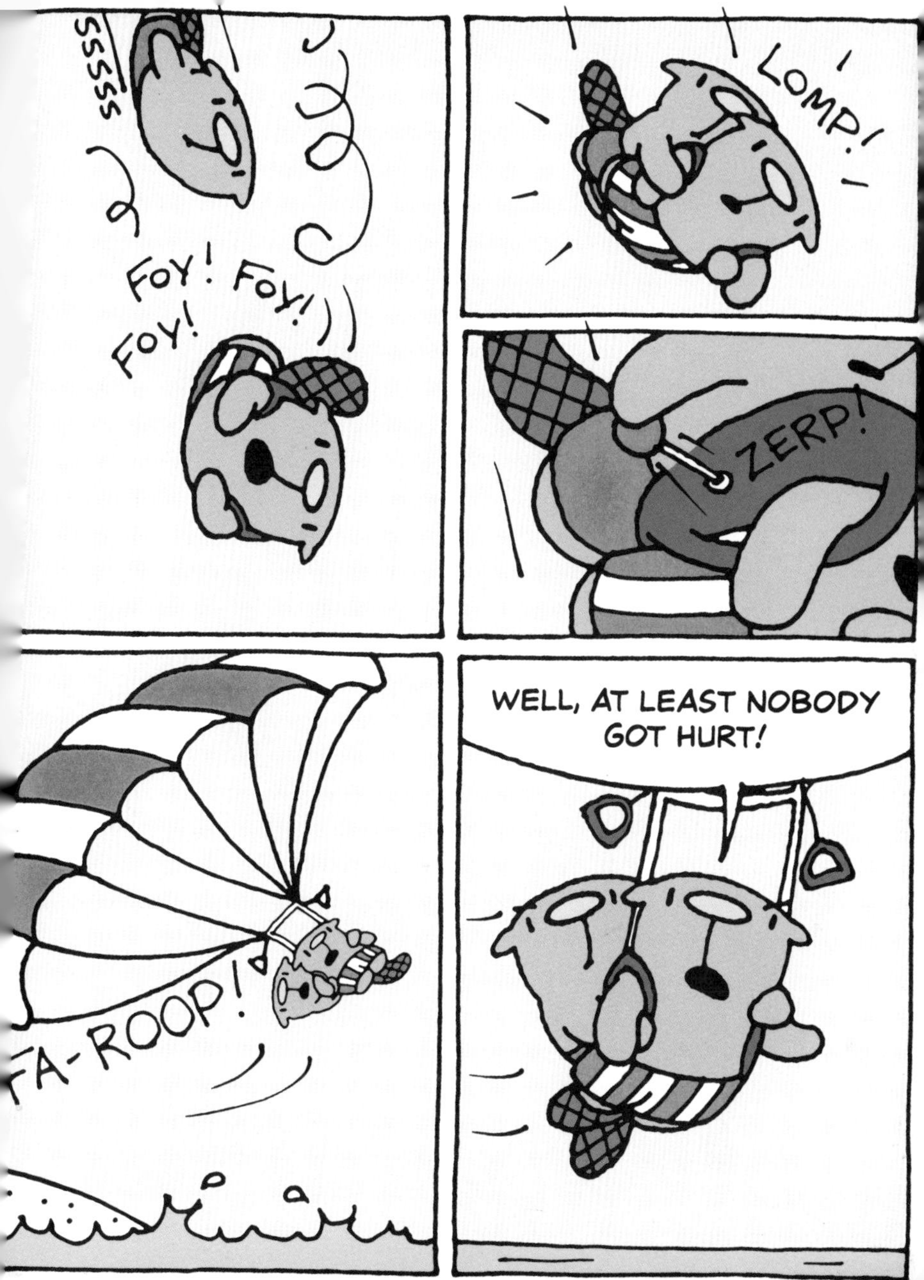
SSSSS
FOY! FOY! FOY!
LOMP!
ZERP!
FA-ROOP!
WELL, AT LEAST NOBODY GOT HURT!

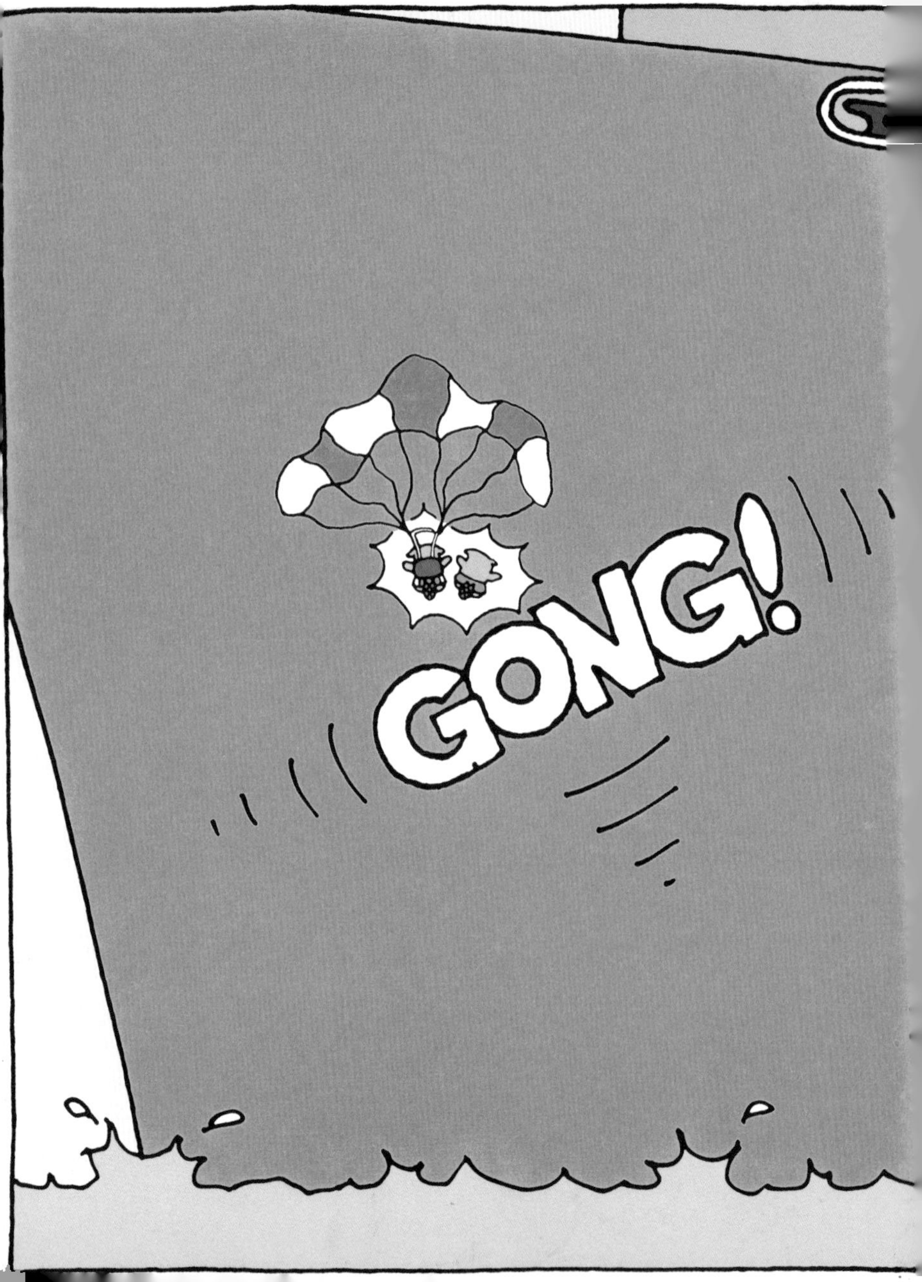
GONG!

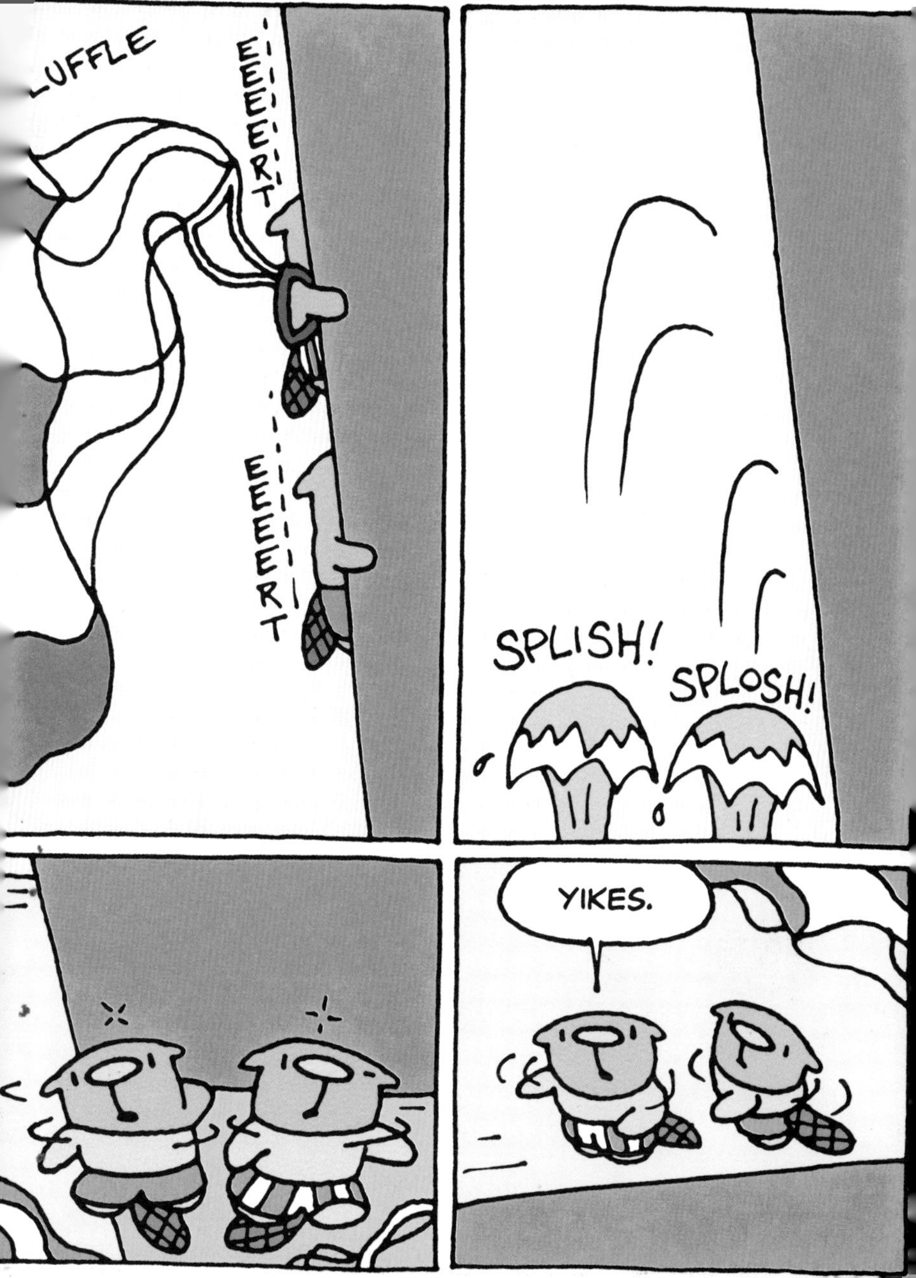

LUFFLE
EEEEERT
EEEEERT
SPLISH!
SPLOSH!
YIKES.

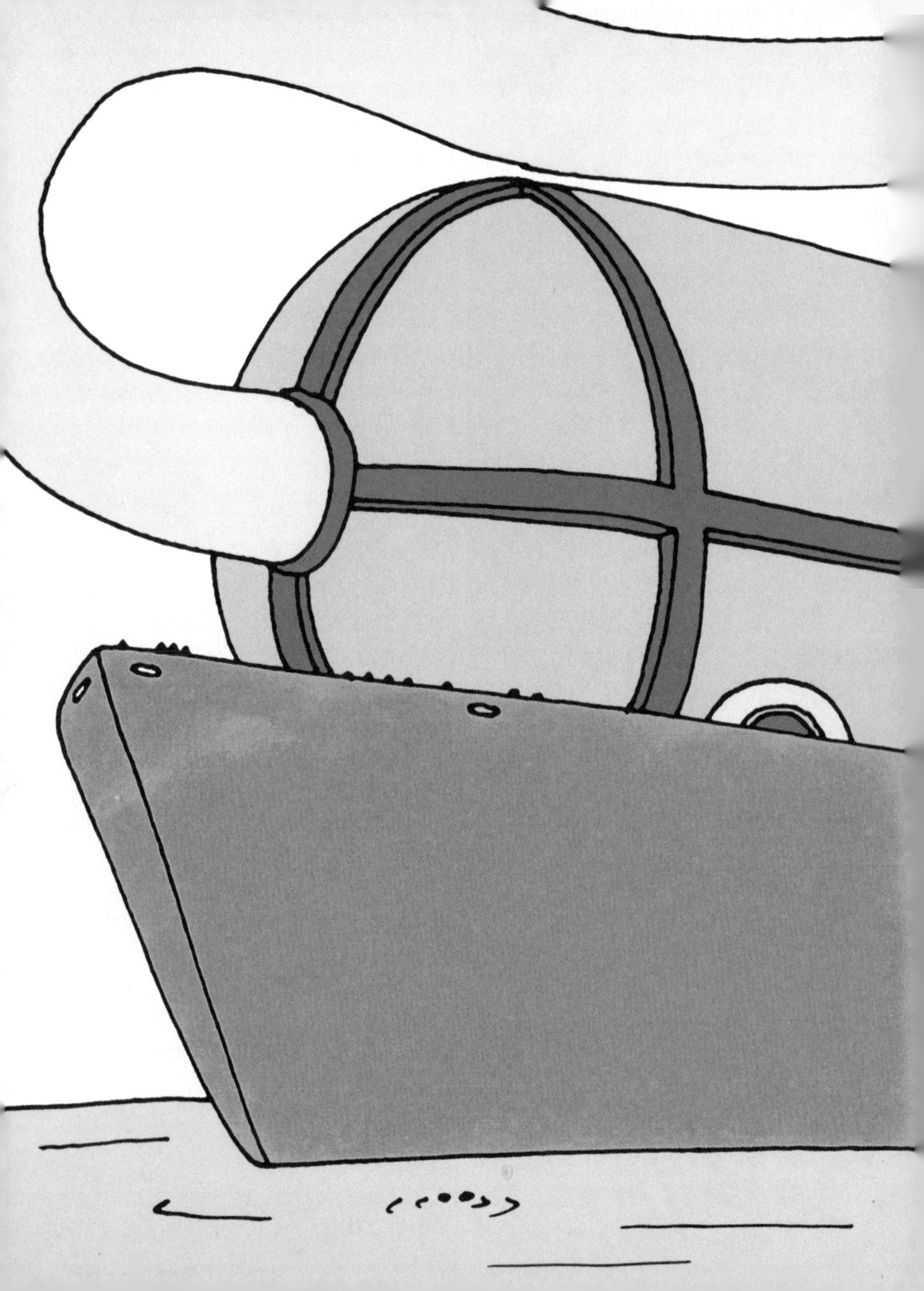

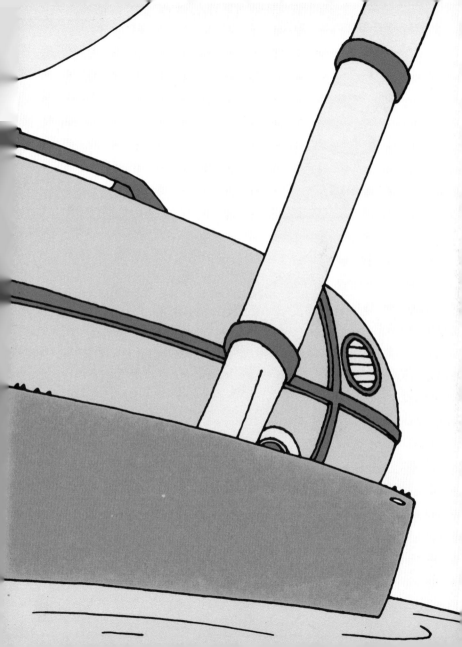

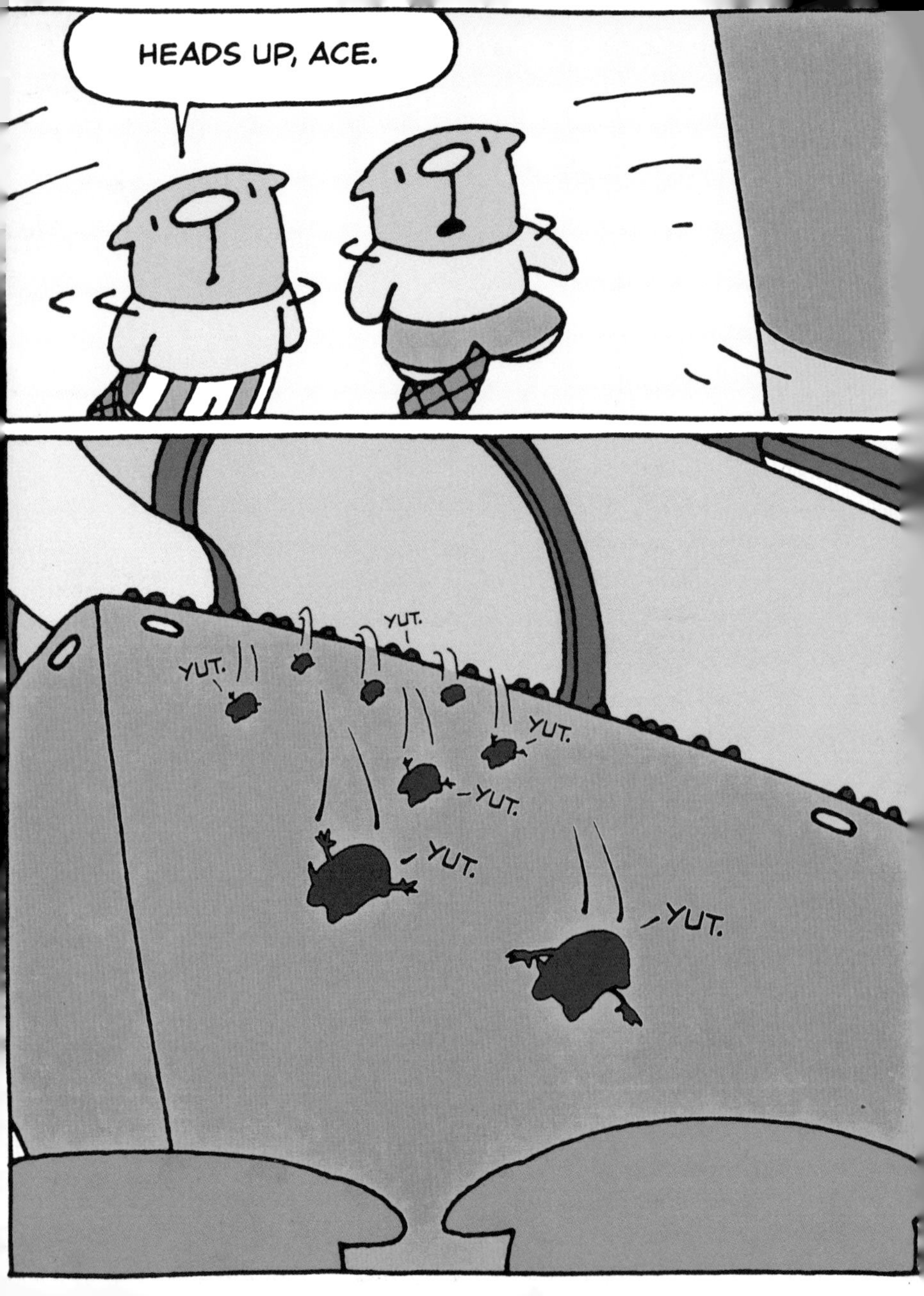
HEADS UP, ACE.
YUT.
YUT.
YUT.
YUT.
YUT.
YUT.

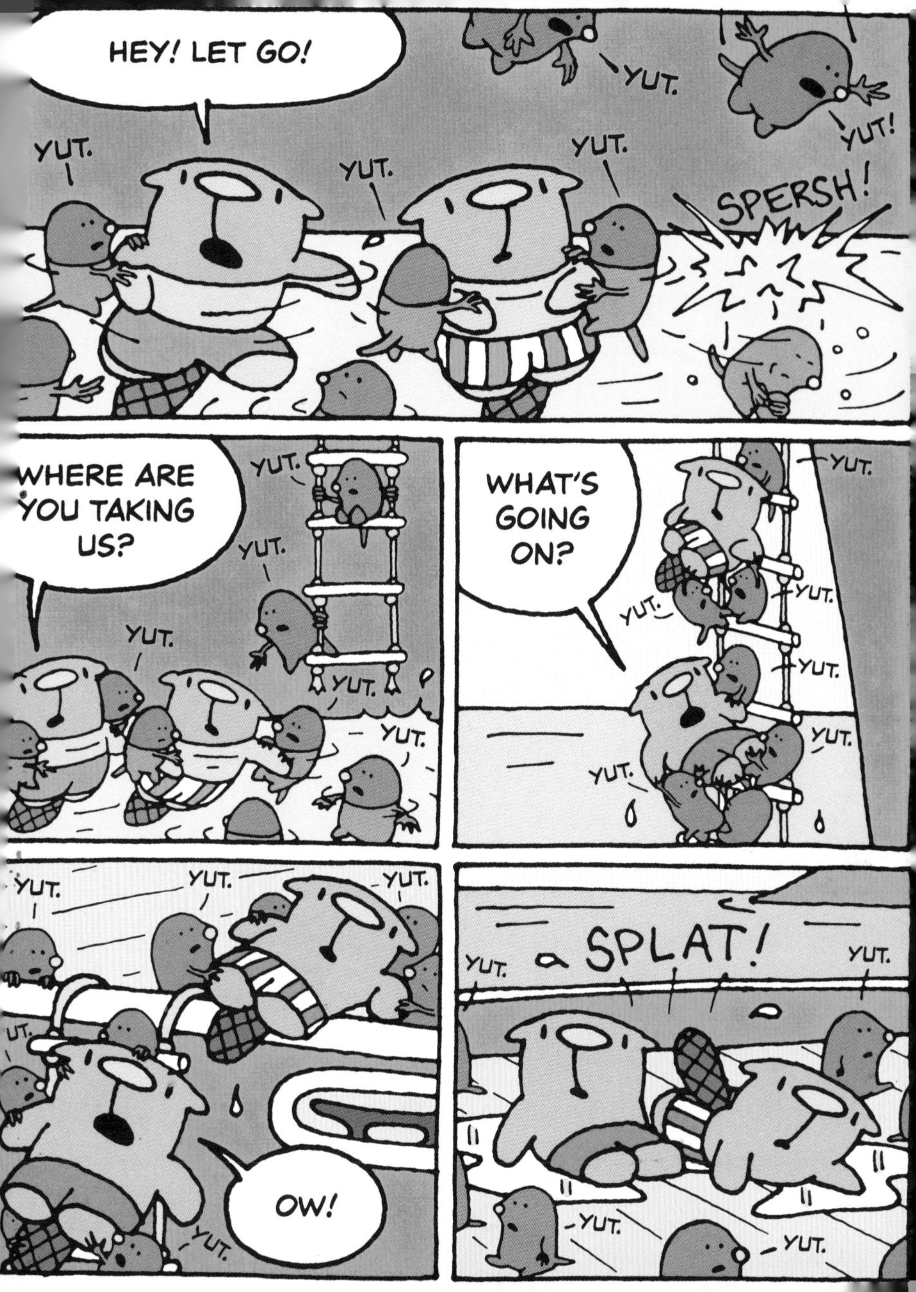
HEY! LET GO!
YUT.
YUT.
YUT.
YUT.
YUT.
YUT!
SPERSH!
WHERE ARE YOU TAKING US?
YUT.
YUT.
YUT.
YUT.
YUT.
WHAT'S GOING ON?
YUT.
YUT.
YUT.
YUT.
YUT.
YUT.
YUT.
YUT.
YUT.
OW!
YUT.
YUT.
SPLAT!
YUT.
YUT.
YUT.

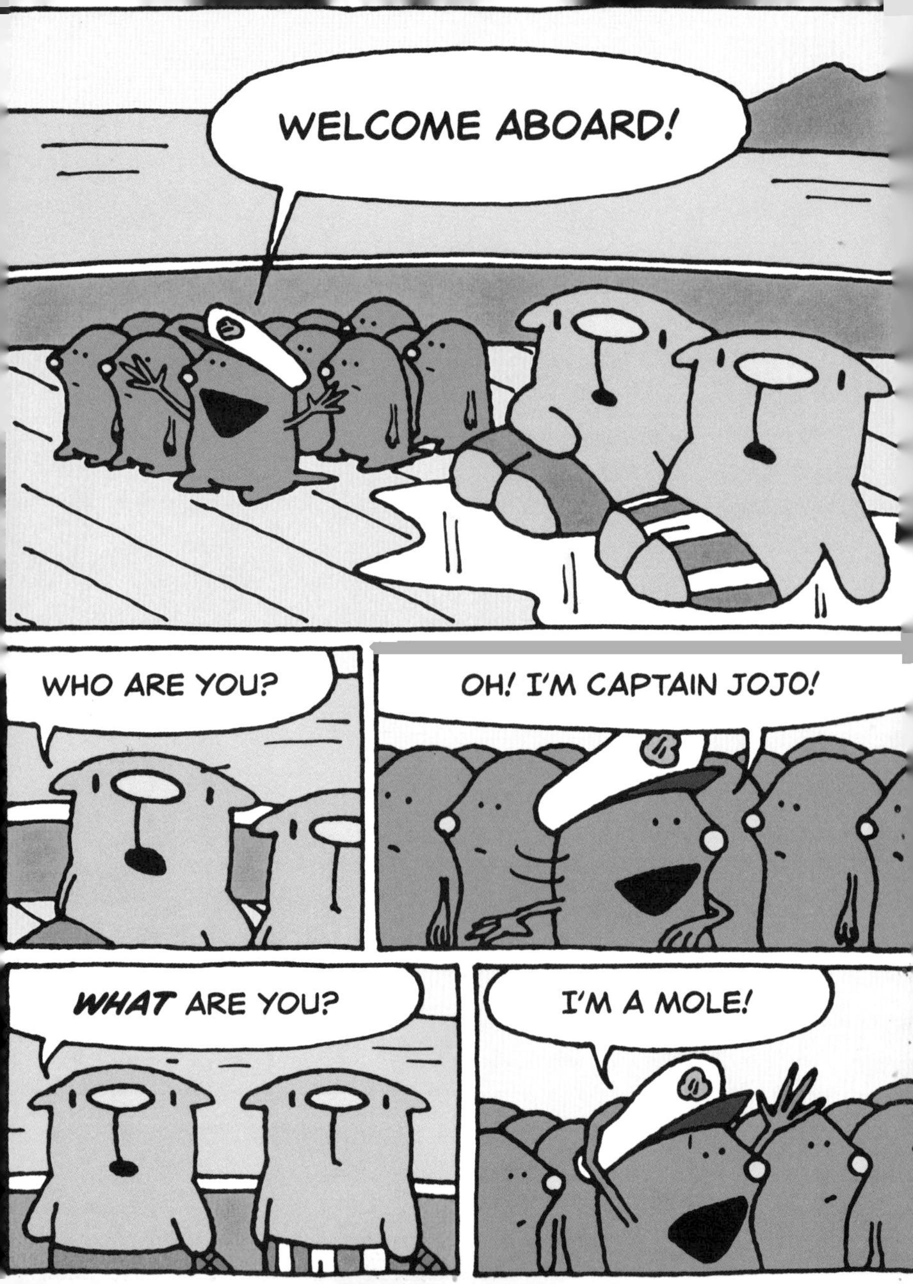
WELCOME ABOARD!
WHO ARE YOU?
OH! I'M CAPTAIN JOJO!
WHAT ARE YOU?
I'M A MOLE!

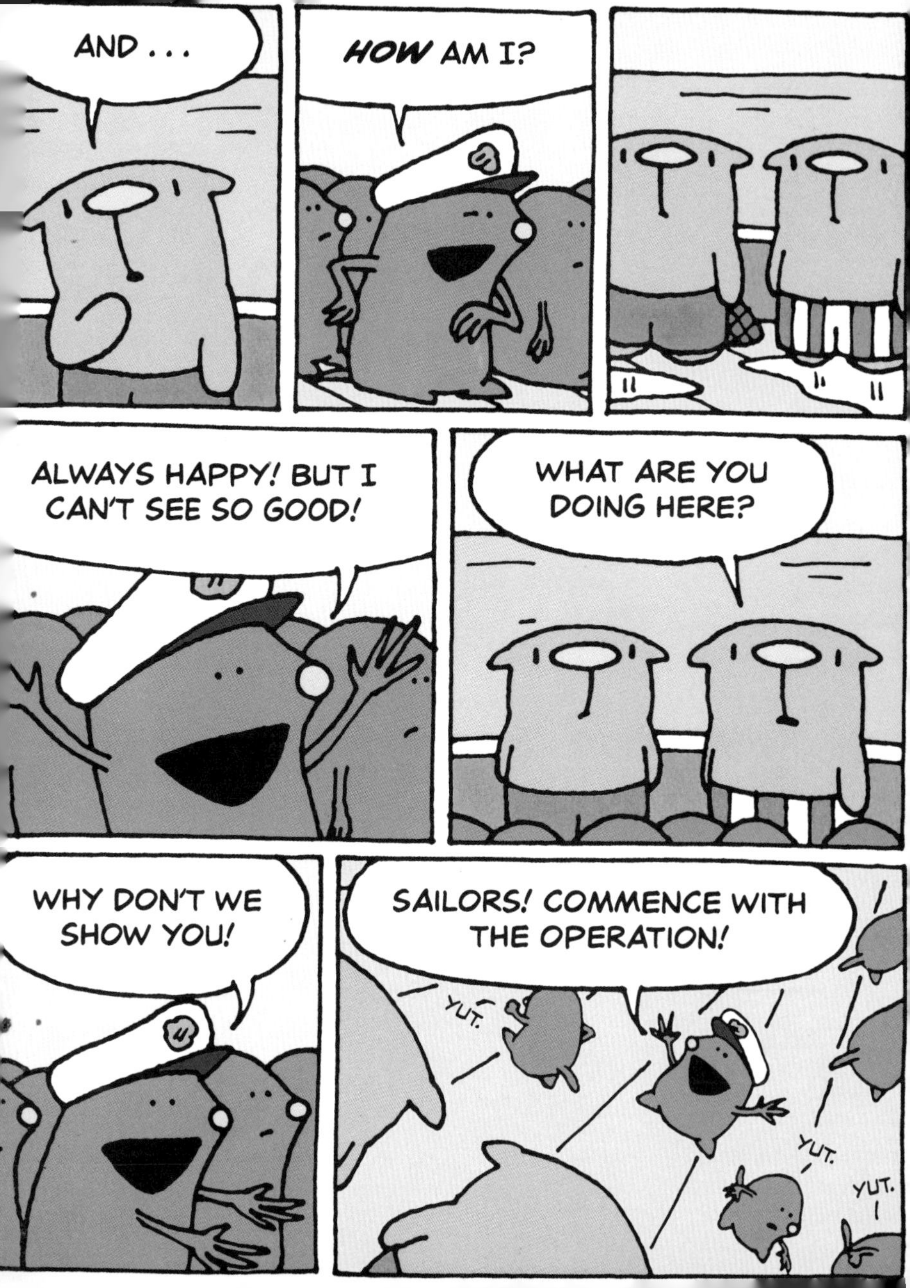
AND . . .
HOW AM I?
ALWAYS HAPPY! BUT I CAN'T SEE SO GOOD!
WHAT ARE YOU DOING HERE?
WHY DON'T WE SHOW YOU!
SAILORS! COMMENCE WITH THE OPERATION!
YUT.
YUT.
YUT.

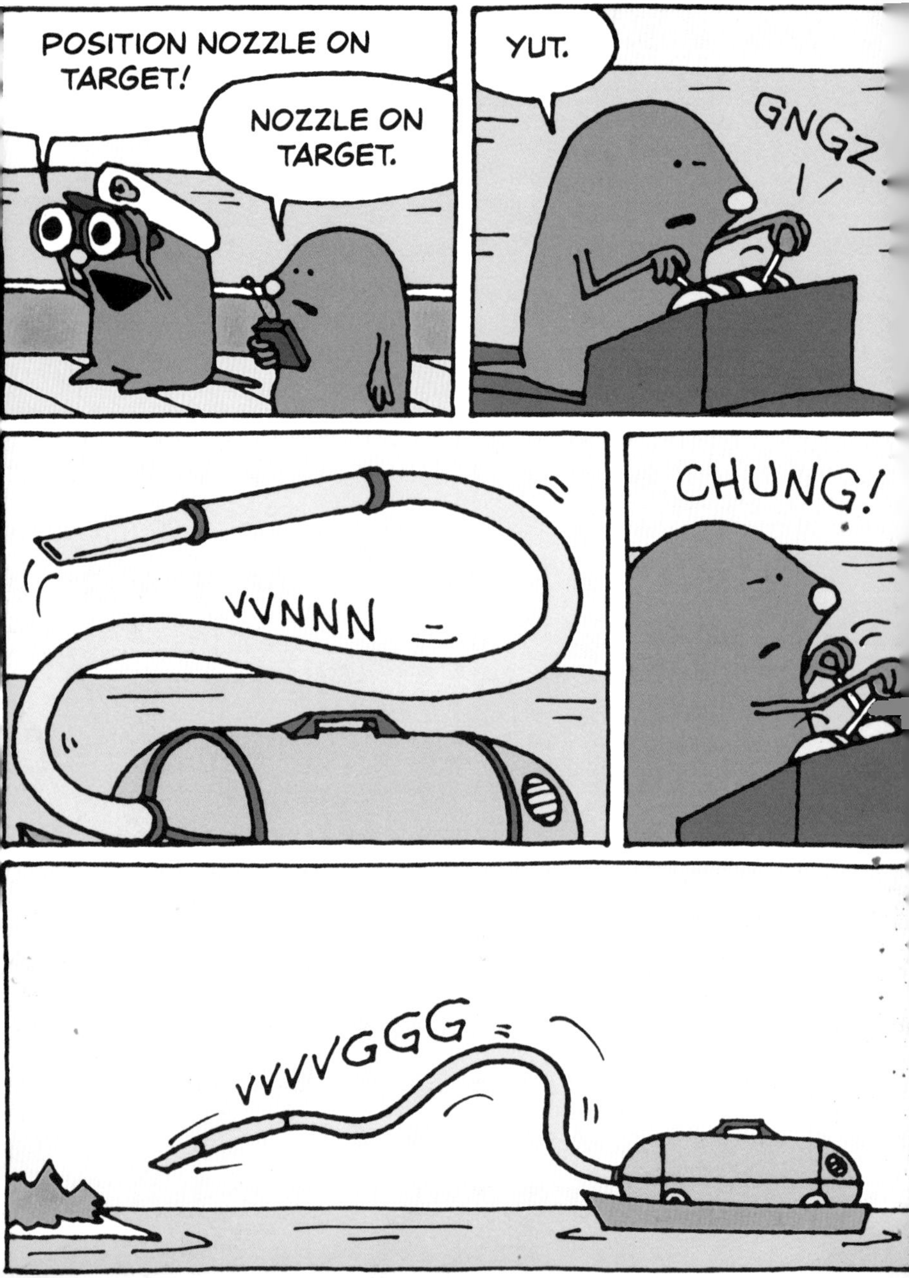
POSITION NOZZLE ON TARGET!
NOZZLE ON TARGET.
YUT.
GNGZ.
VVNNN
CHUNG!
VVVVGGG

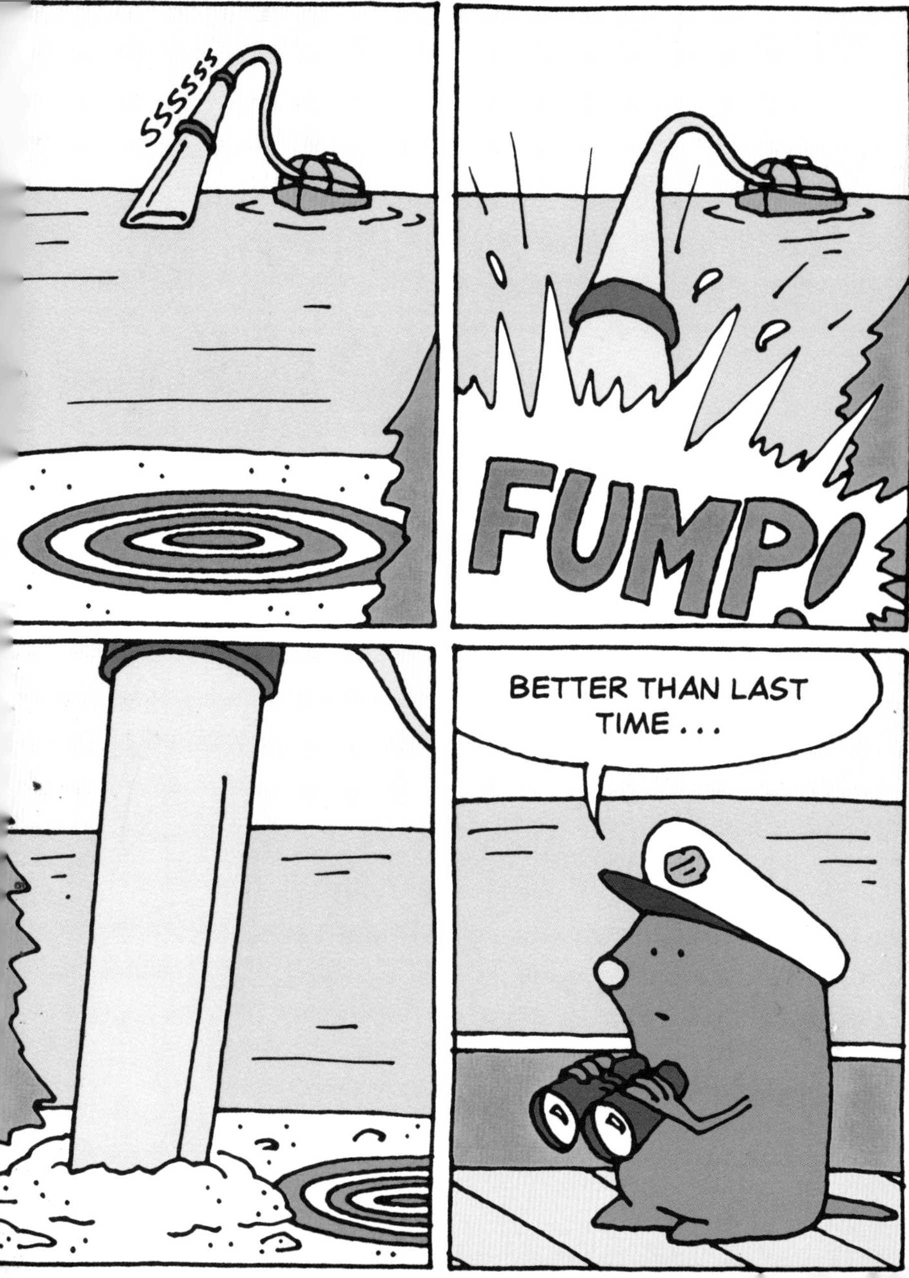
SSSSSS
FUMP!
BETTER THAN LAST TIME . . .

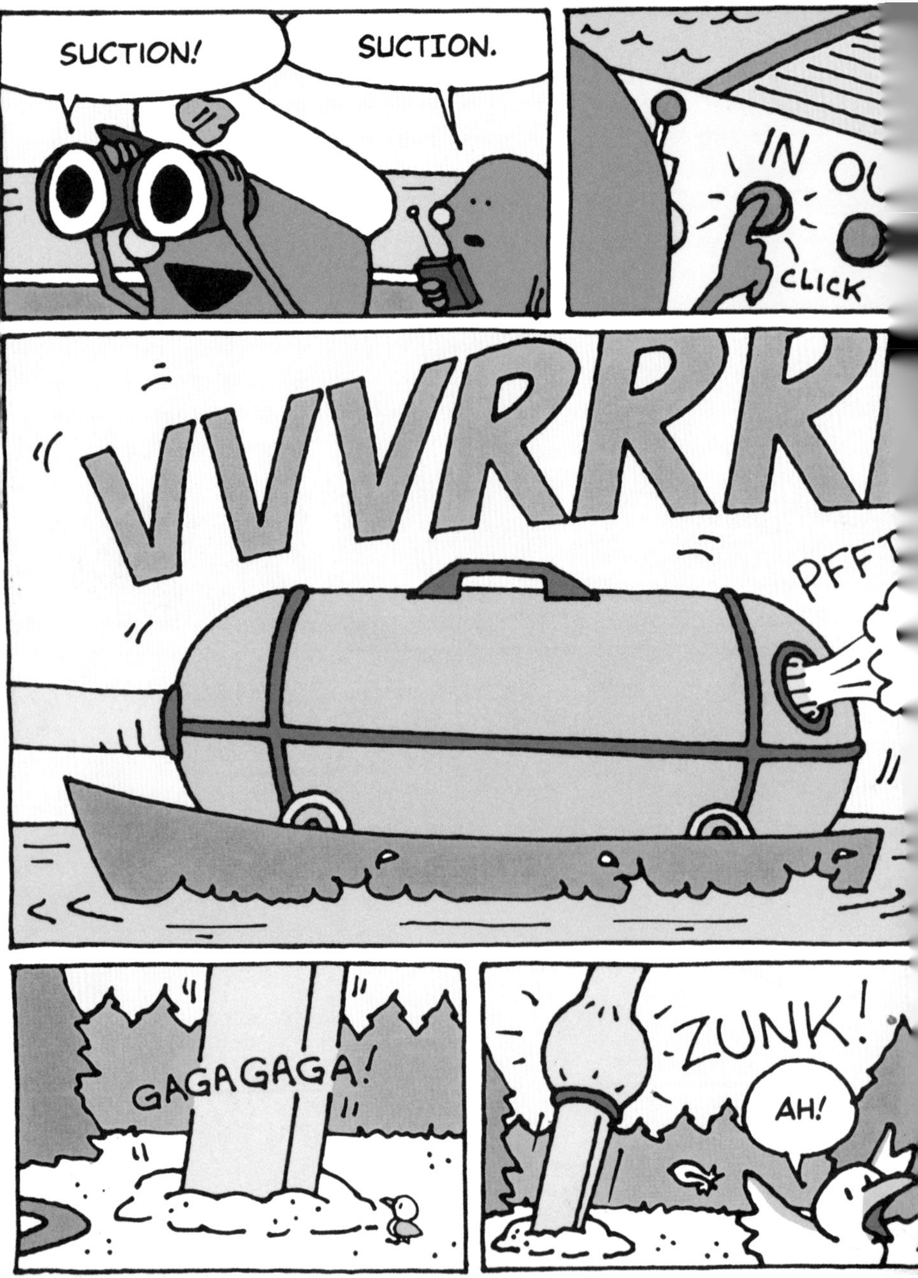
SUCTION!
SUCTION.
IN
OU
CLICK
VVVRRR
PFFT
GAGAGAGA!
ZUNK!
AH!

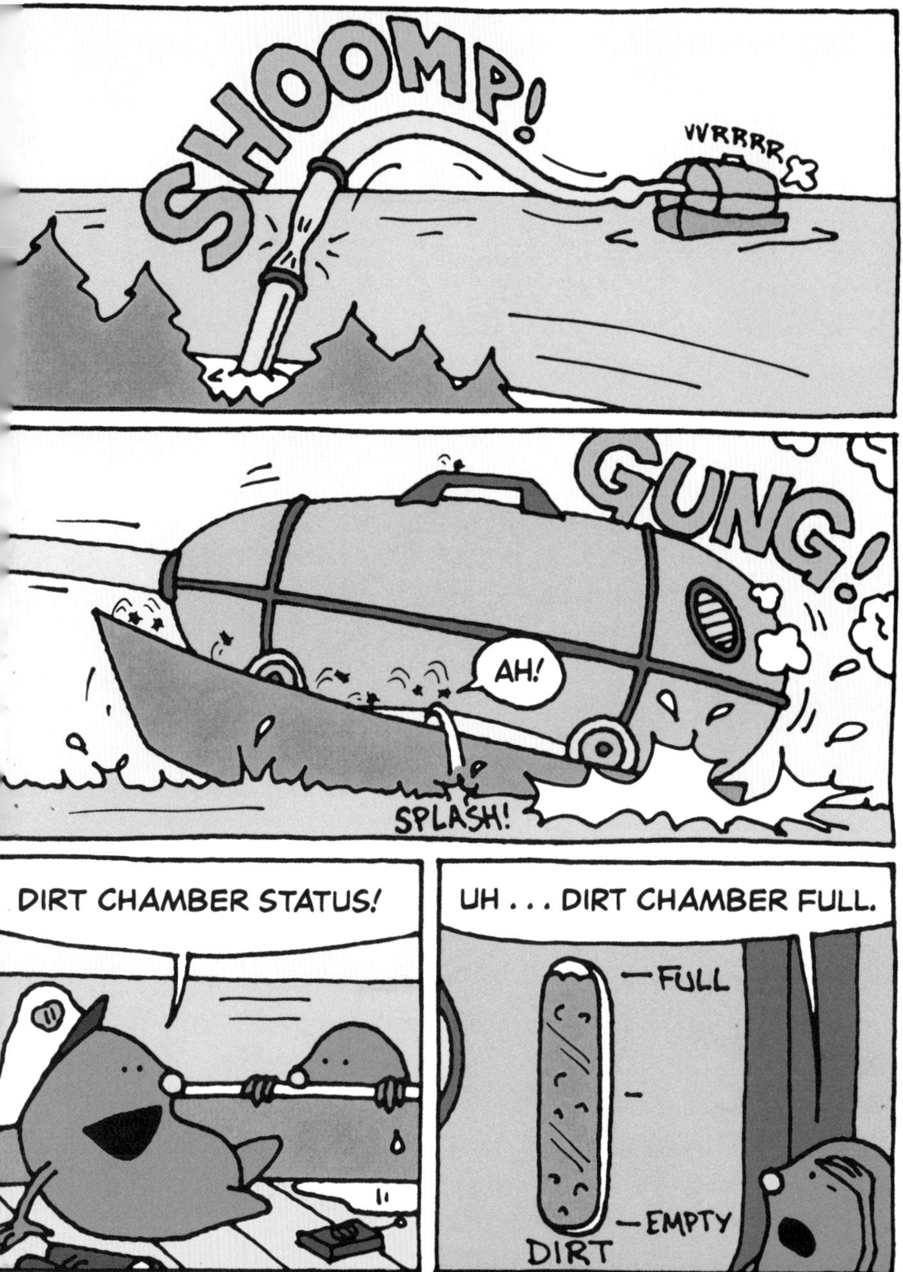
SHOOMP!
VVRRRRR
GUNG!
AH!
SPLASH!
DIRT CHAMBER STATUS!
UH . . . DIRT CHAMBER FULL.
FULL
EMPTY
DIRT

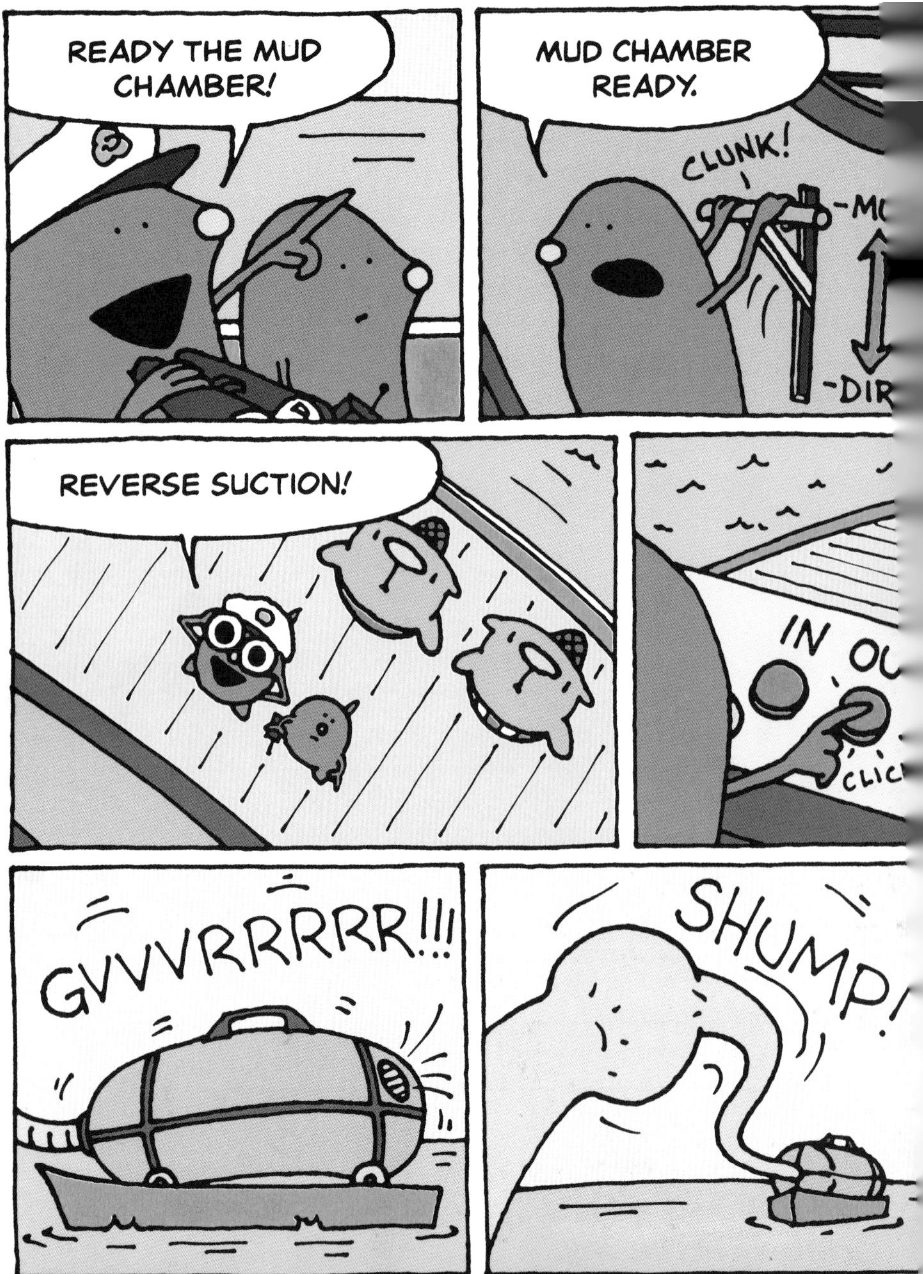
READY THE MUD CHAMBER!
MUD CHAMBER READY.
CLUNK!
REVERSE SUCTION!
IN
GVVVRRRRRR!!!
SHUMP!

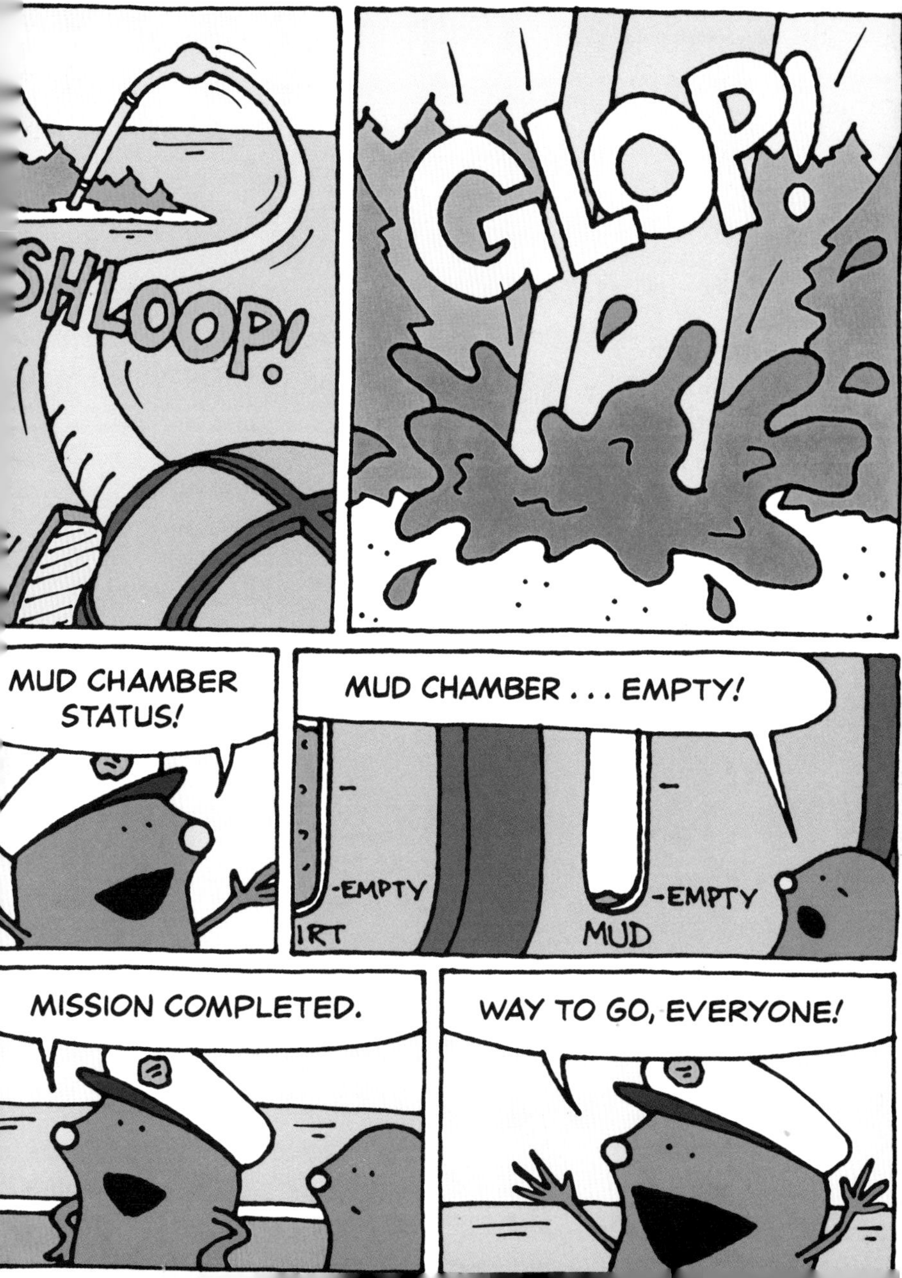
SHLOOP!
GLOP!
MUD CHAMBER STATUS!
MUD CHAMBER . . . EMPTY!
-EMPTY
IRT
-EMPTY
MUD
MISSION COMPLETED.
WAY TO GO, EVERYONE!

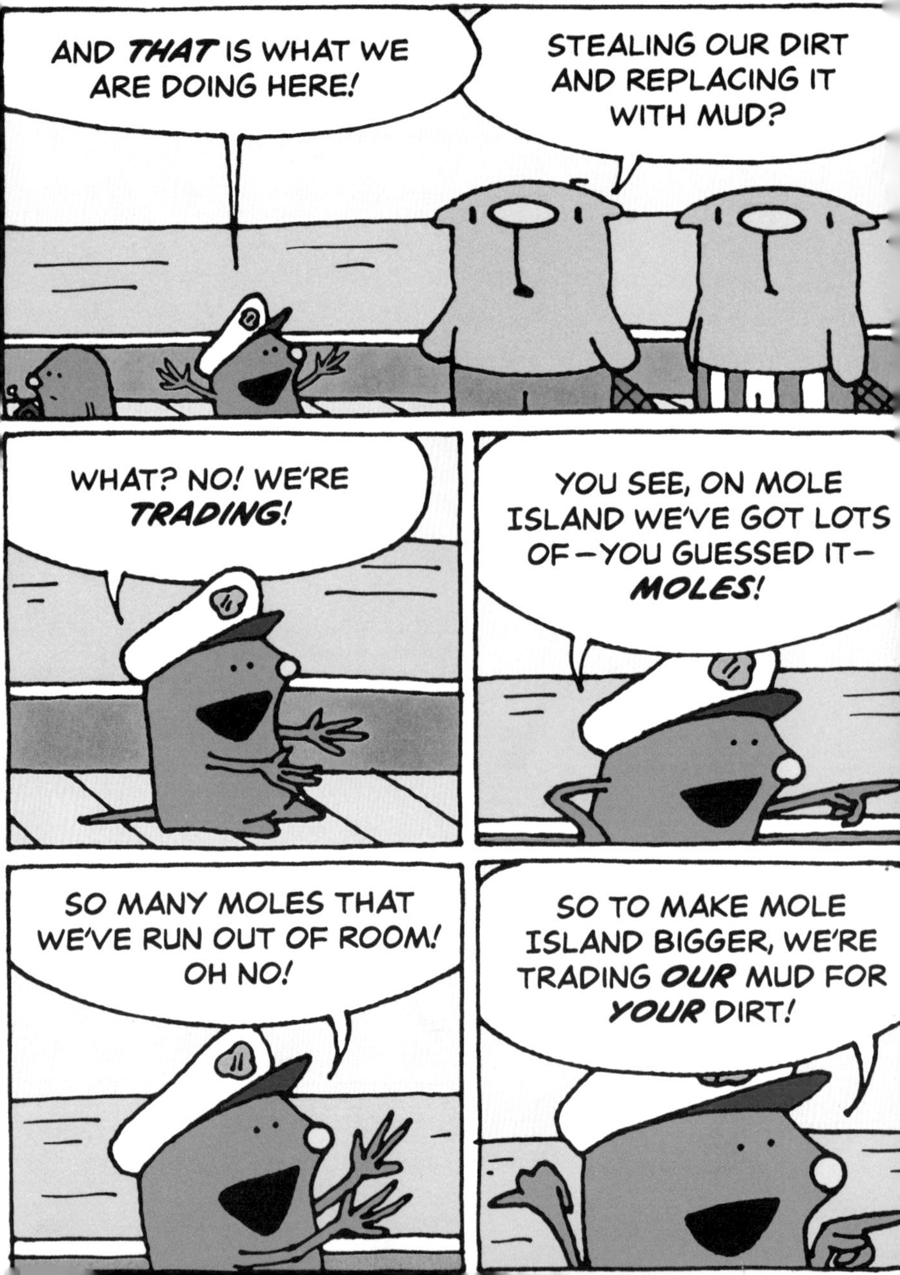
AND THAT IS WHAT WE ARE DOING HERE!
STEALING OUR DIRT AND REPLACING IT WITH MUD?
WHAT? NO! WE'RE TRADING!
YOU SEE, ON MOLE ISLAND WE'VE GOT LOTS OF—YOU GUESSED IT—MOLES!
SO MANY MOLES THAT WE'VE RUN OUT OF ROOM! OH NO!
SO TO MAKE MOLE ISLAND BIGGER, WE'RE TRADING OUR MUD FOR YOUR DIRT!

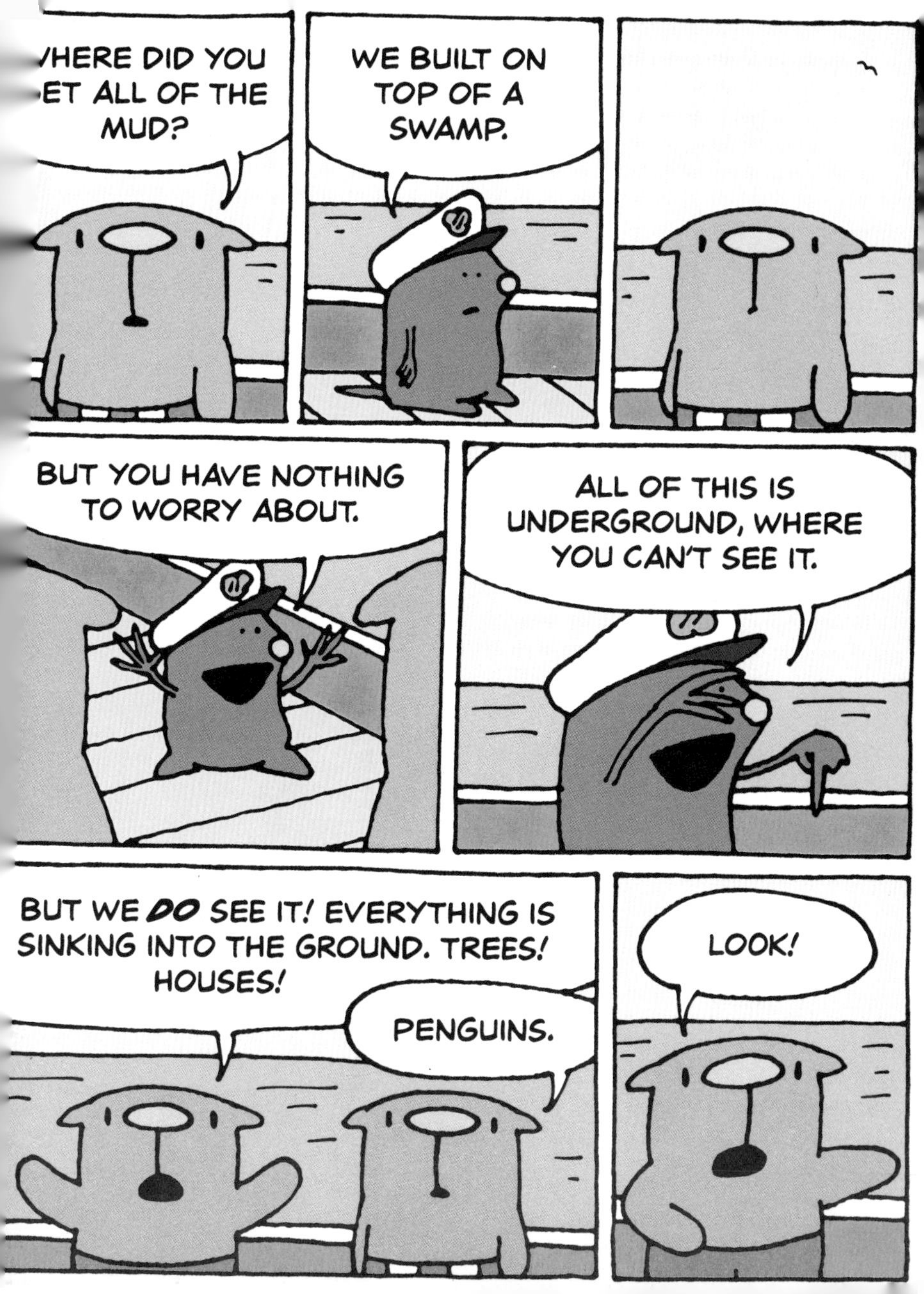
WHERE DID YOU GET ALL OF THE MUD?
WE BUILT ON TOP OF A SWAMP.
BUT YOU HAVE NOTHING TO WORRY ABOUT.
ALL OF THIS IS UNDERGROUND, WHERE YOU CAN'T SEE IT.
BUT WE *DO* SEE IT! EVERYTHING IS SINKING INTO THE GROUND. TREES! HOUSES!
PENGUINS.
LOOK!

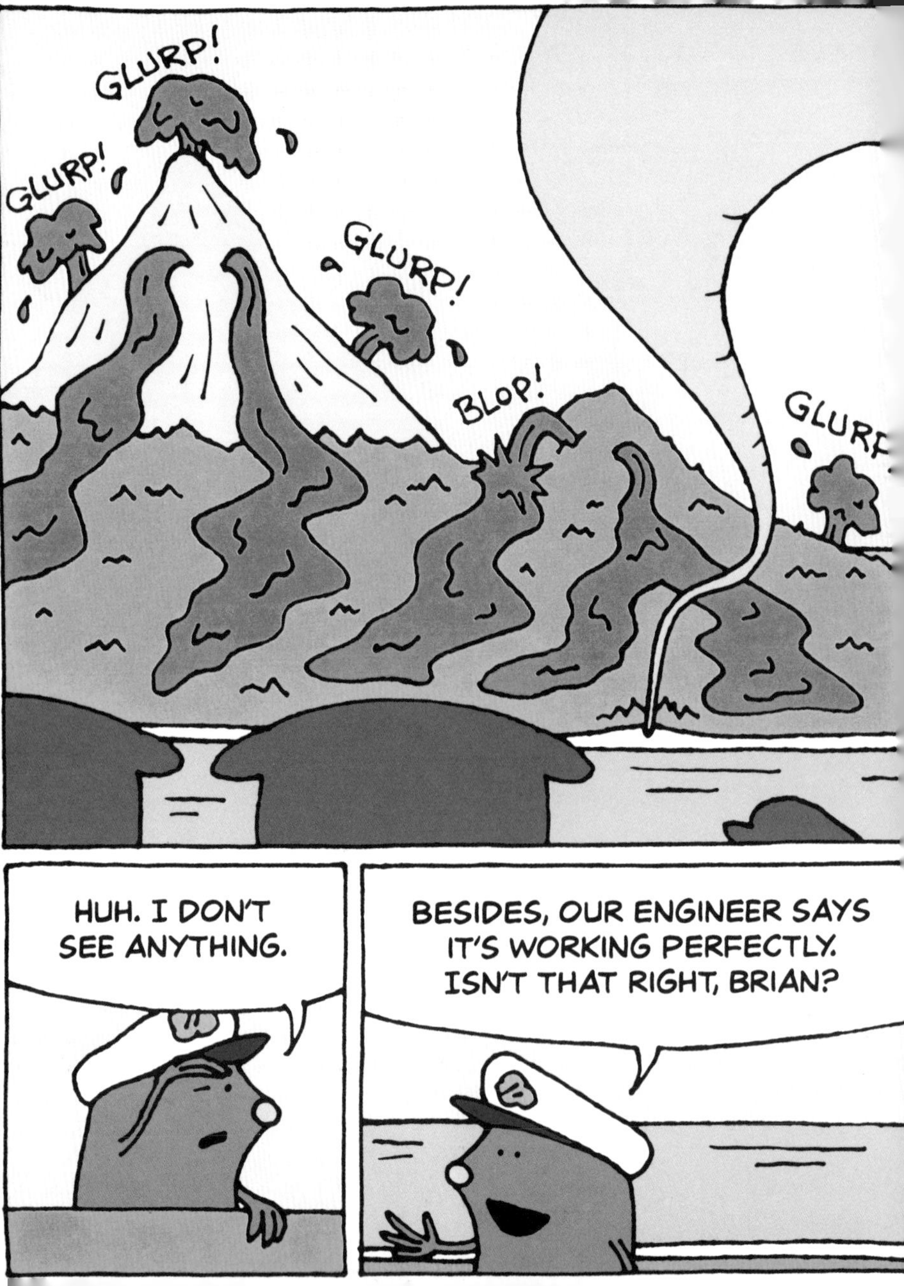
GLURP!
GLURP!
GLURP!
BLOP!
GLURP
HUH. I DON'T SEE ANYTHING.
BESIDES, OUR ENGINEER SAYS IT'S WORKING PERFECTLY. ISN'T THAT RIGHT, BRIAN?

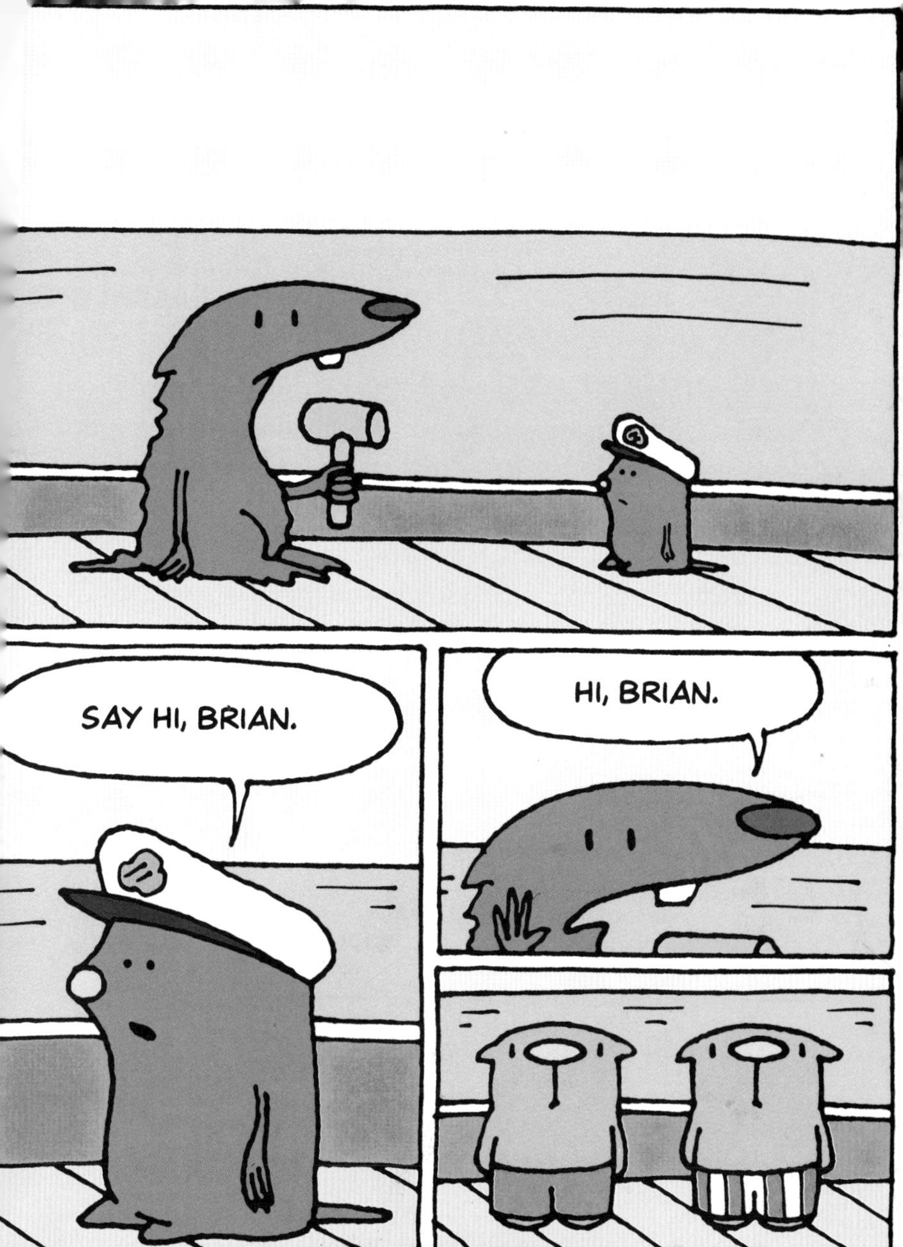
SAY HI, BRIAN.
HI, BRIAN.

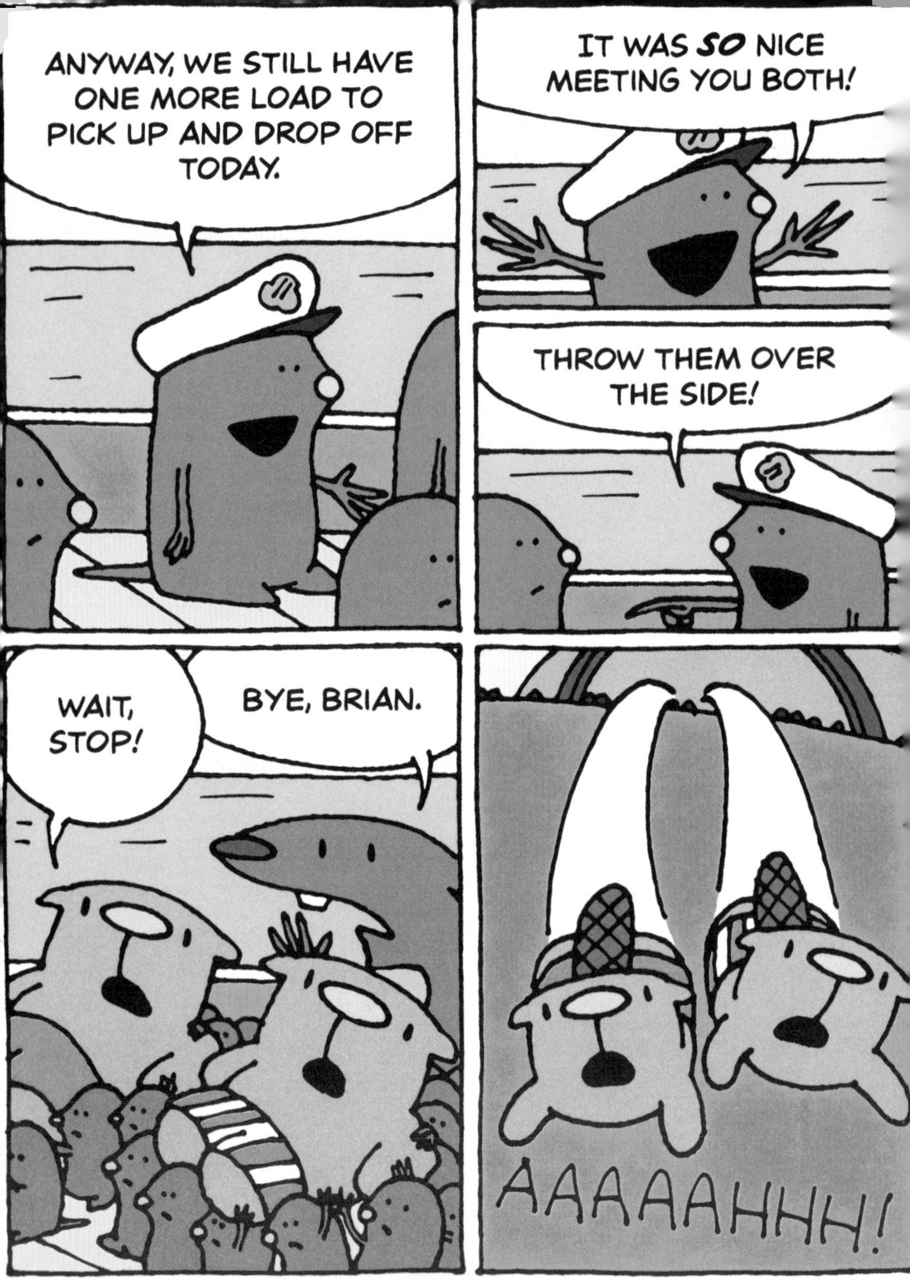
ANYWAY, WE STILL HAVE ONE MORE LOAD TO PICK UP AND DROP OFF TODAY.
IT WAS *SO* NICE MEETING YOU BOTH!
THROW THEM OVER THE SIDE!
WAIT, STOP!
BYE, BRIAN.
AAAAAHHH!

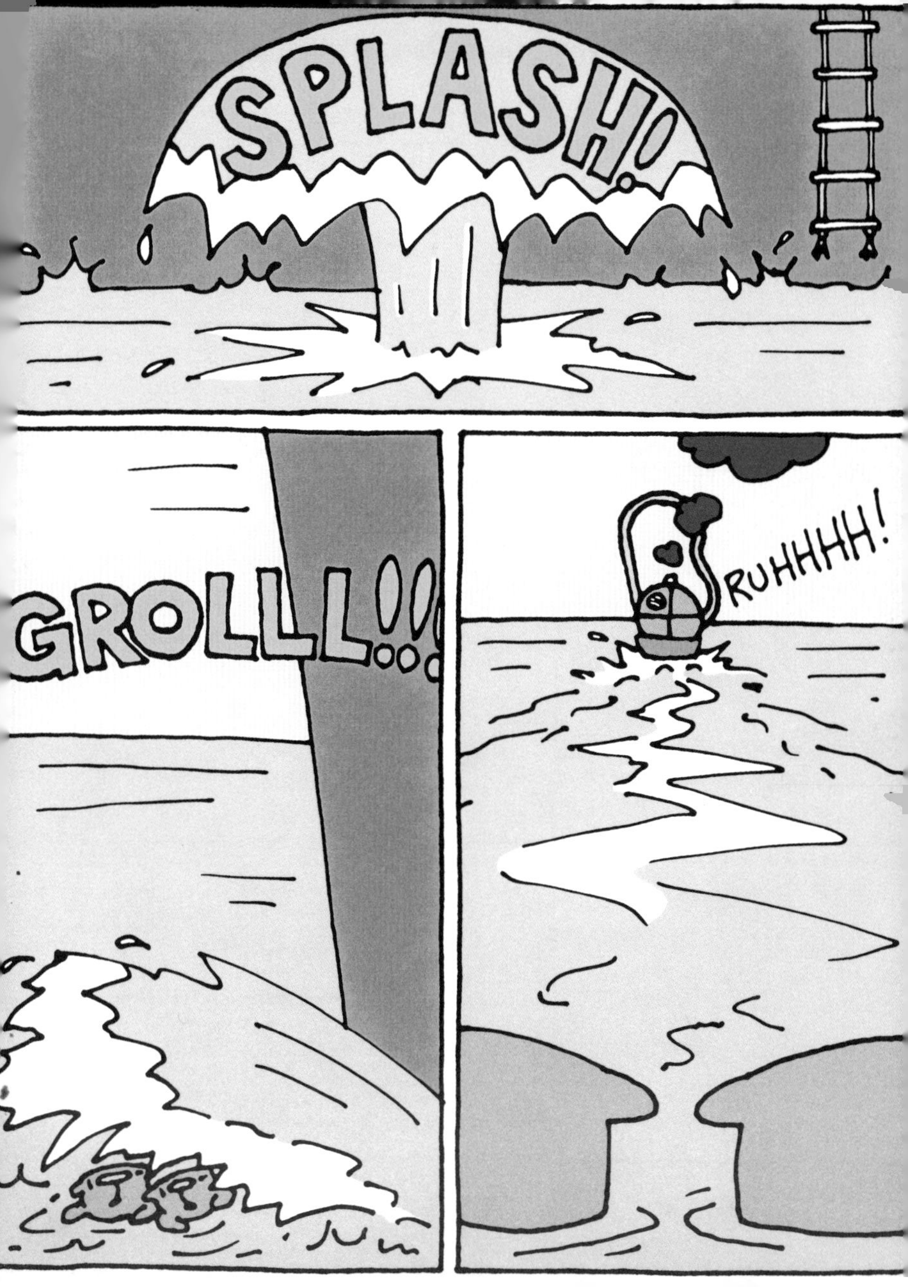
SPLASH!
GROLLL!!!
RUHHHH!

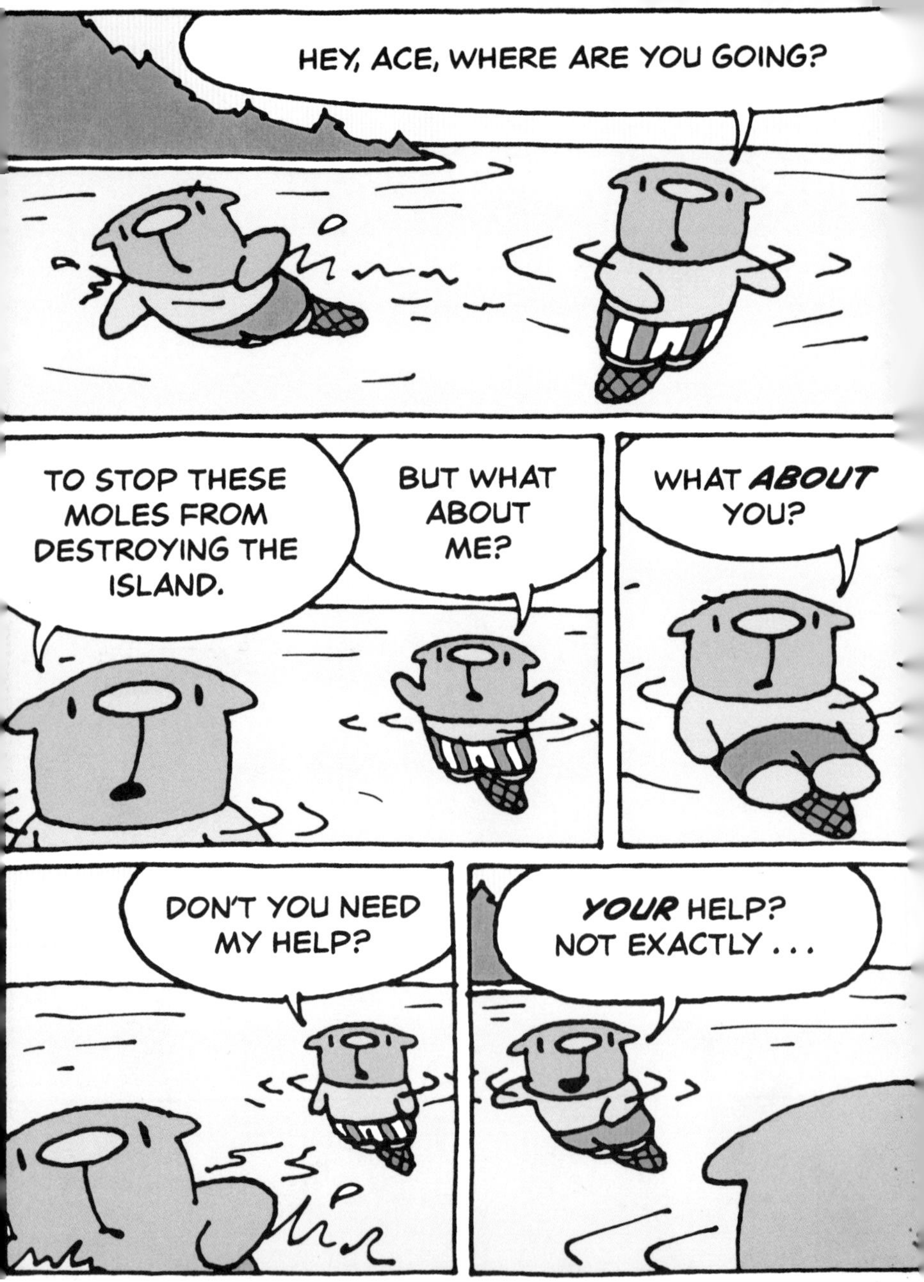
HEY, ACE, WHERE ARE YOU GOING?
TO STOP THESE MOLES FROM DESTROYING THE ISLAND.
BUT WHAT ABOUT ME?
WHAT ABOUT YOU?
DON'T YOU NEED MY HELP?
YOUR HELP? NOT EXACTLY . . .

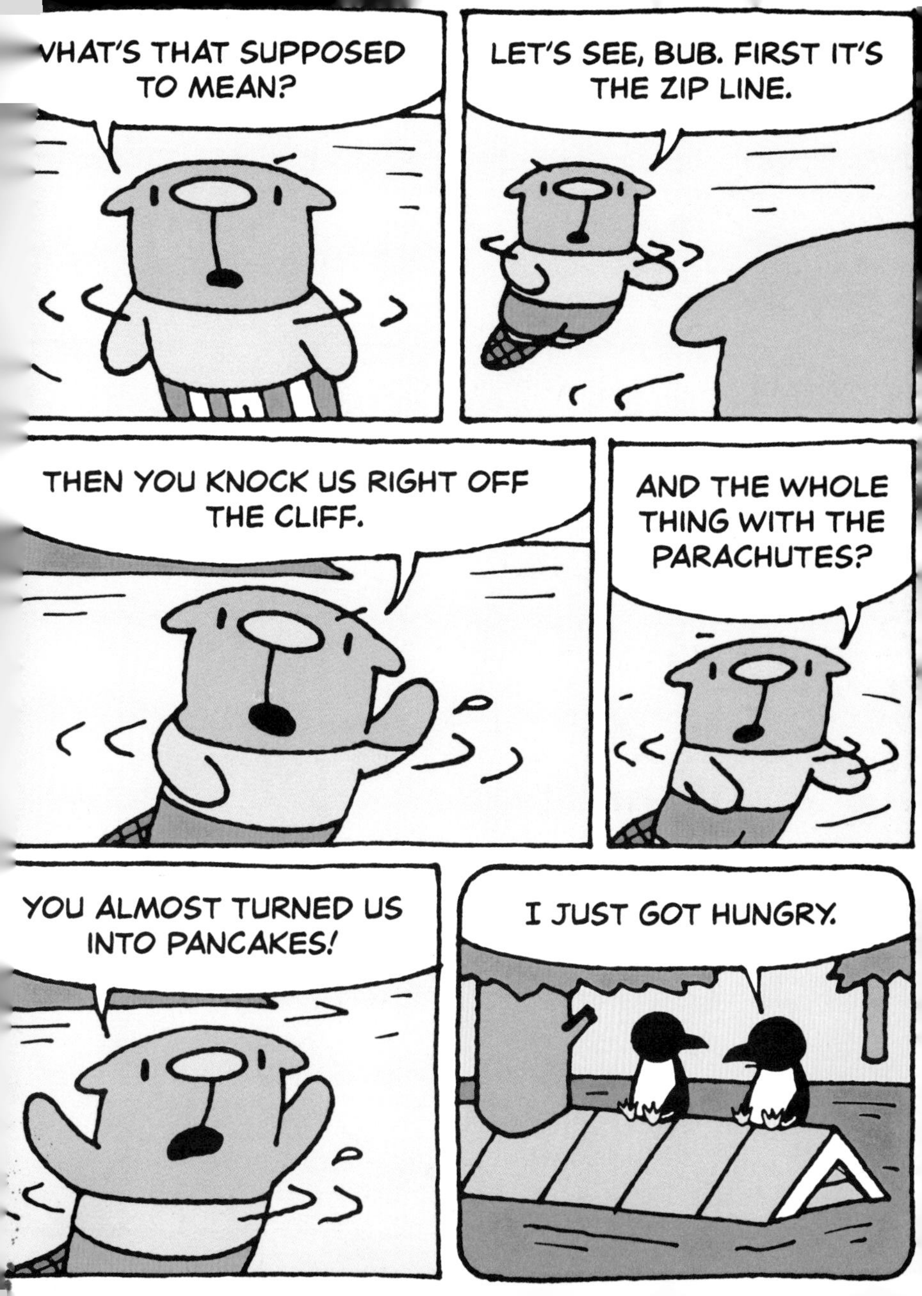
WHAT'S THAT SUPPOSED TO MEAN?
LET'S SEE, BUB. FIRST IT'S THE ZIP LINE.
THEN YOU KNOCK US RIGHT OFF THE CLIFF.
AND THE WHOLE THING WITH THE PARACHUTES?
YOU ALMOST TURNED US INTO PANCAKES!
I JUST GOT HUNGRY.

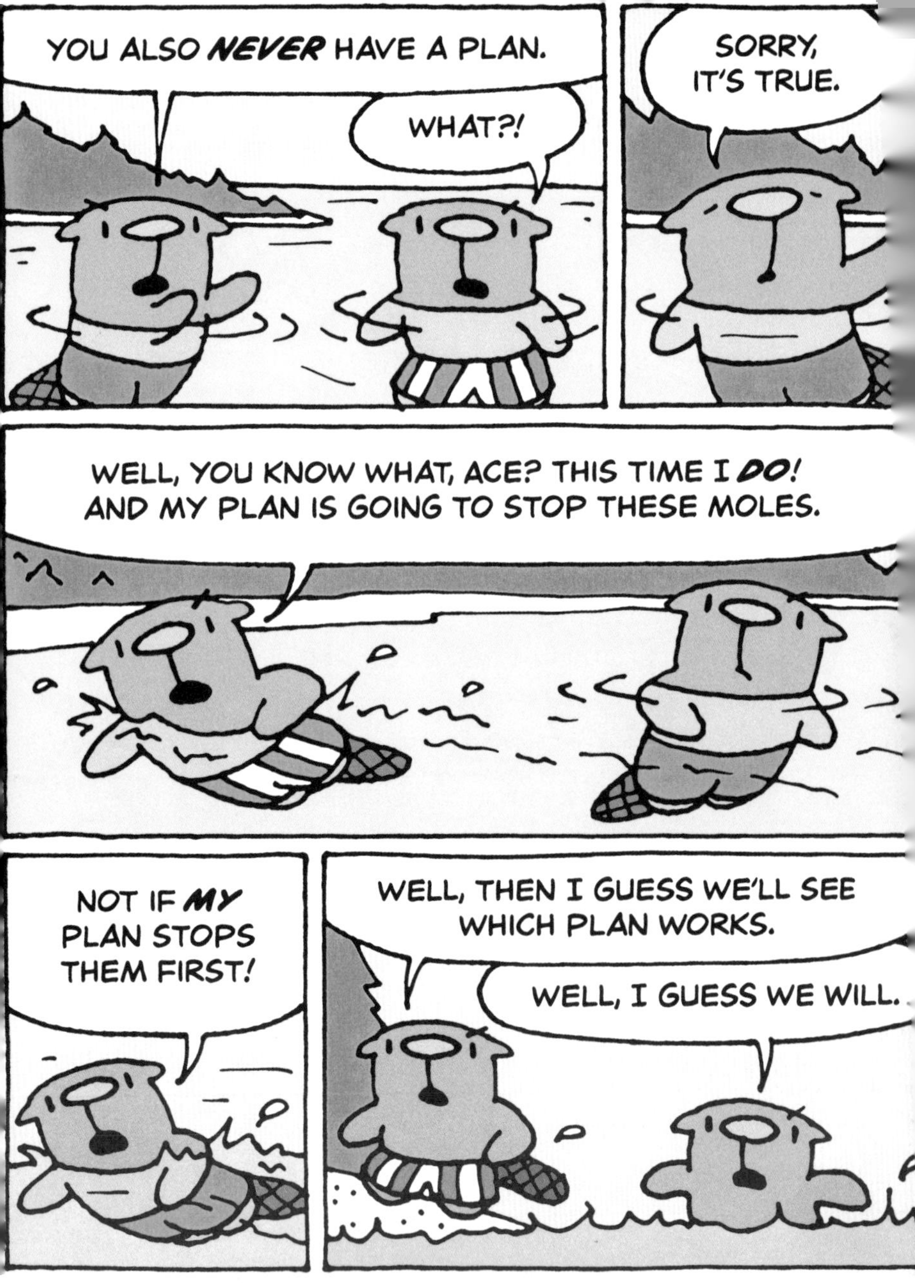
YOU ALSO NEVER HAVE A PLAN.
WHAT?!
SORRY, IT'S TRUE.
WELL, YOU KNOW WHAT, ACE? THIS TIME I DO! AND MY PLAN IS GOING TO STOP THESE MOLES.
NOT IF MY PLAN STOPS THEM FIRST!
WELL, THEN I GUESS WE'LL SEE WHICH PLAN WORKS.
WELL, I GUESS WE WILL.

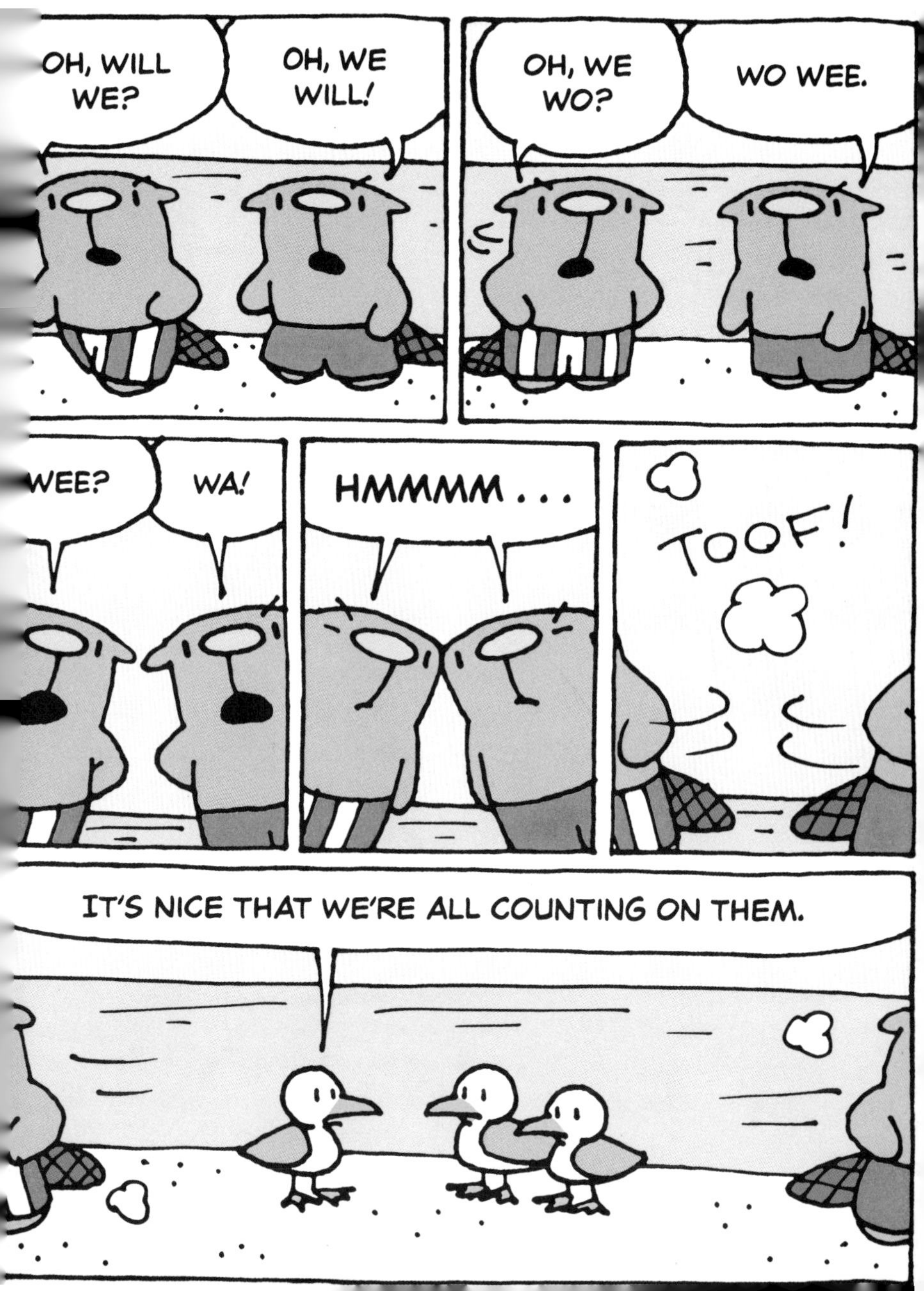
OH, WILL WE?
OH, WE WILL!
OH, WE WO?
WO WEE.
WEE?
WA!
HMMMM . . .
TOOF!
IT'S NICE THAT WE'RE ALL COUNTING ON THEM.

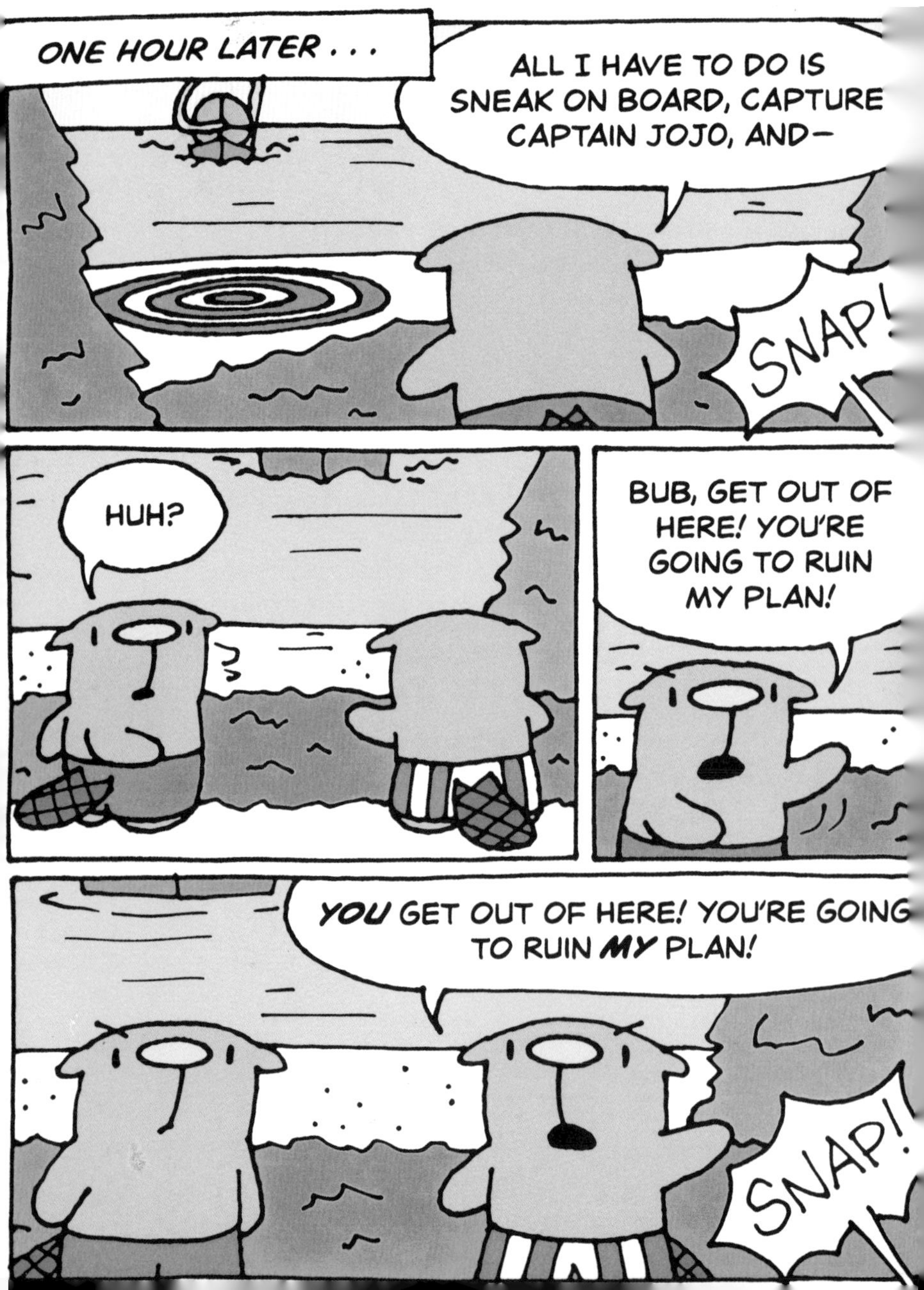
ONE HOUR LATER . . .
ALL I HAVE TO DO IS SNEAK ON BOARD, CAPTURE CAPTAIN JOJO, AND—
SNAP!
HUH?
BUB, GET OUT OF HERE! YOU'RE GOING TO RUIN MY PLAN!
YOU GET OUT OF HERE! YOU'RE GOING TO RUIN *MY* PLAN!
SNAP!

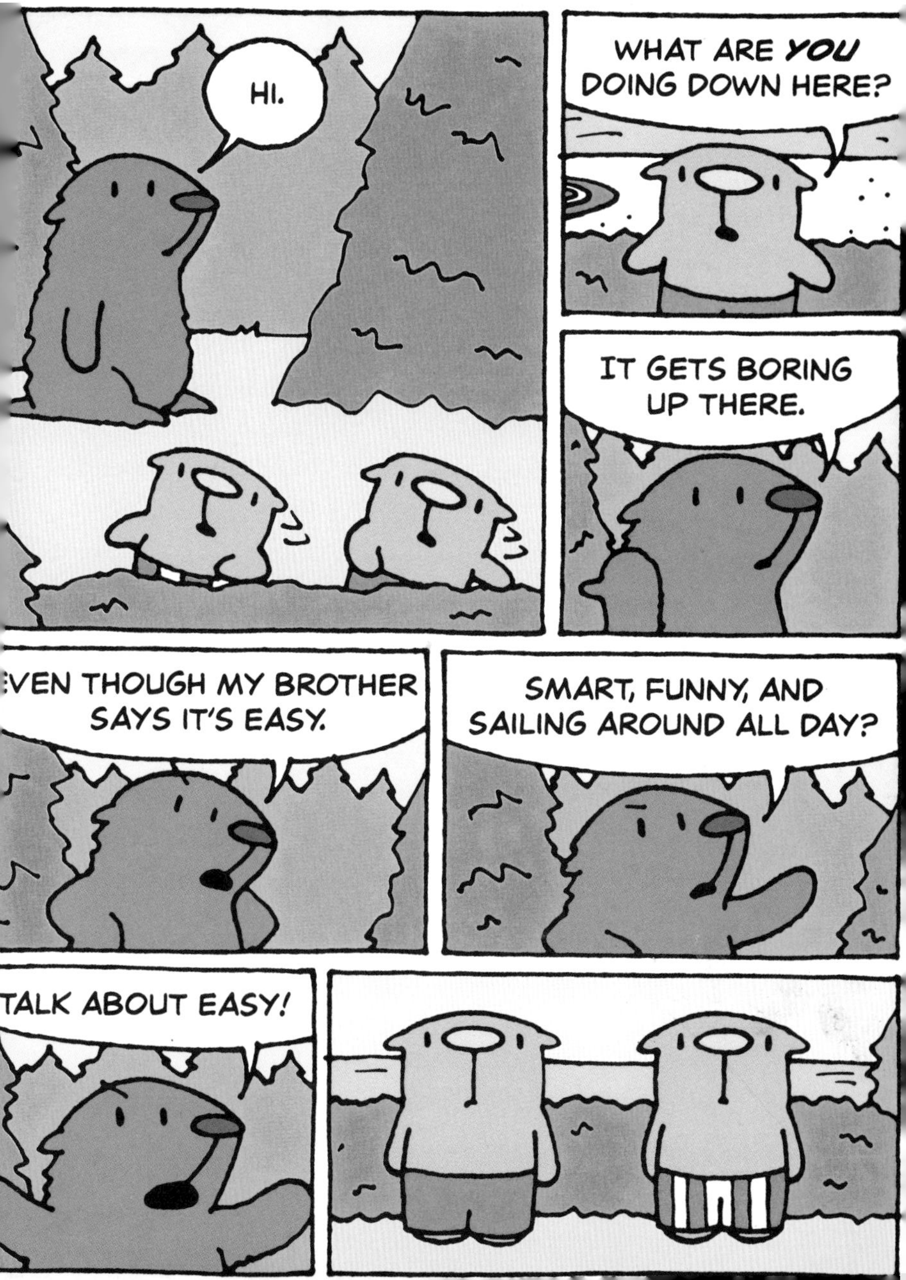
HI.
WHAT ARE *YOU* DOING DOWN HERE?
IT GETS BORING UP THERE.
EVEN THOUGH MY BROTHER SAYS IT'S EASY.
SMART, FUNNY, AND SAILING AROUND ALL DAY?
TALK ABOUT EASY!

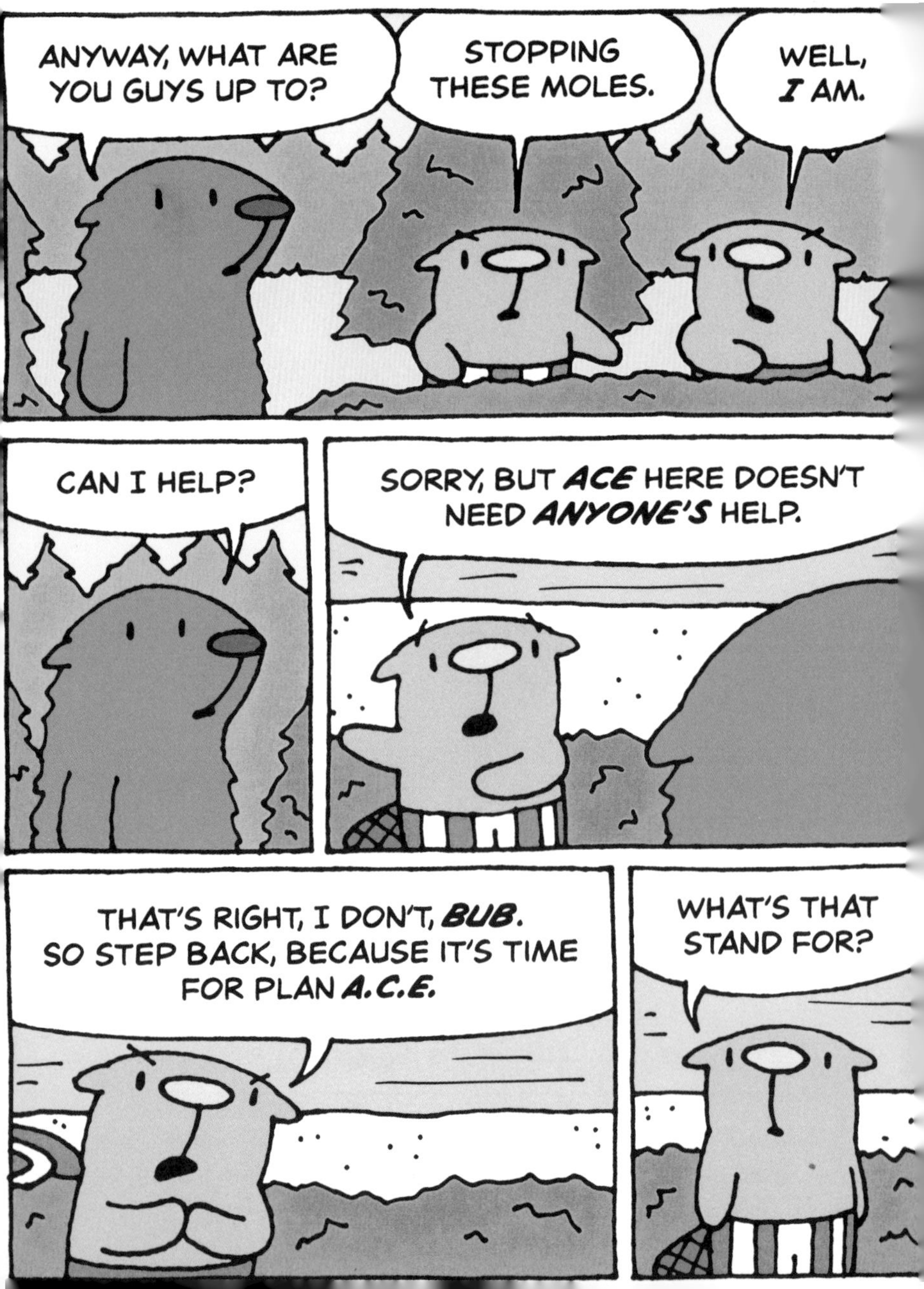
ANYWAY, WHAT ARE YOU GUYS UP TO?
STOPPING THESE MOLES.
WELL, *I* AM.
CAN I HELP?
SORRY, BUT ***ACE*** HERE DOESN'T NEED ***ANYONE'S*** HELP.
THAT'S RIGHT, I DON'T, ***BUB.*** SO STEP BACK, BECAUSE IT'S TIME FOR PLAN ***A.C.E.***
WHAT'S THAT STAND FOR?

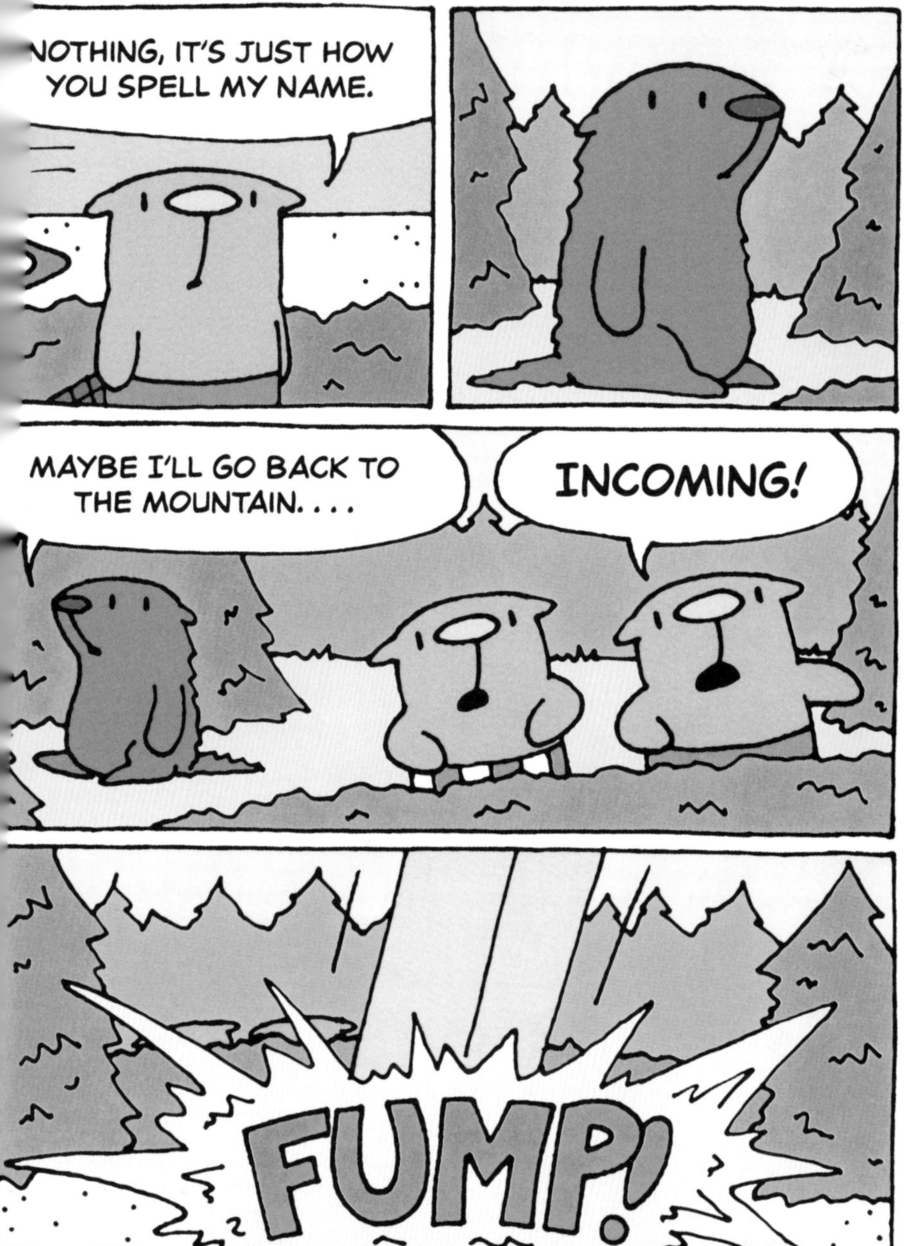
NOTHING, IT'S JUST HOW YOU SPELL MY NAME.
MAYBE I'LL GO BACK TO THE MOUNTAIN. . . .
INCOMING!
FUMP!

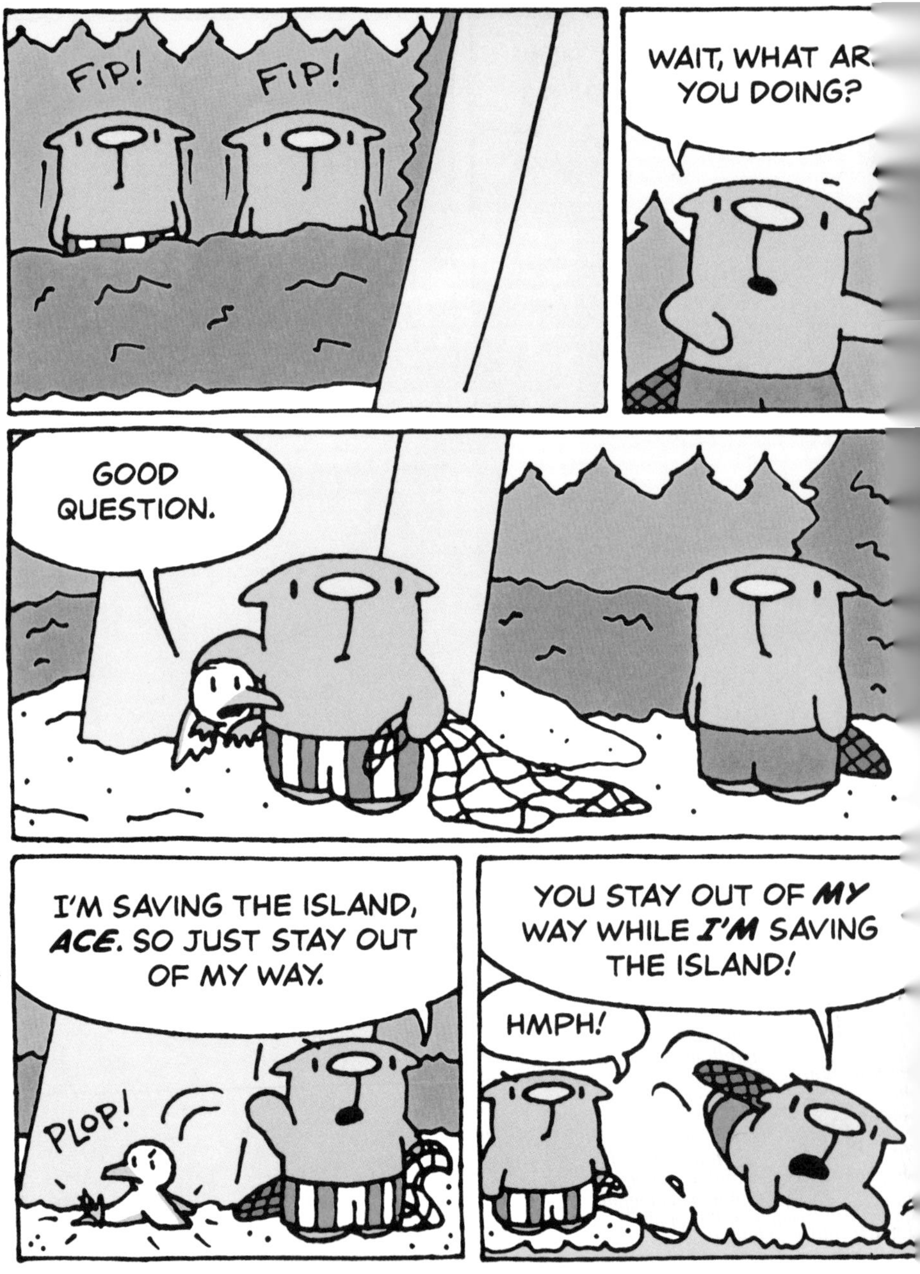
FIP!
FIP!
WAIT, WHAT AR
YOU DOING?
GOOD QUESTION.
I'M SAVING THE ISLAND, ***ACE***. SO JUST STAY OUT OF MY WAY.
PLOP!
YOU STAY OUT OF ***MY*** WAY WHILE ***I'M*** SAVING THE ISLAND!
HMPH!

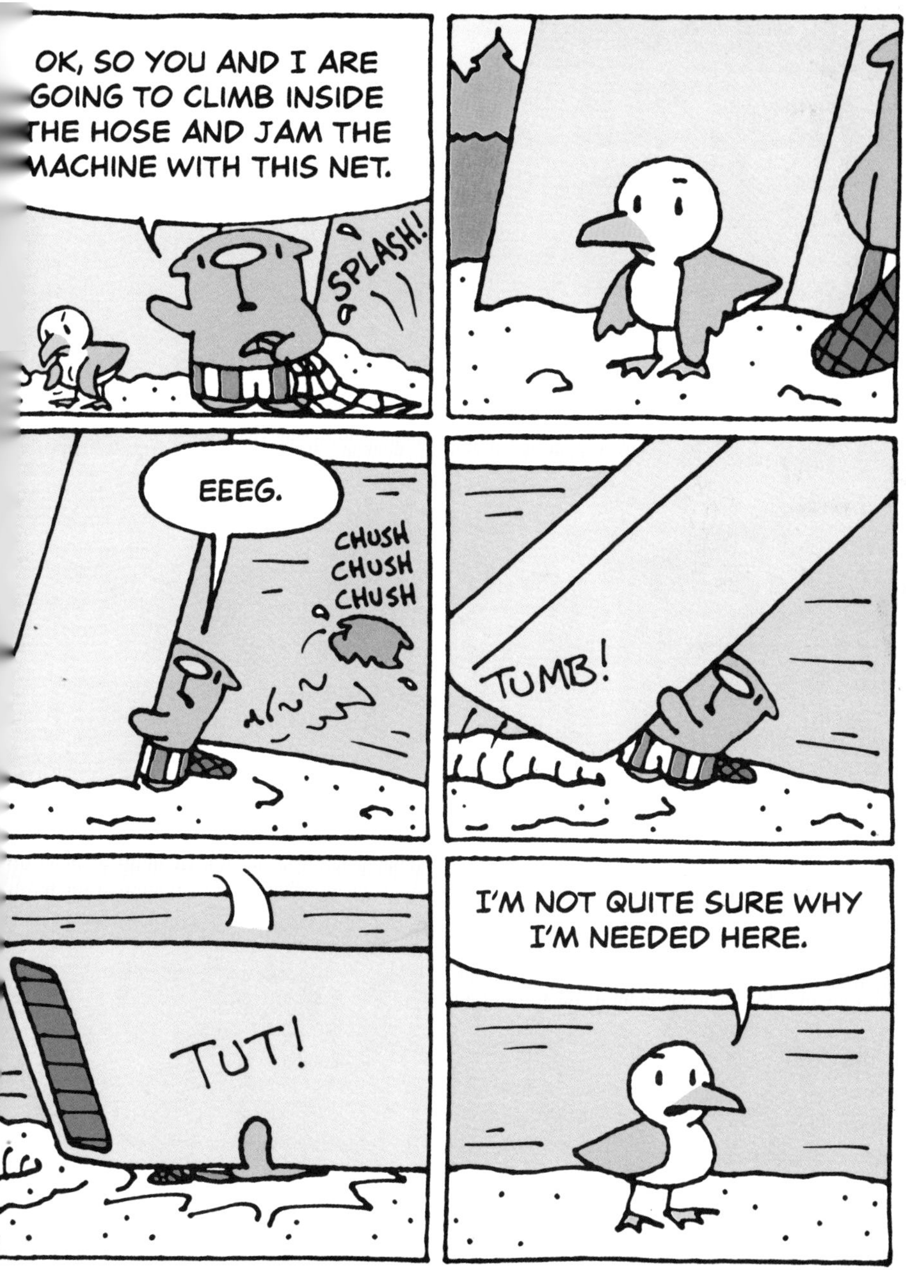
OK, SO YOU AND I ARE GOING TO CLIMB INSIDE THE HOSE AND JAM THE MACHINE WITH THIS NET.
SPLASH!
EEEG.
CHUSH CHUSH CHUSH
TUMB!
TUT!
I'M NOT QUITE SURE WHY I'M NEEDED HERE.

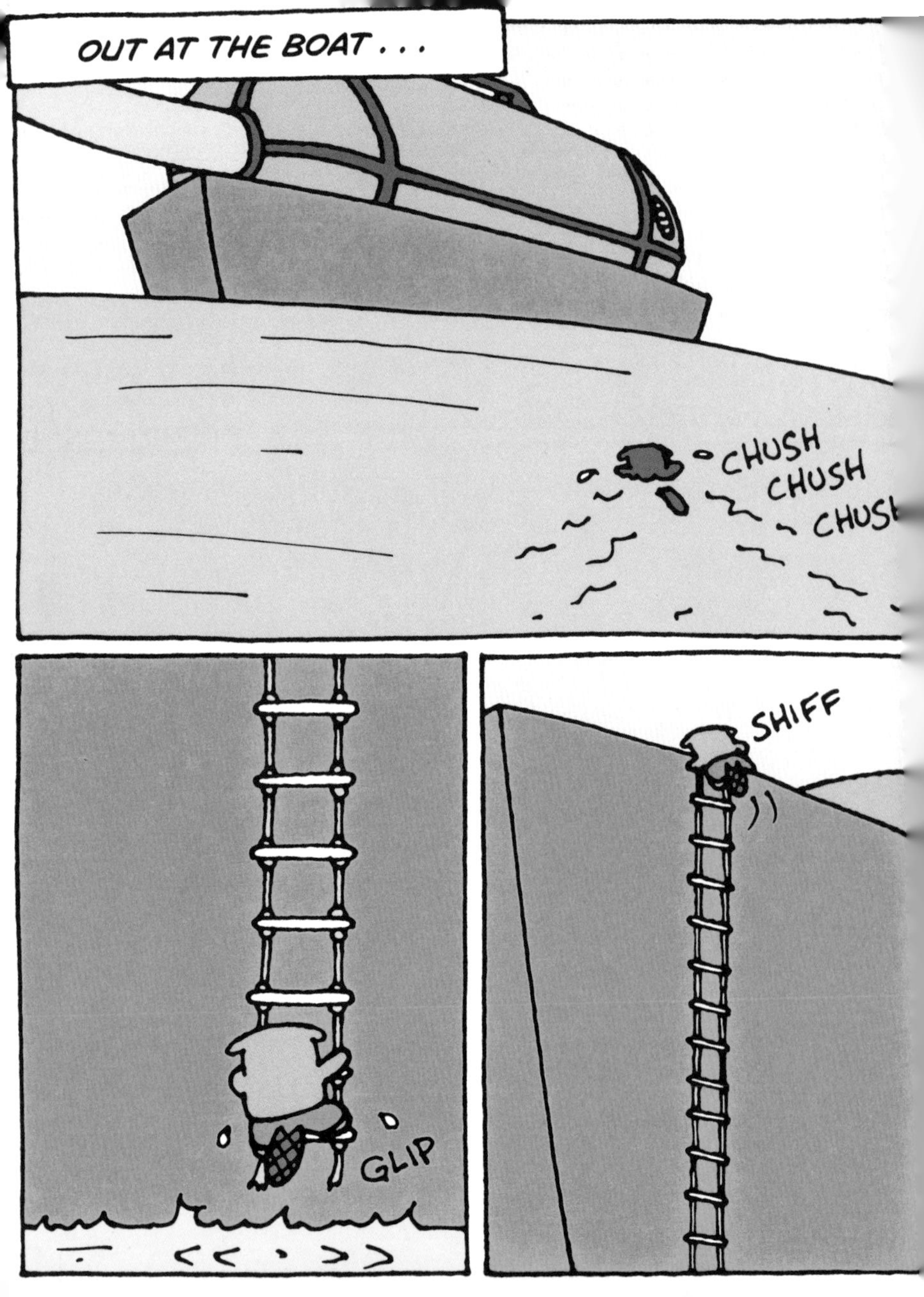
OUT AT THE BOAT . . .
CHUSH
CHUSH
CHUSH
GLIP
SHIFF

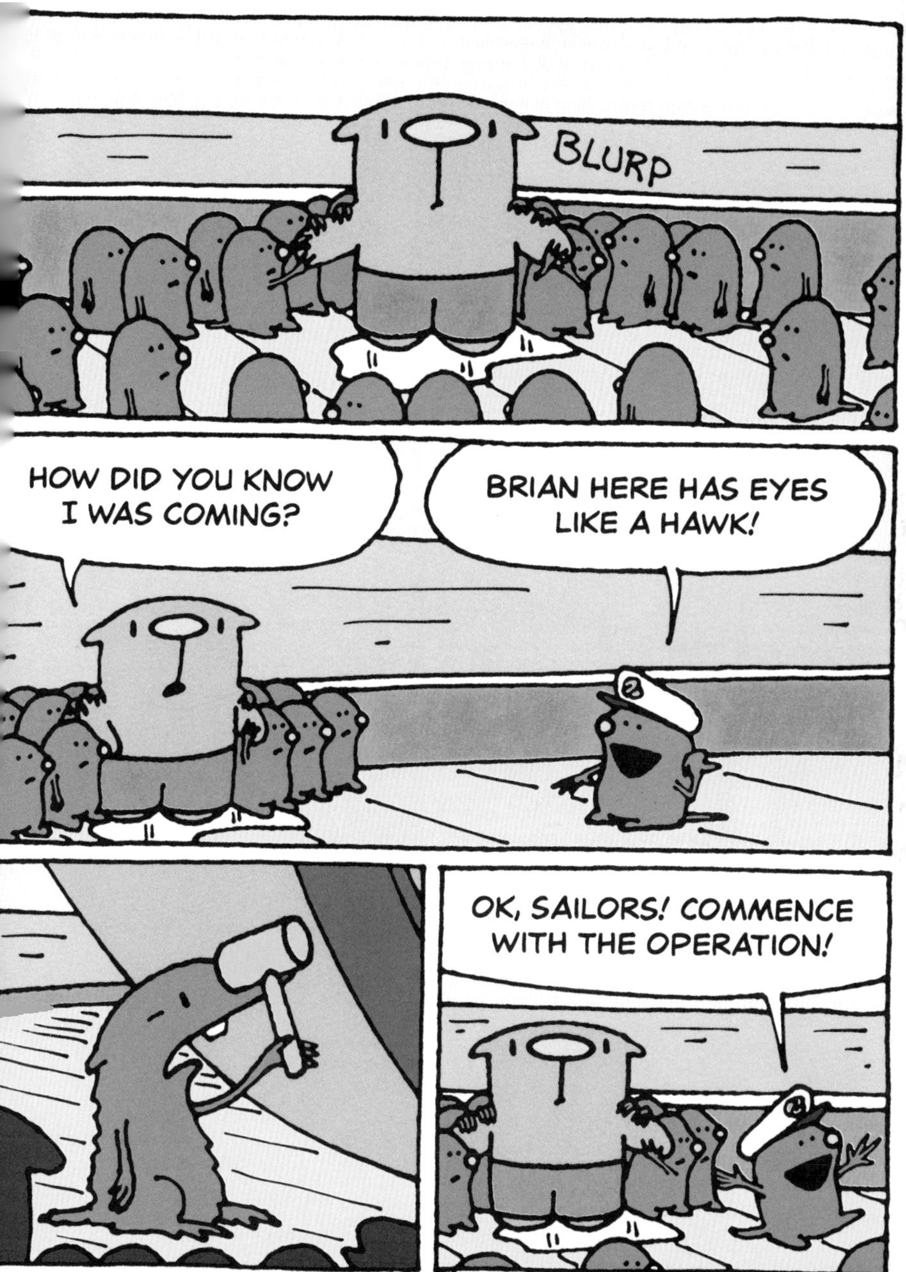
BLURP
HOW DID YOU KNOW I WAS COMING?
BRIAN HERE HAS EYES LIKE A HAWK!
OK, SAILORS! COMMENCE WITH THE OPERATION!

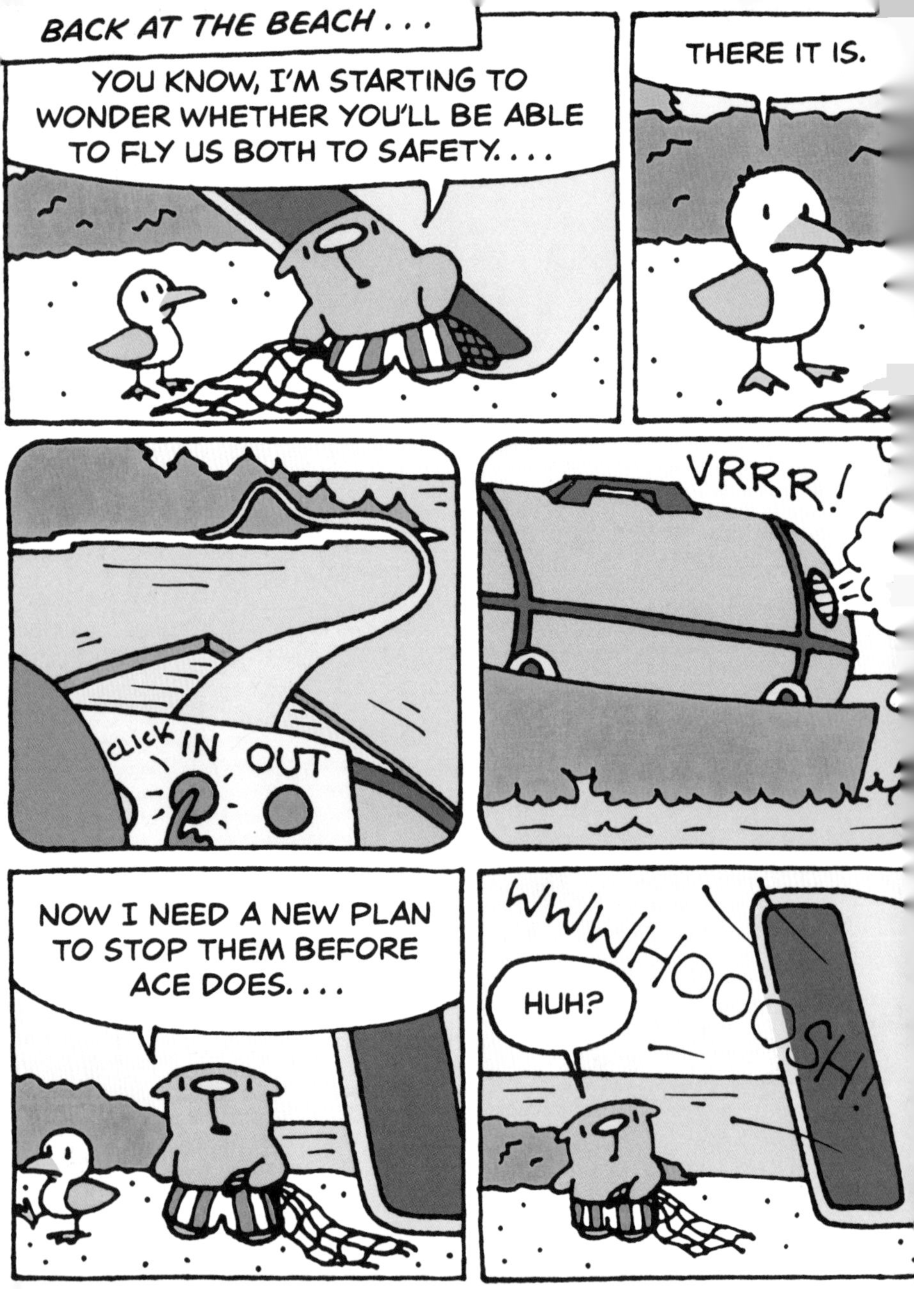

BACK AT THE BEACH . . .
YOU KNOW, I'M STARTING TO WONDER WHETHER YOU'LL BE ABLE TO FLY US BOTH TO SAFETY. . . .
THERE IT IS.
CLICK
IN
OUT
VRRRR!
NOW I NEED A NEW PLAN TO STOP THEM BEFORE ACE DOES. . . .
WWWHOOOOSH!
HUH?

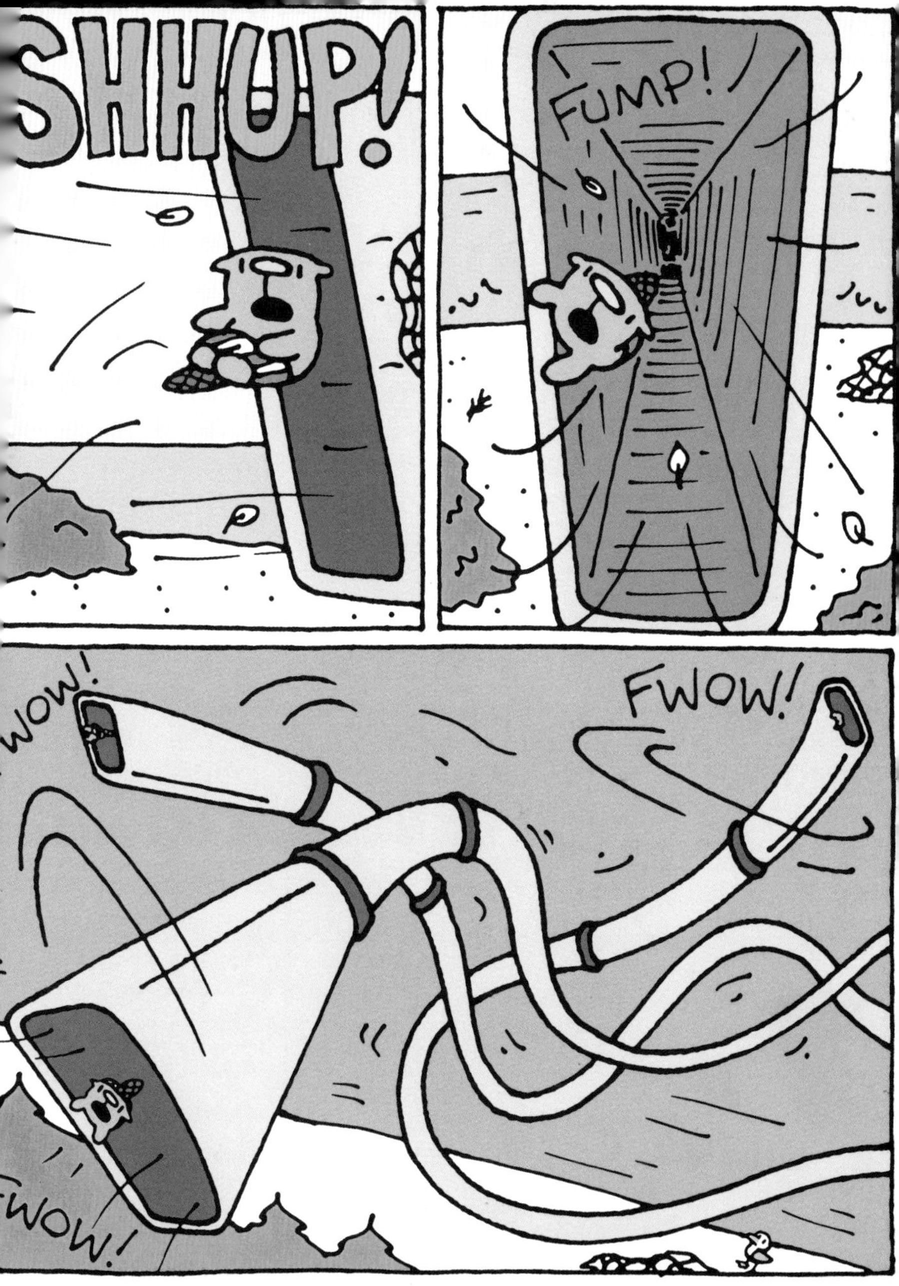
SHHUP!
FUMP!
WOW!
FWOW!
FWOW!

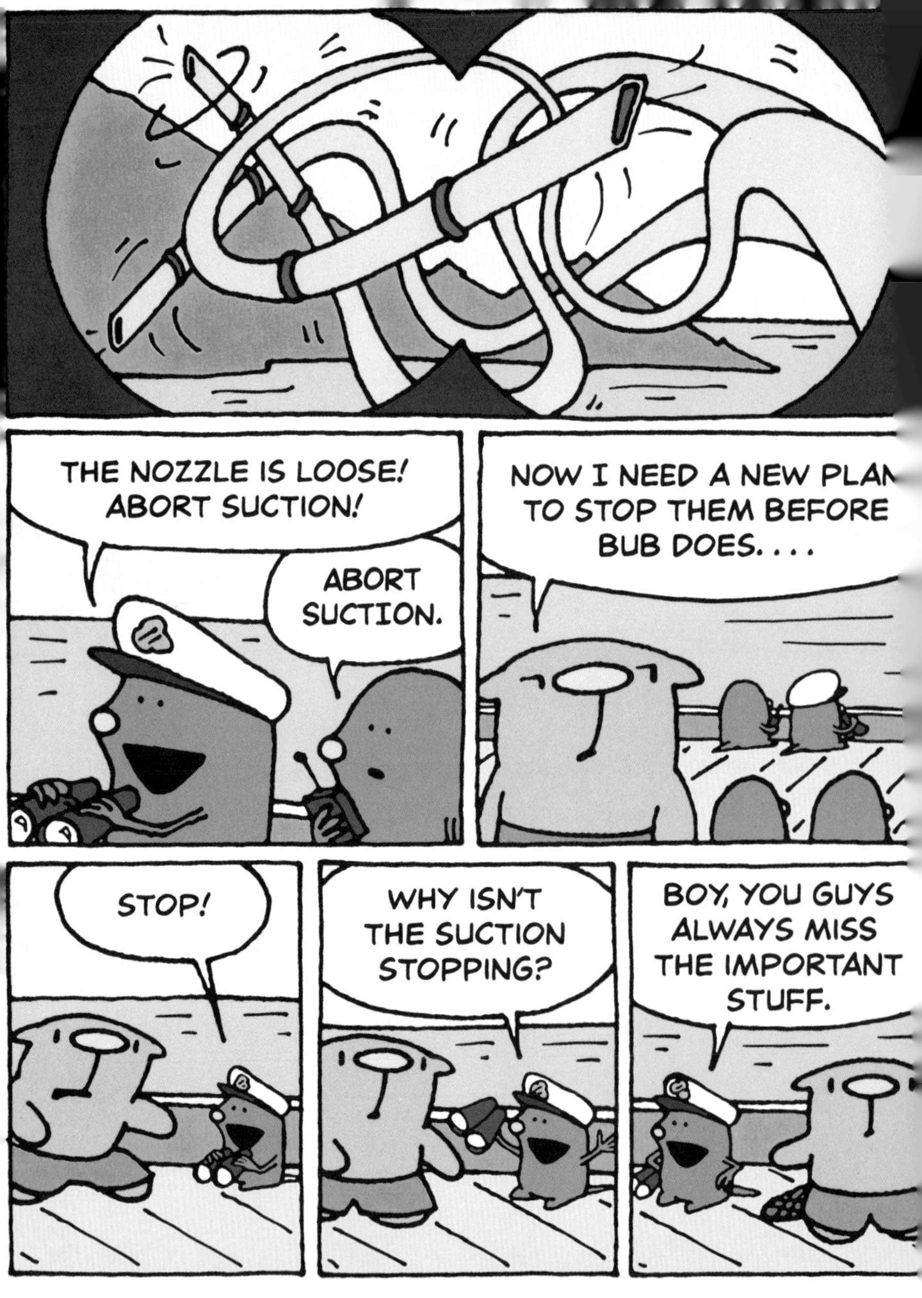
THE NOZZLE IS LOOSE! ABORT SUCTION!
ABORT SUCTION.
NOW I NEED A NEW PLAN TO STOP THEM BEFORE BUB DOES. . . .
STOP!
WHY ISN'T THE SUCTION STOPPING?
BOY, YOU GUYS ALWAYS MISS THE IMPORTANT STUFF.

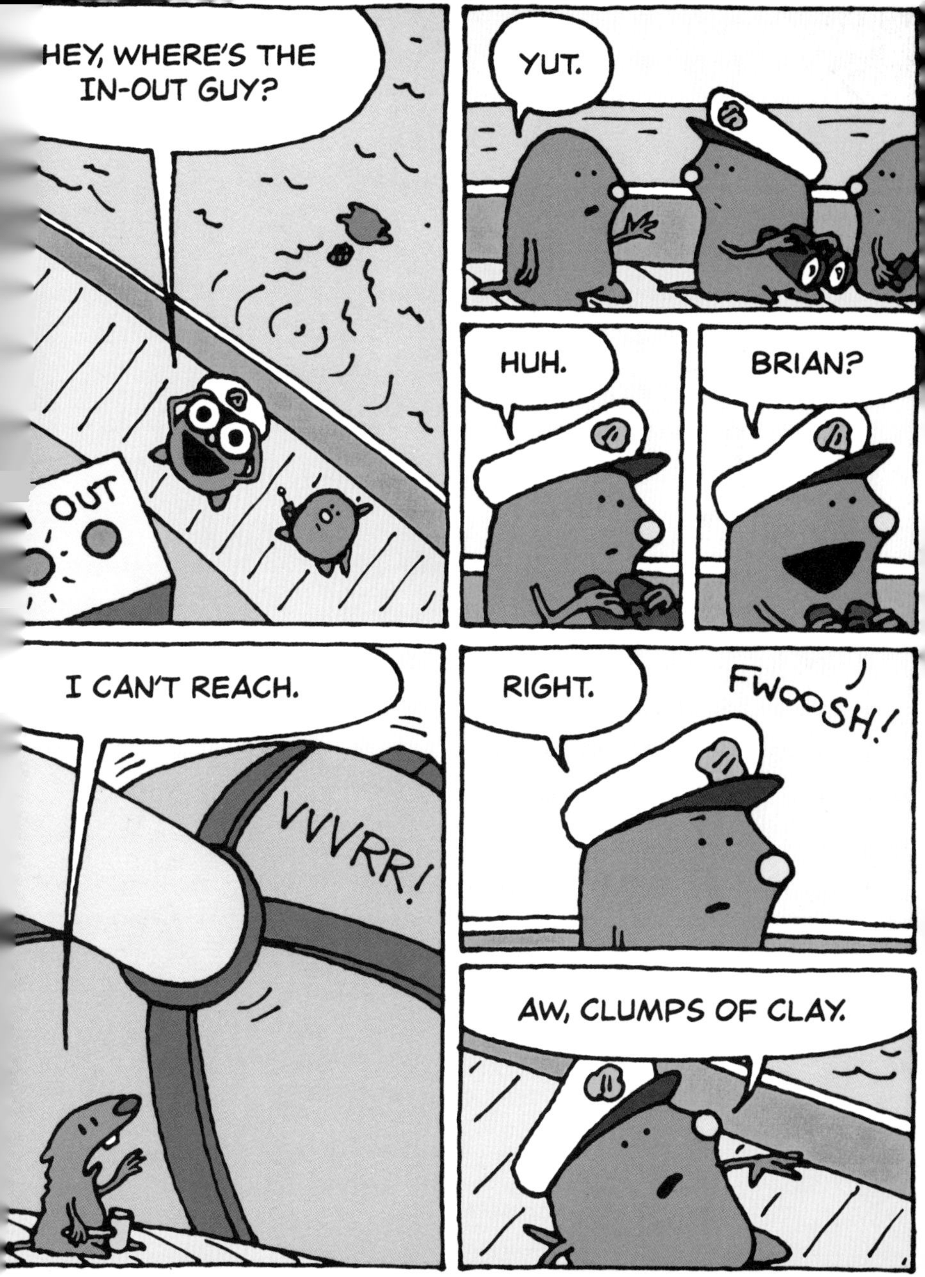

HEY, WHERE'S THE IN-OUT GUY?
OUT
YUT.
HUH.
BRIAN?
I CAN'T REACH.
VVVRR!
RIGHT.
FWOOSH!
AW, CLUMPS OF CLAY.

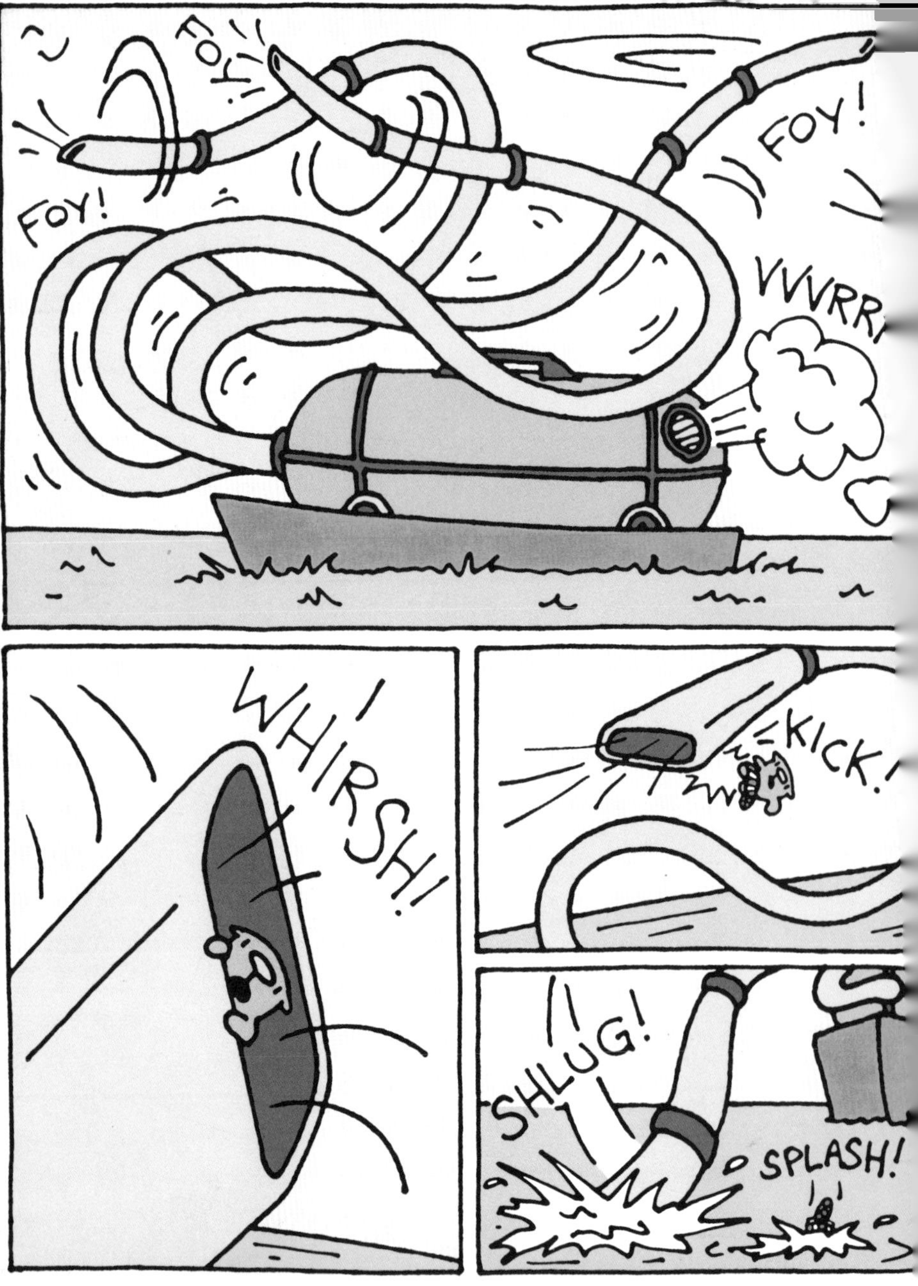
FOY!
FOY!
FOY!
VVVRRR
WHIRSH!
KICK!
SHLUG!
SPLASH!

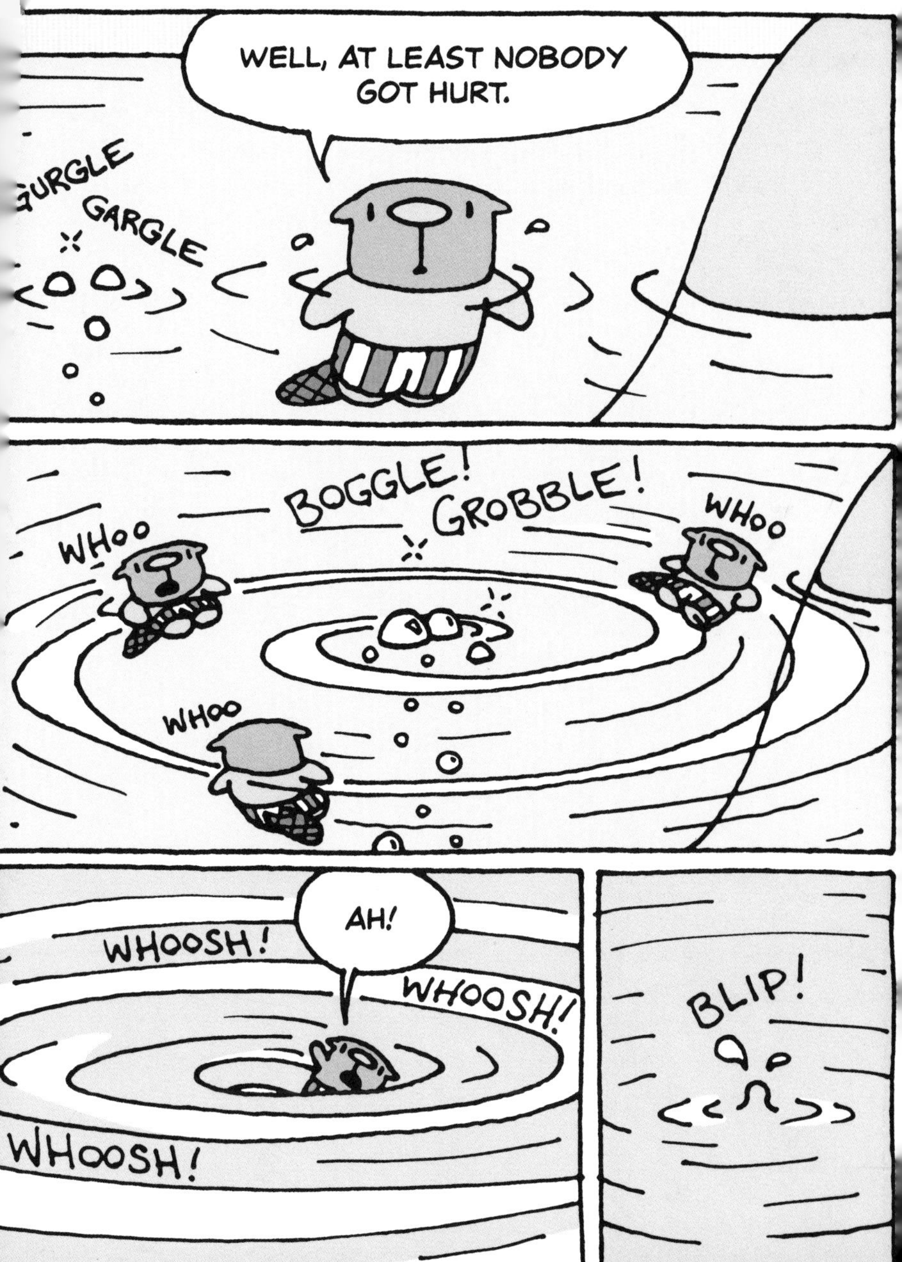
WELL, AT LEAST NOBODY GOT HURT.
GURGLE
GARGLE
BOGGLE!
GROBBLE!
WHOO
WHOO
WHOO
WHOOSH!
AH!
WHOOSH!
WHOOSH!
BLIP!

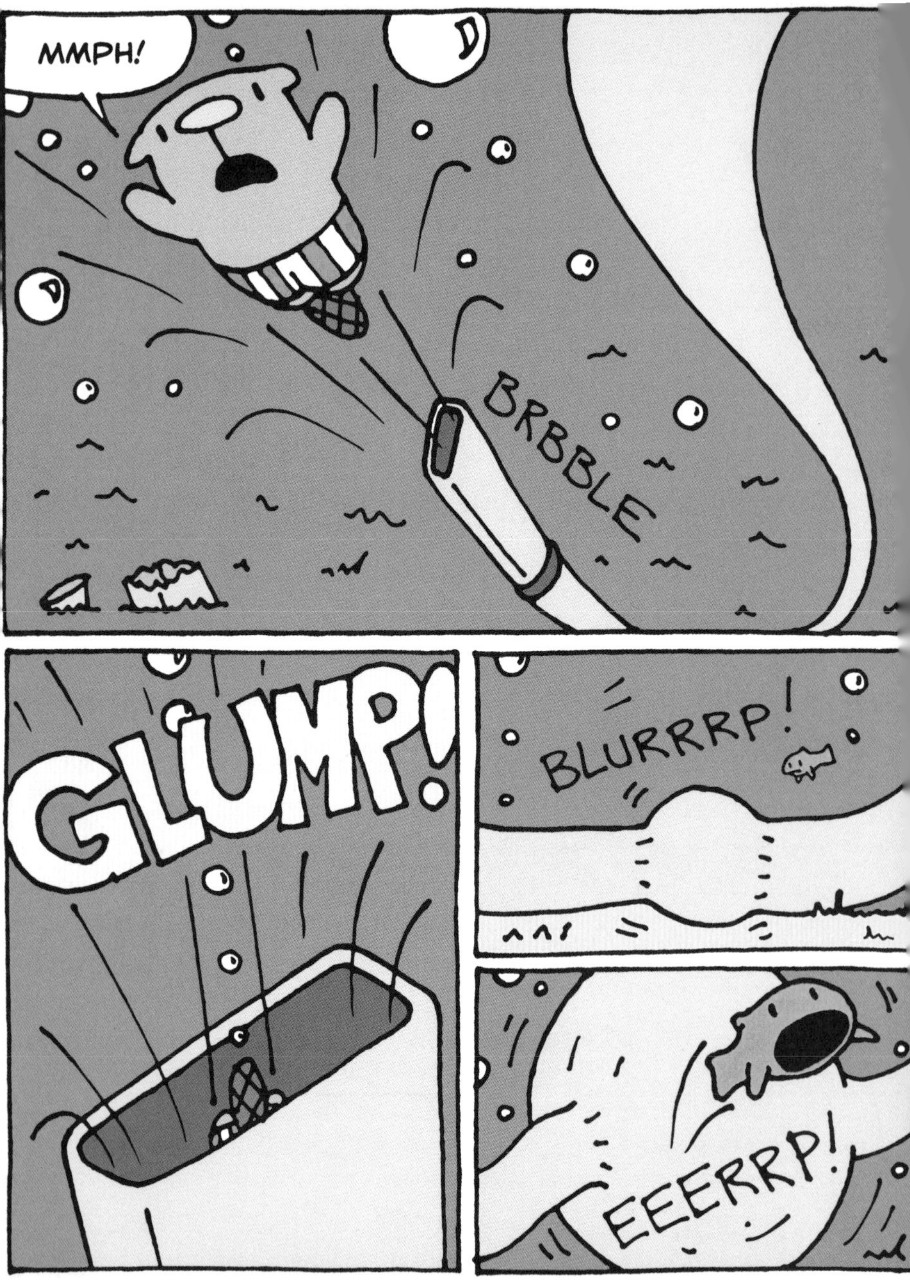
MMPH!
BRBBLE
GLUMP!
BLURRRP!
EEERRP!

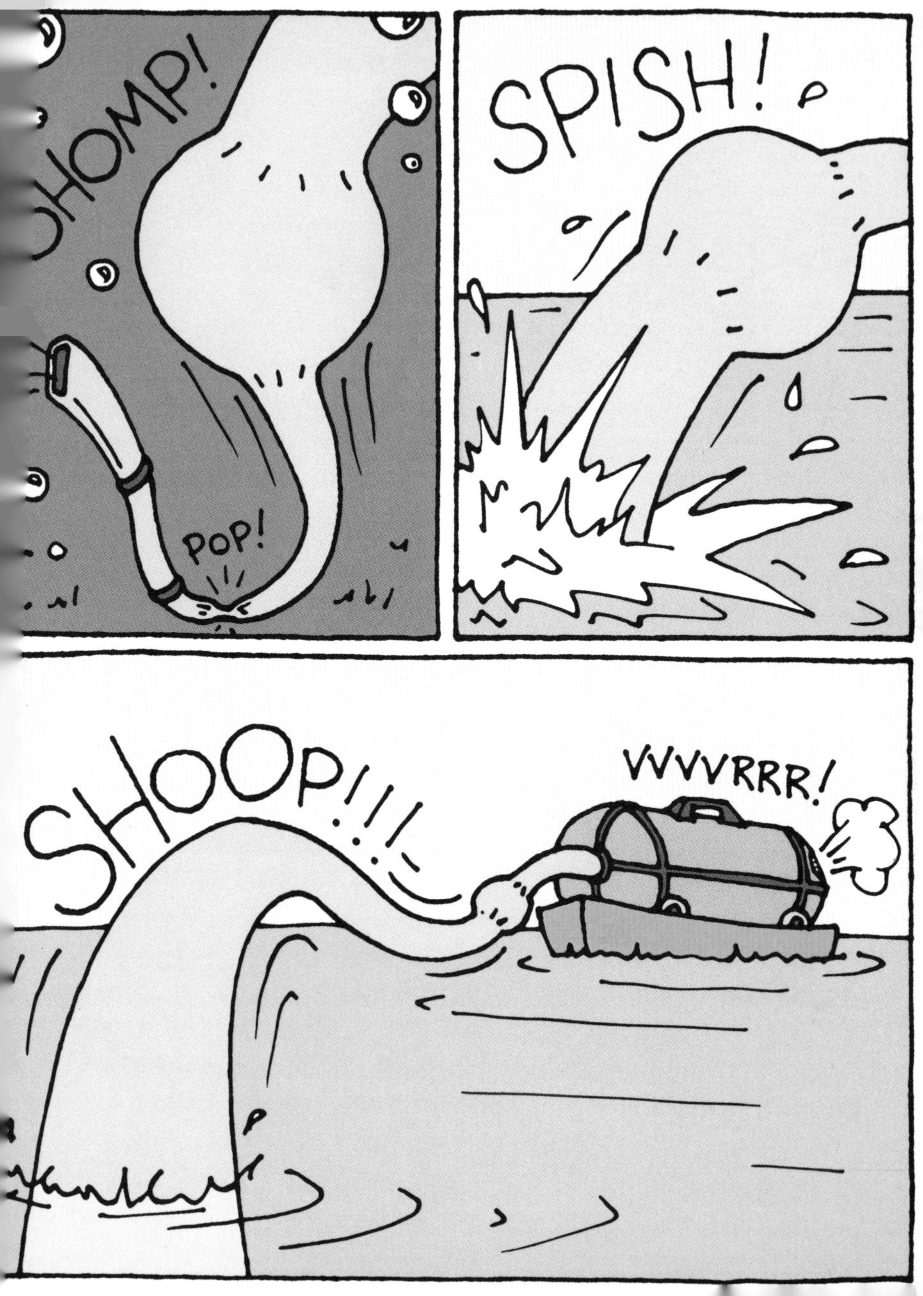

CHOMP!
POP!
SPISH!
SHOOP!!!!
VVVVRRR!

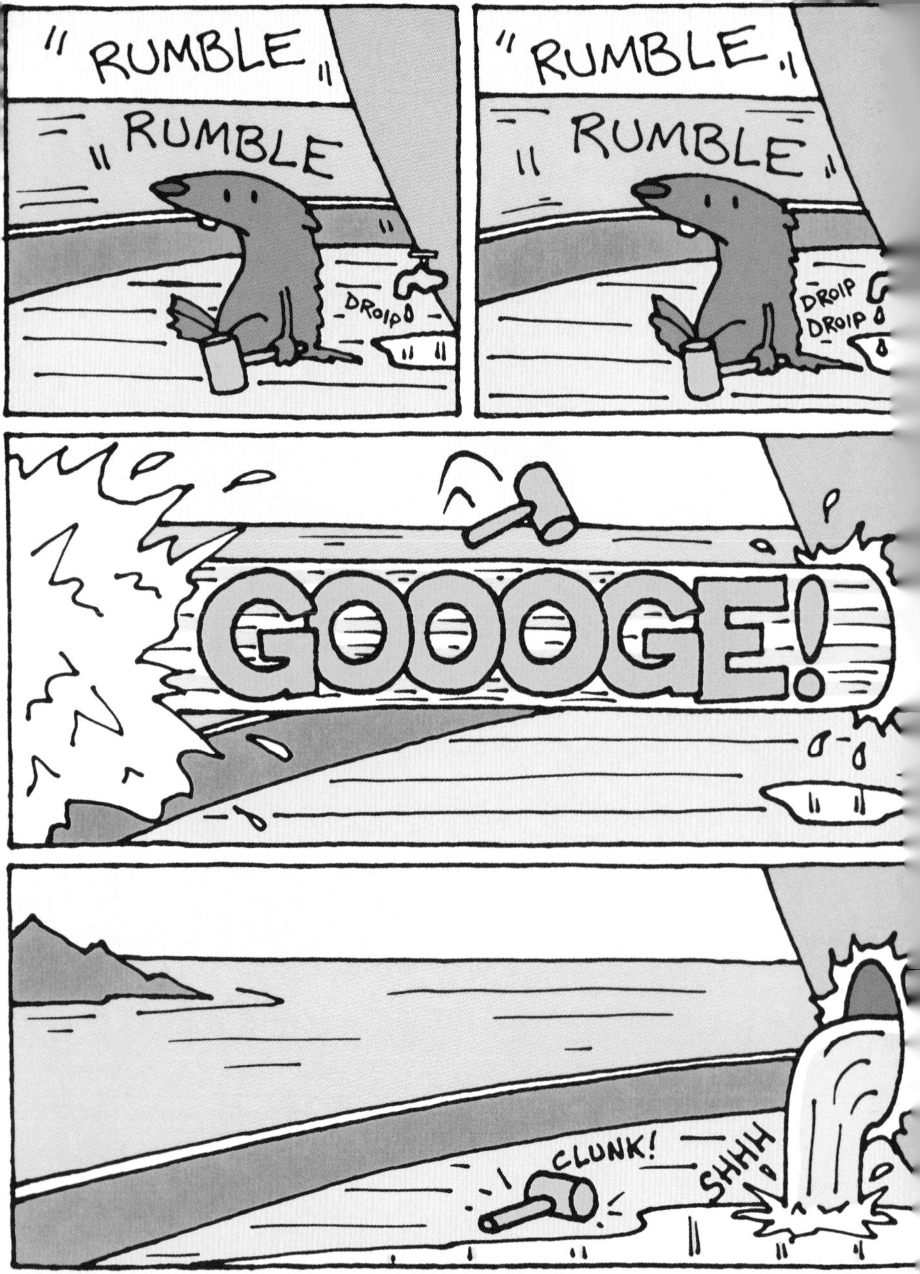
"RUMBLE"
"RUMBLE"
DROIP
"RUMBLE"
"RUMBLE"
DROIP
DROIP
GOOOGE!
CLUNK!
SHHH

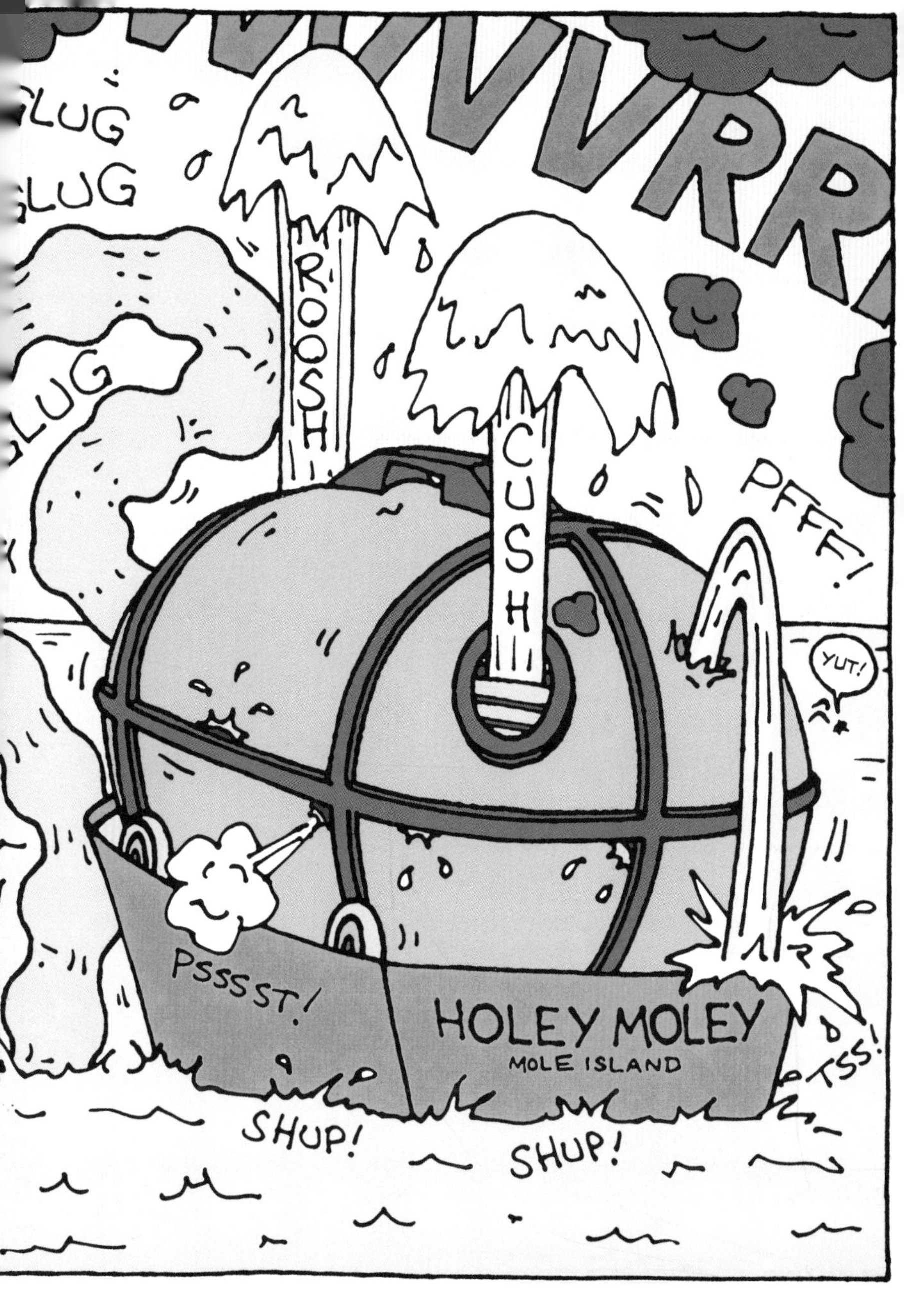
VVVRR
GLUG
GLUG
GLUG
ROOSH
CUSH
PFFFF!
YUT!
PSSSST!
HOLEY MOLEY
MOLE ISLAND
TSS!
SHUP!
SHUP!

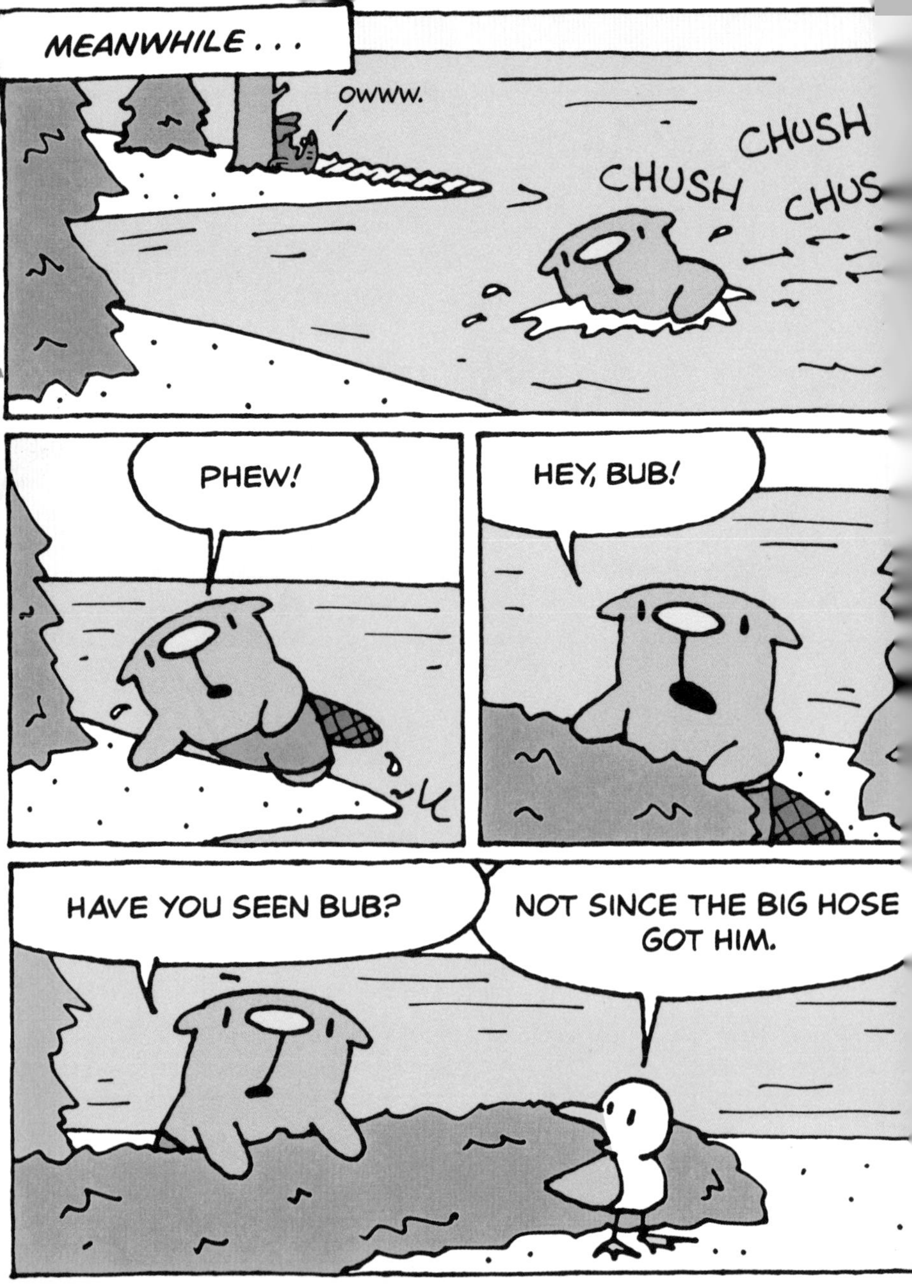
MEANWHILE . . .
OWWW.
CHUSH
CHUSH
CHUS
PHEW!
HEY, BUB!
HAVE YOU SEEN BUB?
NOT SINCE THE BIG HOSE GOT HIM.

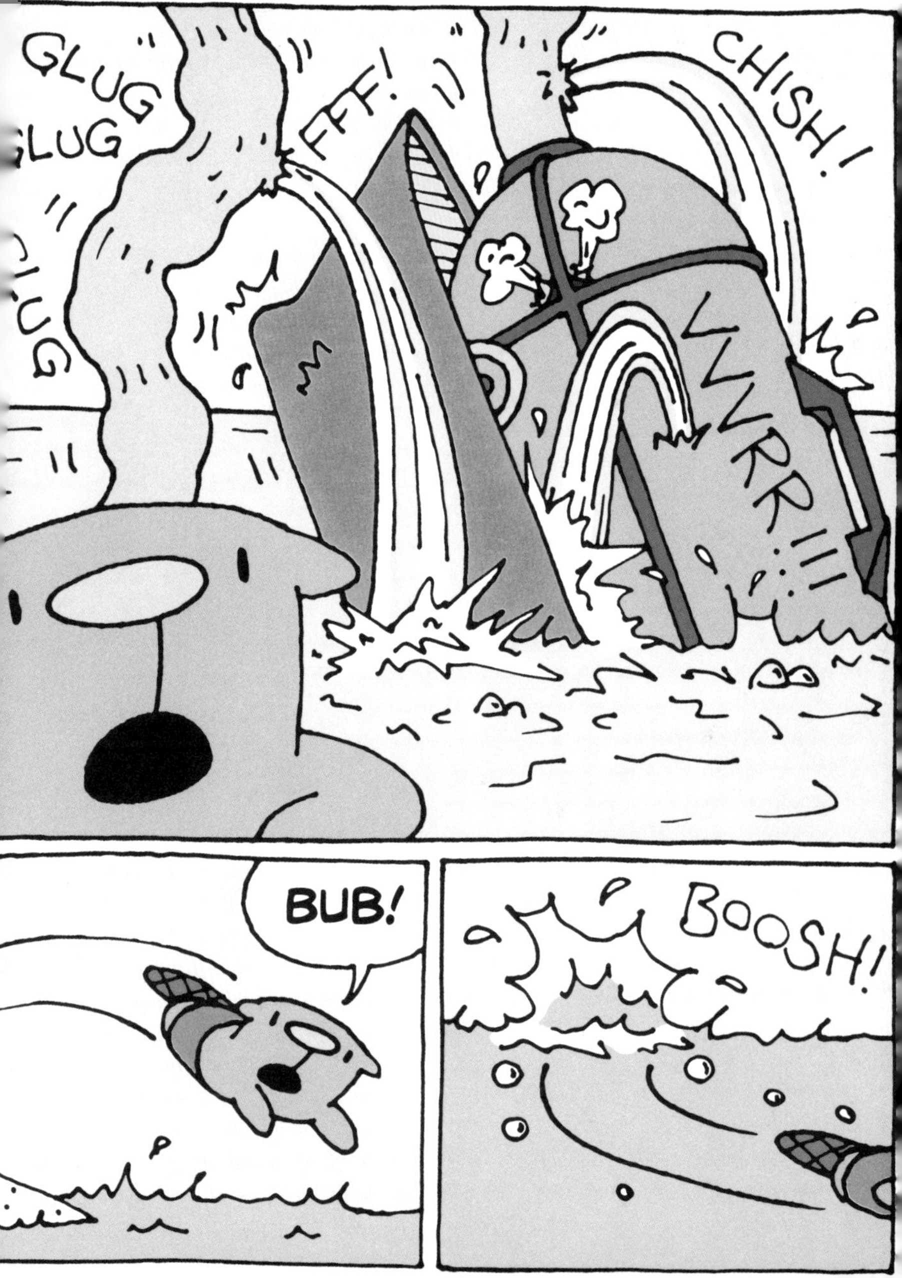
GLUG
GLUG
LUG
FFF!
CHISH!
VVVRR!
BUB!
BOOSH!

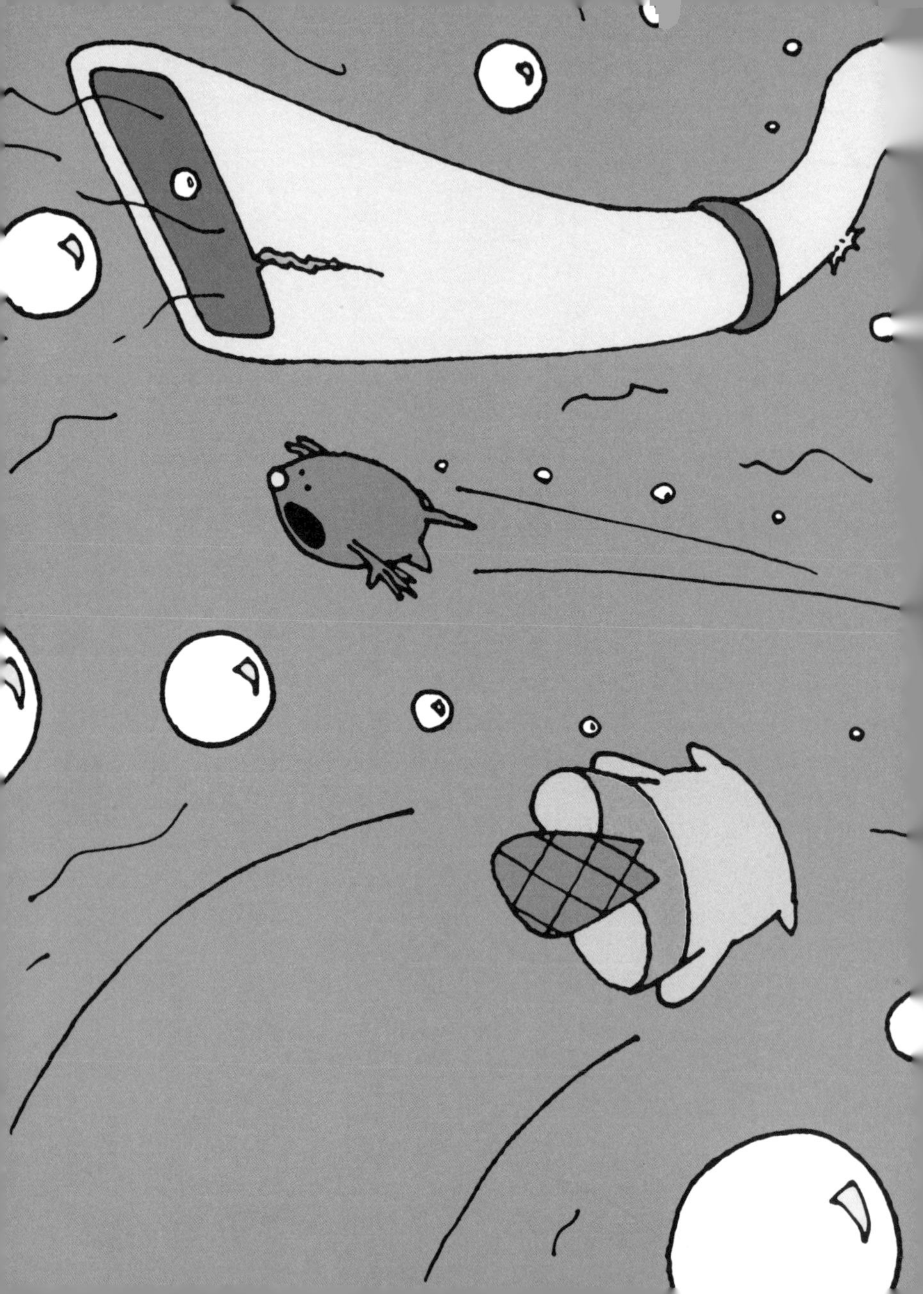

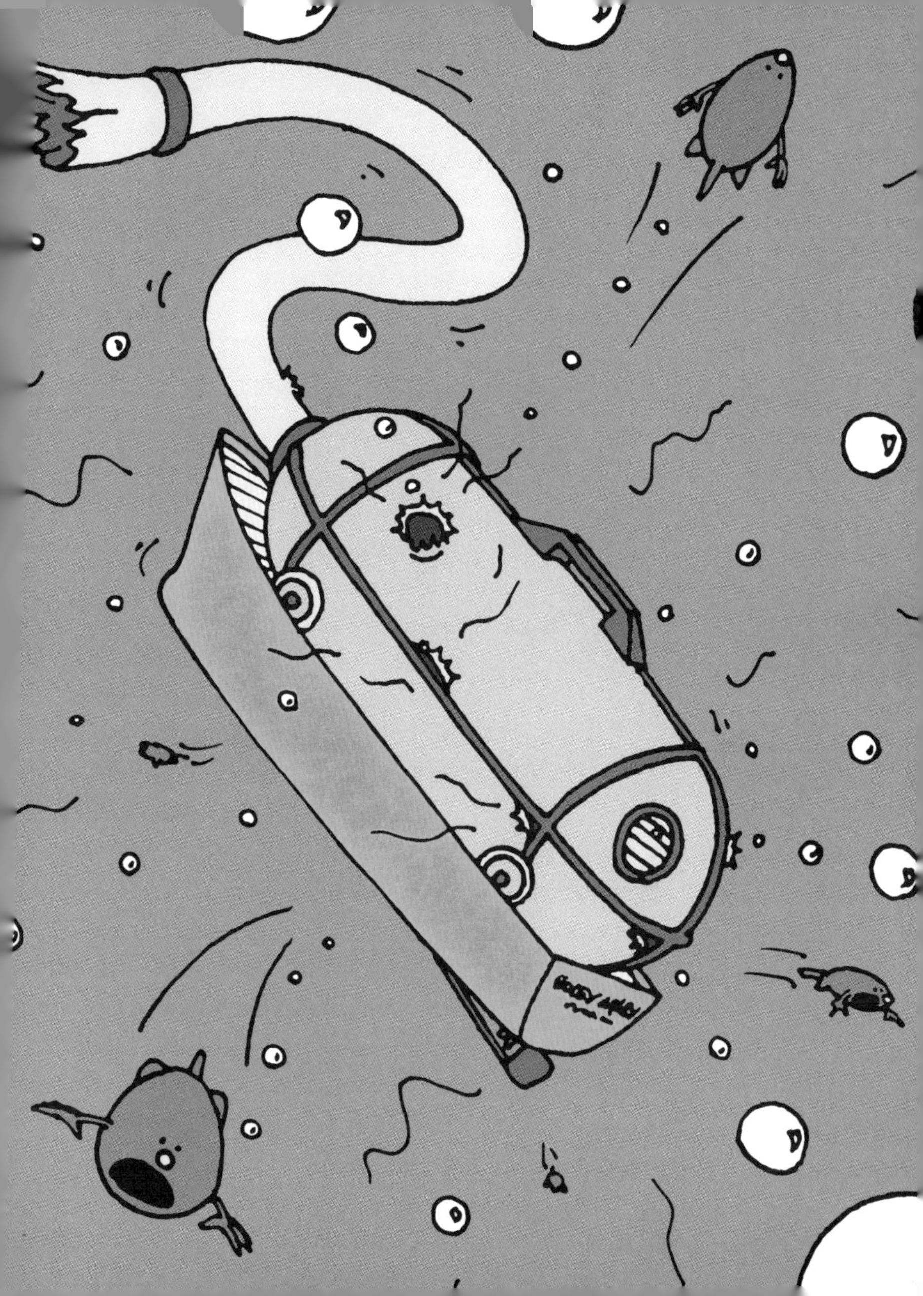

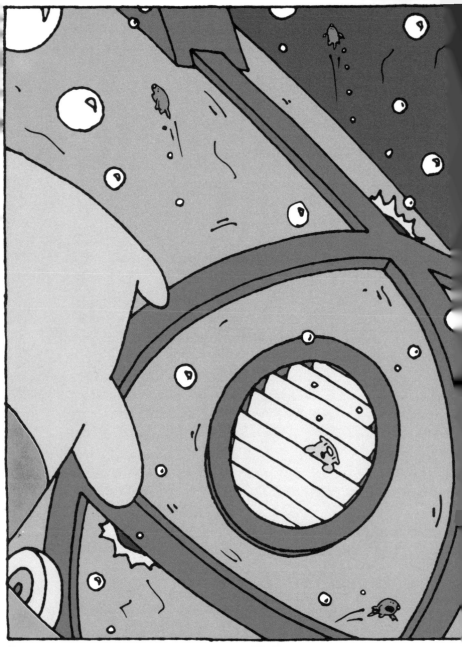

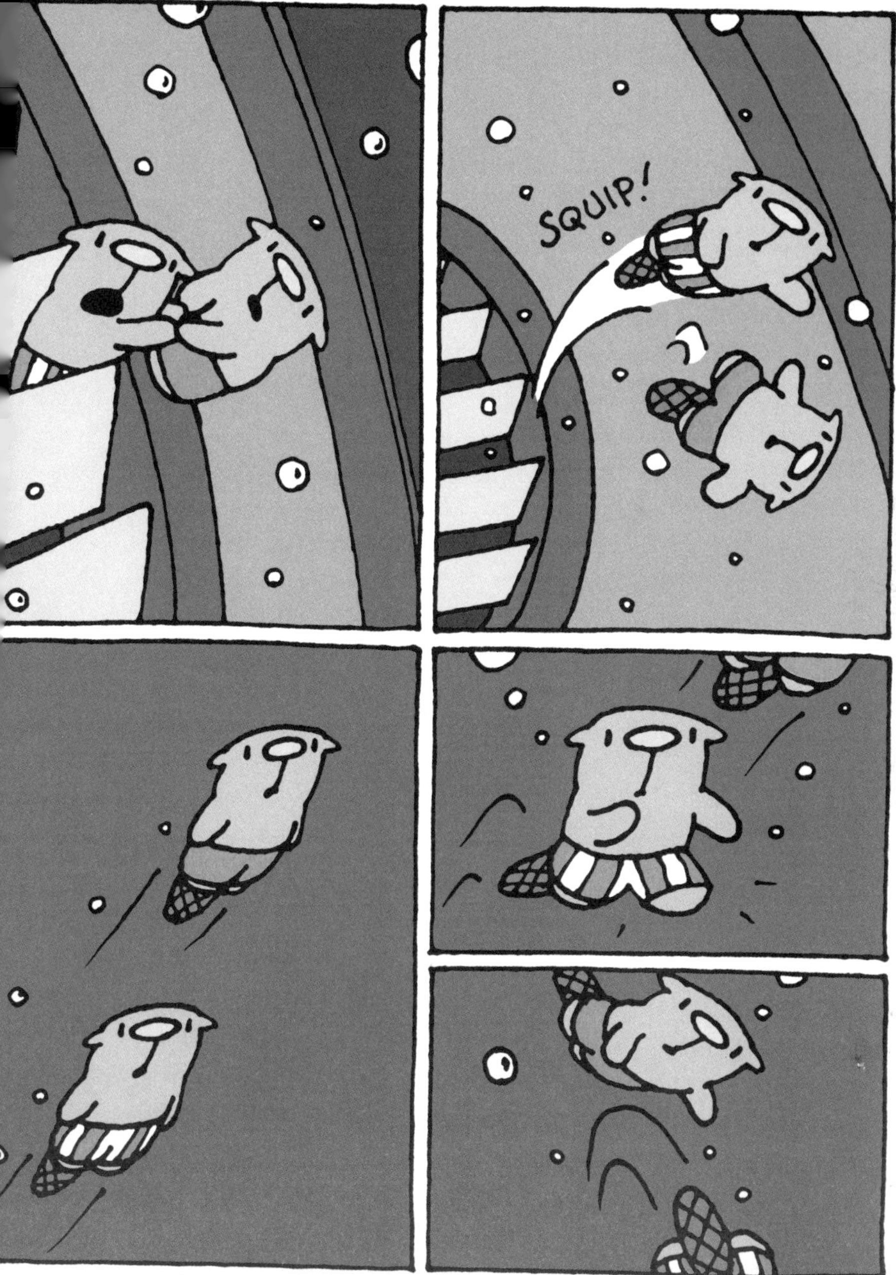
SQUIP!

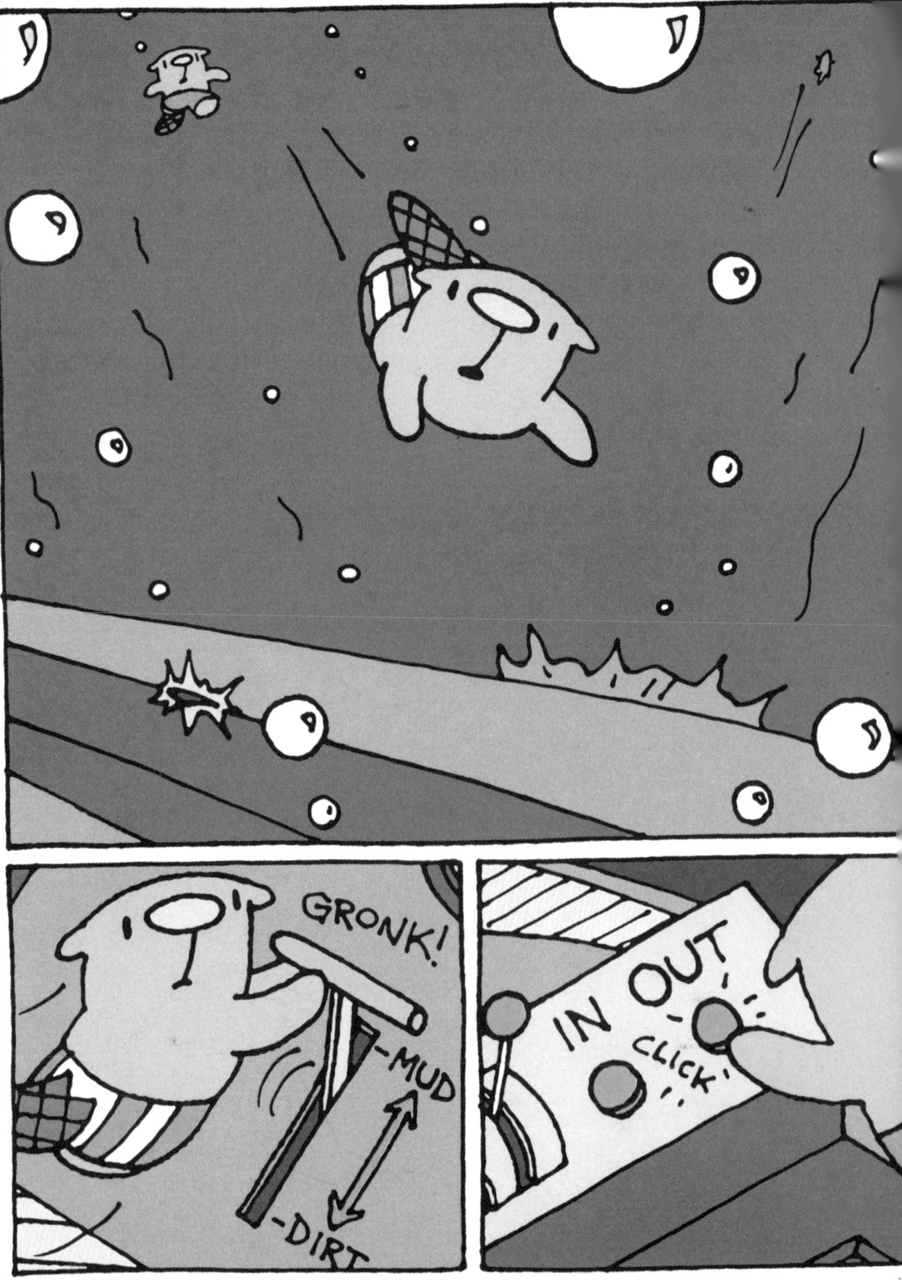
GRONK!
-MUD
-DIRT
IN OUT
CLICK

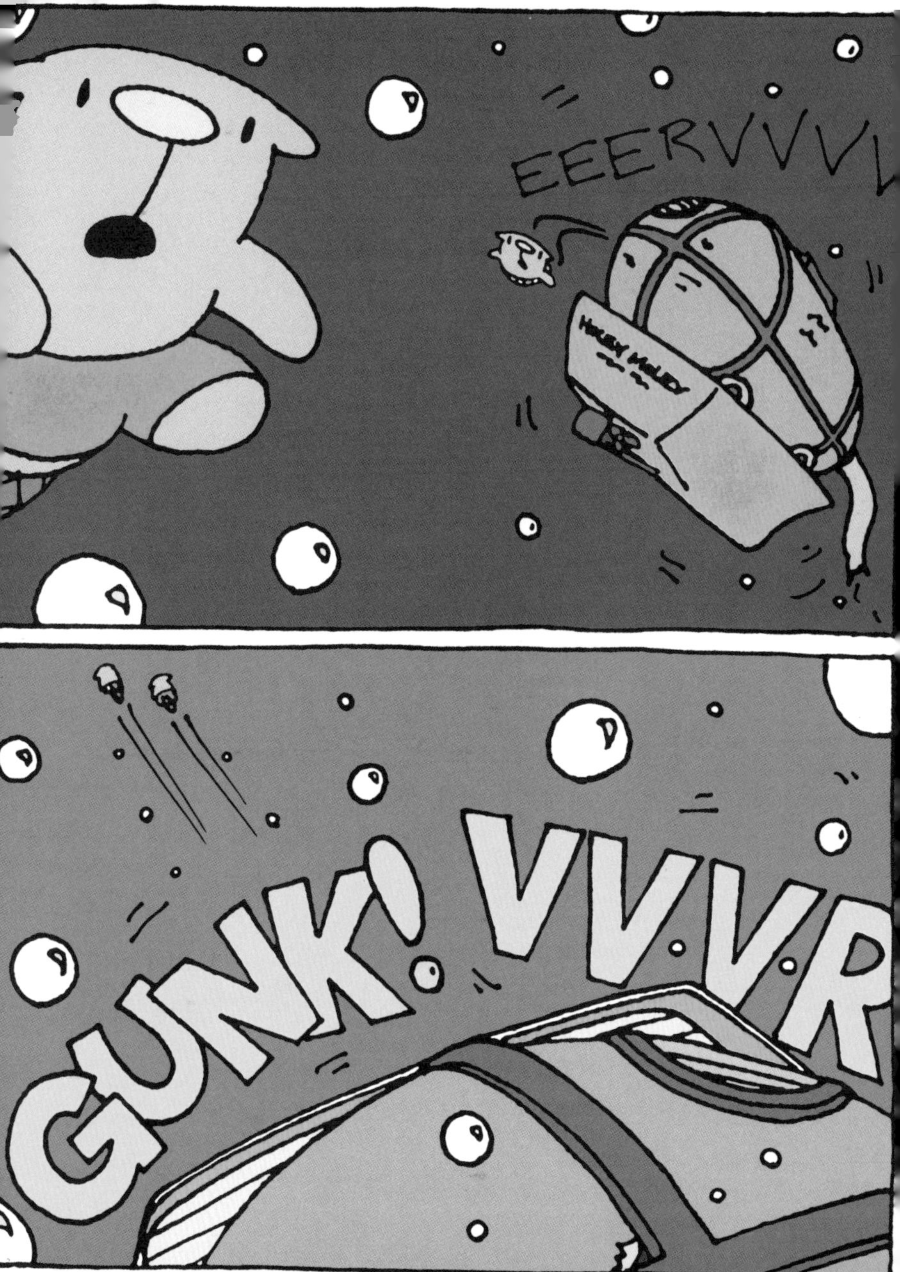
EEERVVVV
GUNK! VVVR

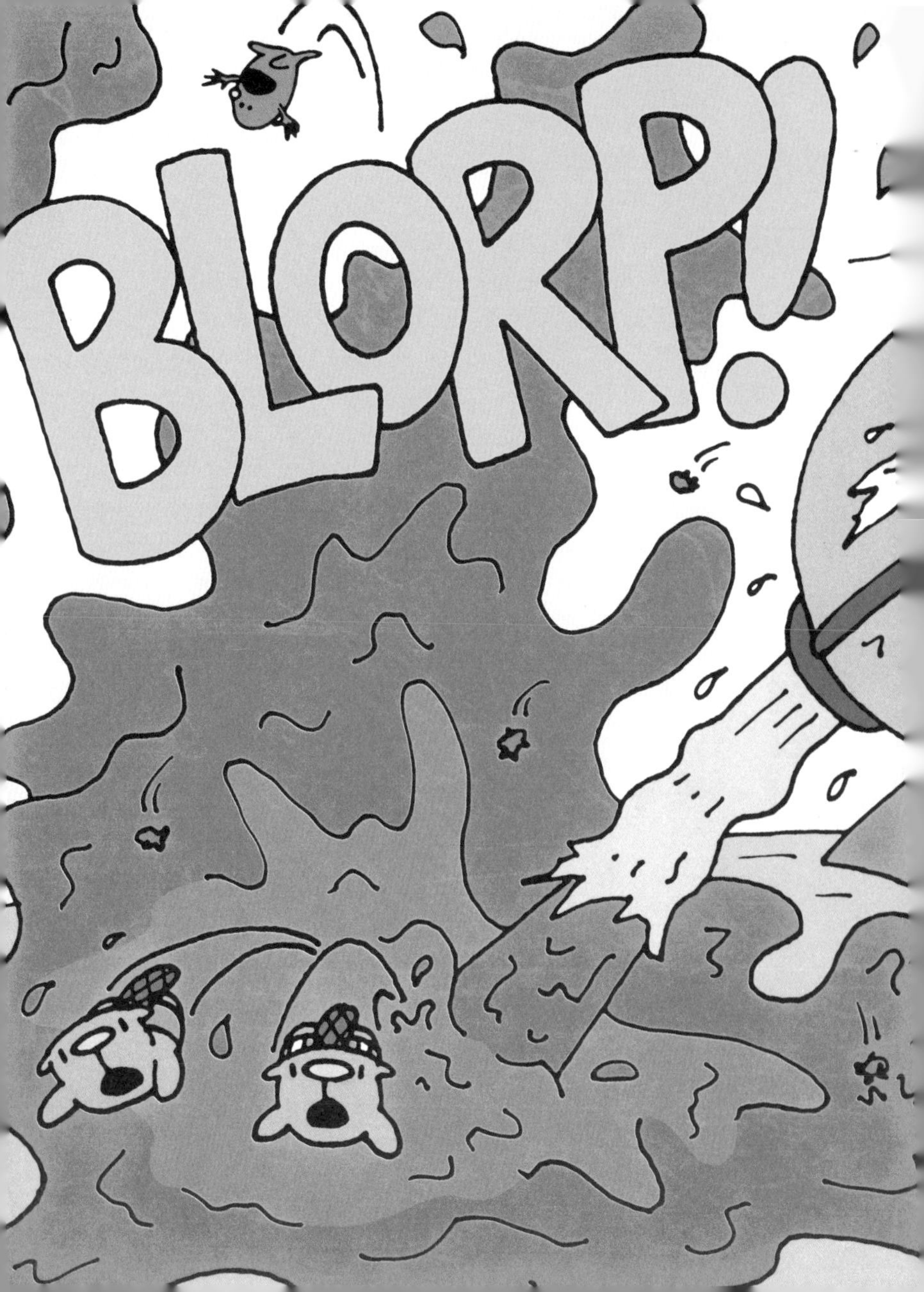
BLORP!

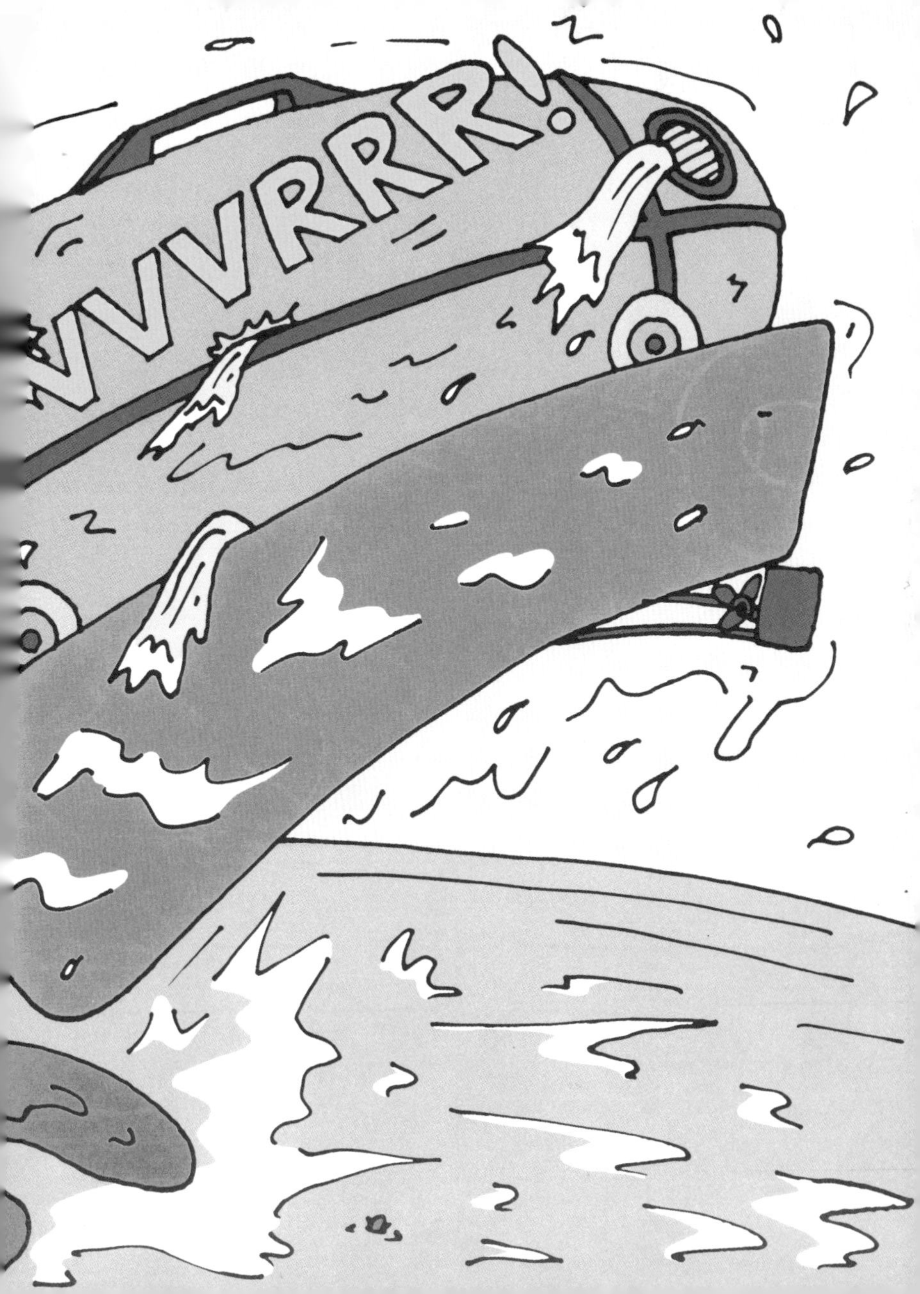
VVVRRR!

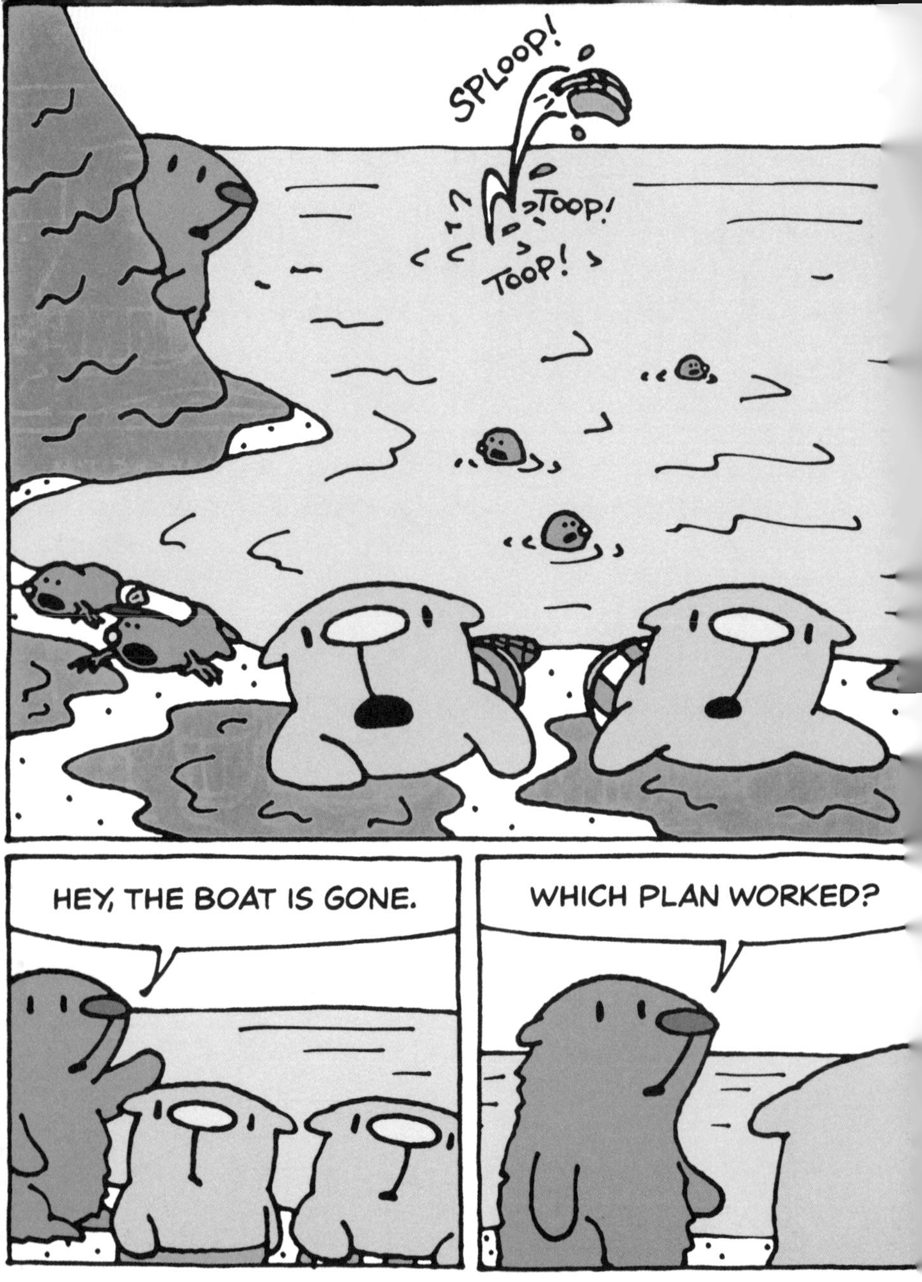
SPLOOP!
TOOP!
TOOP!
HEY, THE BOAT IS GONE.
WHICH PLAN WORKED?

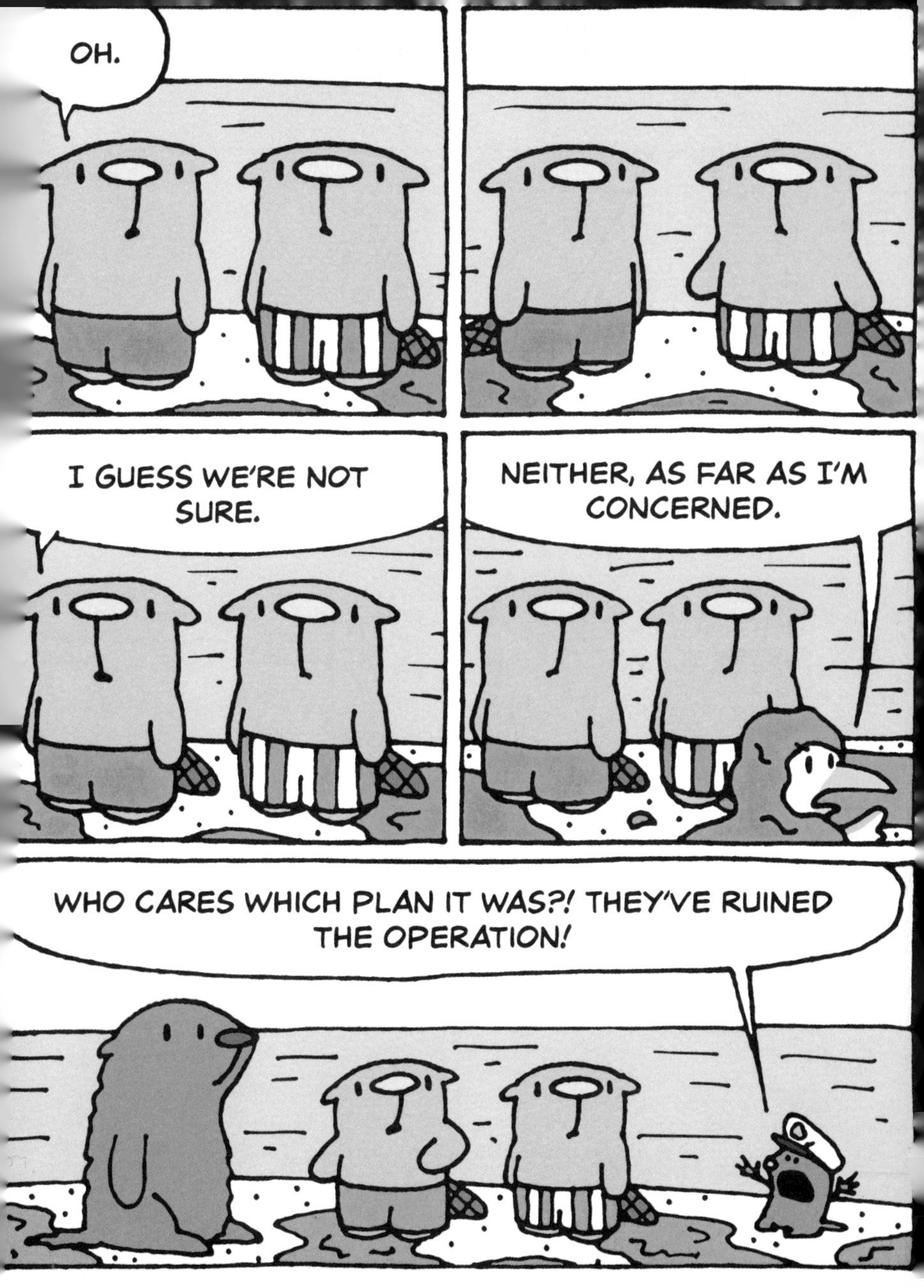
OH.
I GUESS WE'RE NOT SURE.
NEITHER, AS FAR AS I'M CONCERNED.
WHO CARES WHICH PLAN IT WAS?! THEY'VE RUINED THE OPERATION!

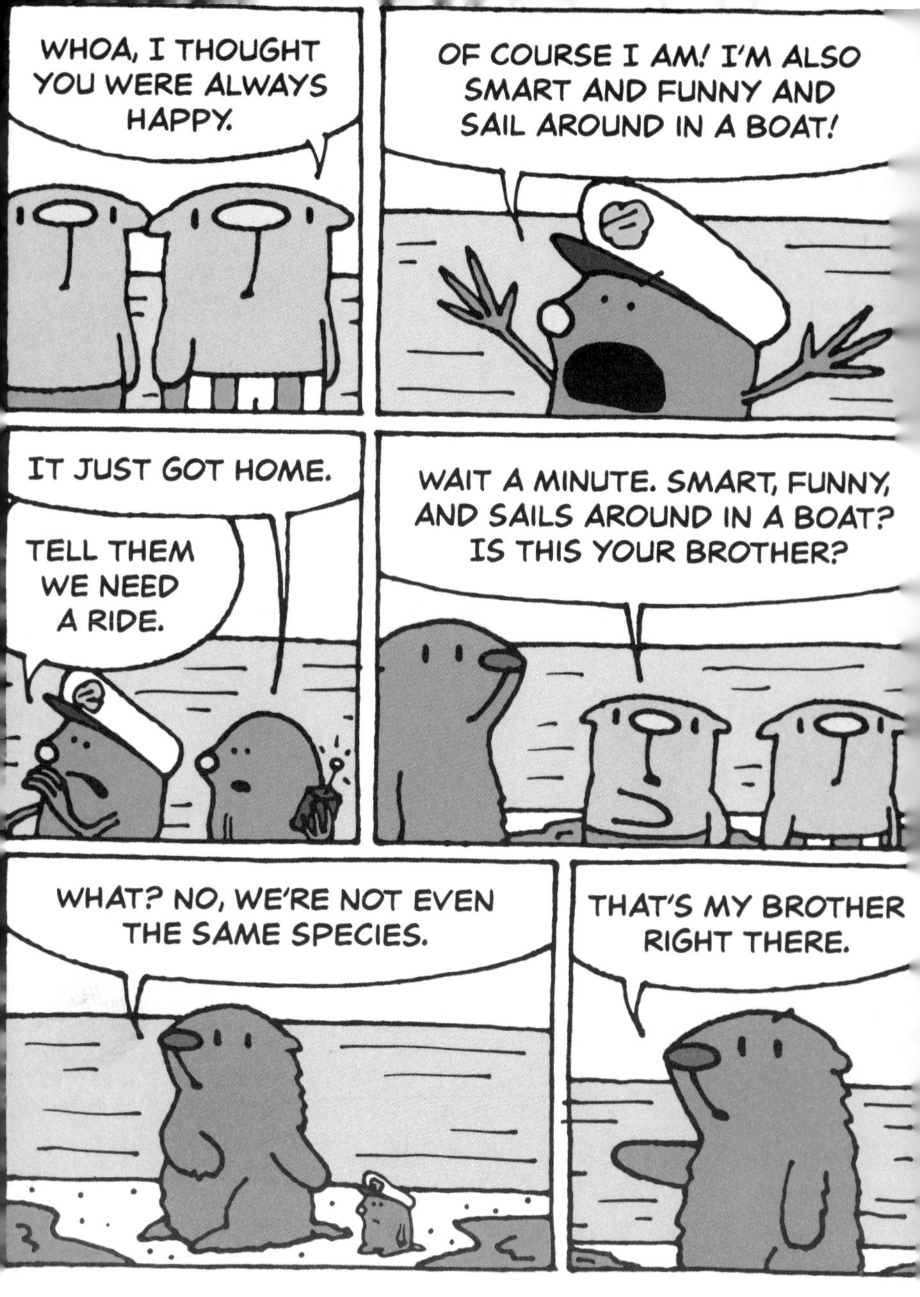
WHOA, I THOUGHT YOU WERE ALWAYS HAPPY.
OF COURSE I AM! I'M ALSO SMART AND FUNNY AND SAIL AROUND IN A BOAT!
IT JUST GOT HOME.
TELL THEM WE NEED A RIDE.
WAIT A MINUTE. SMART, FUNNY, AND SAILS AROUND IN A BOAT? IS THIS YOUR BROTHER?
WHAT? NO, WE'RE NOT EVEN THE SAME SPECIES.
THAT'S MY BROTHER RIGHT THERE.

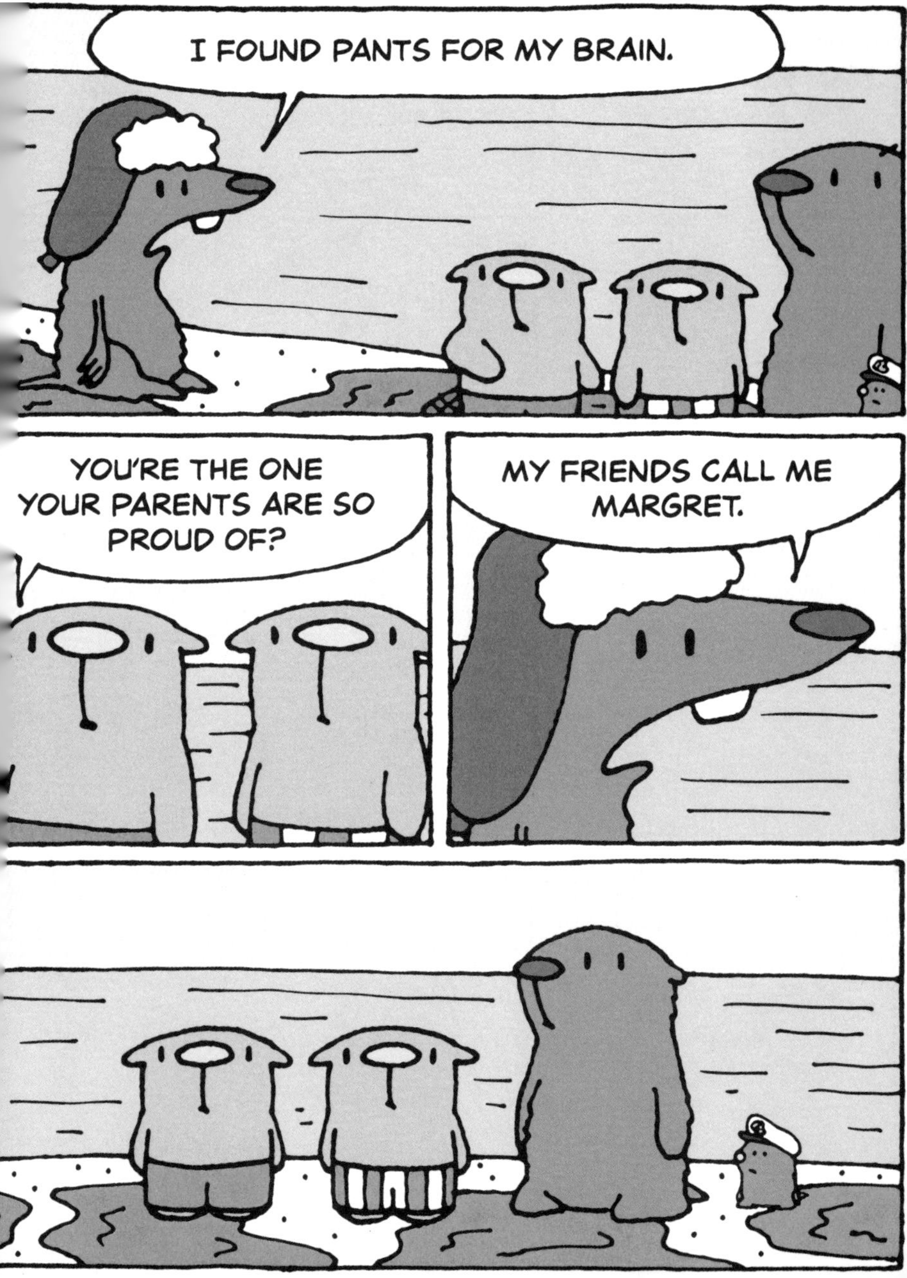
I FOUND PANTS FOR MY BRAIN.
YOU'RE THE ONE YOUR PARENTS ARE SO PROUD OF?
MY FRIENDS CALL ME MARGRET.

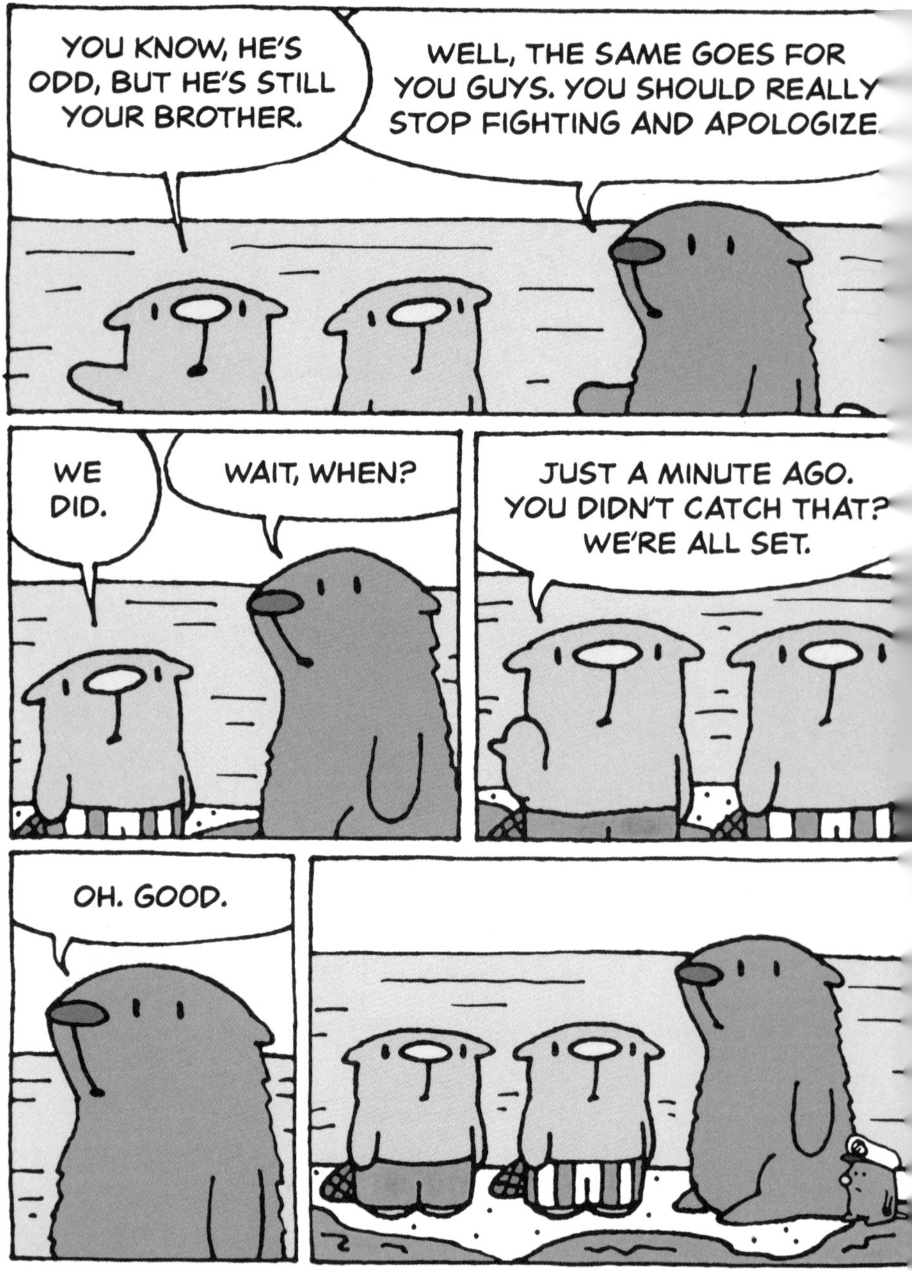
YOU KNOW, HE'S ODD, BUT HE'S STILL YOUR BROTHER.
WELL, THE SAME GOES FOR YOU GUYS. YOU SHOULD REALLY STOP FIGHTING AND APOLOGIZE.
WE DID.
WAIT, WHEN?
JUST A MINUTE AGO. YOU DIDN'T CATCH THAT? WE'RE ALL SET.
OH. GOOD.

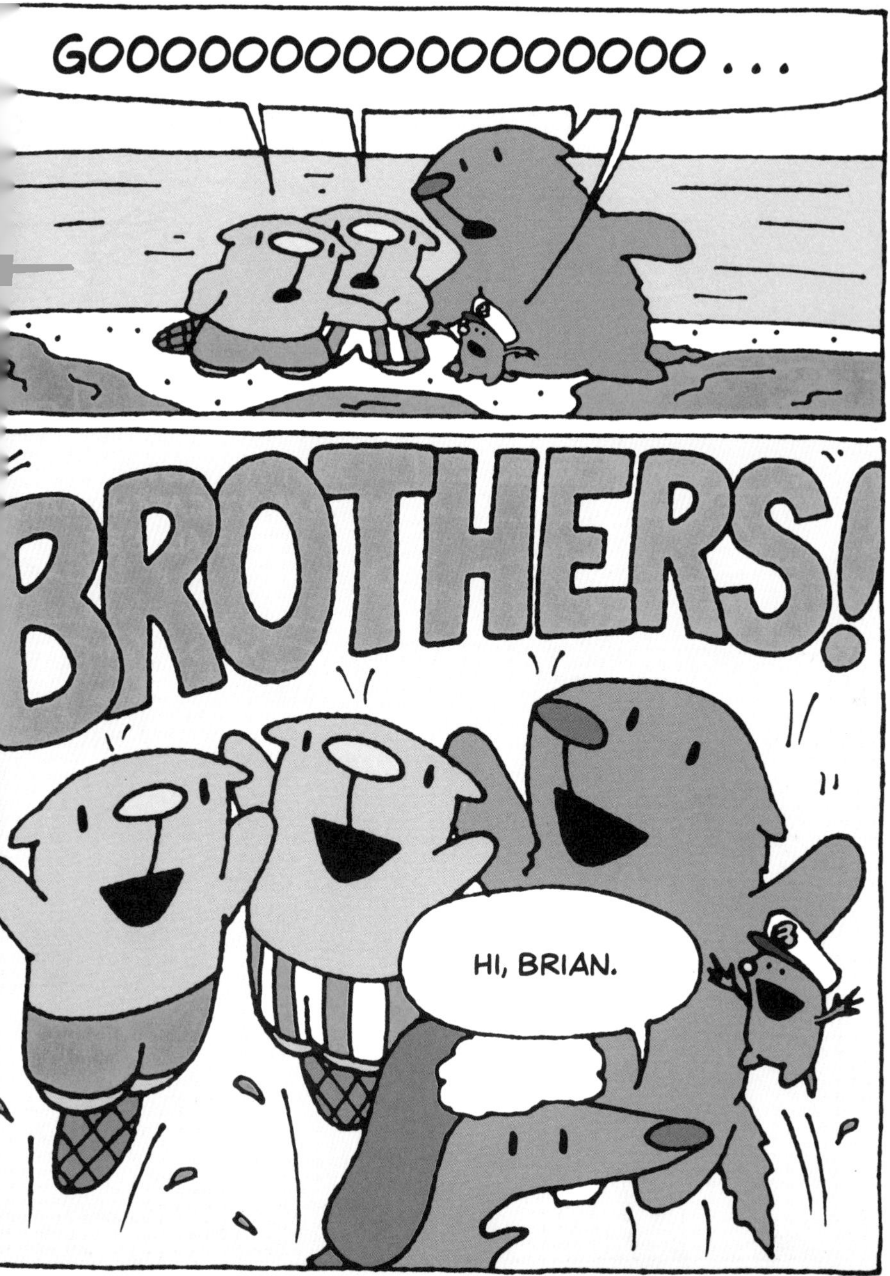
GOOOOOOOOOOOOOOOOOOOO . . .
BROTHERS!
HI, BRIAN.

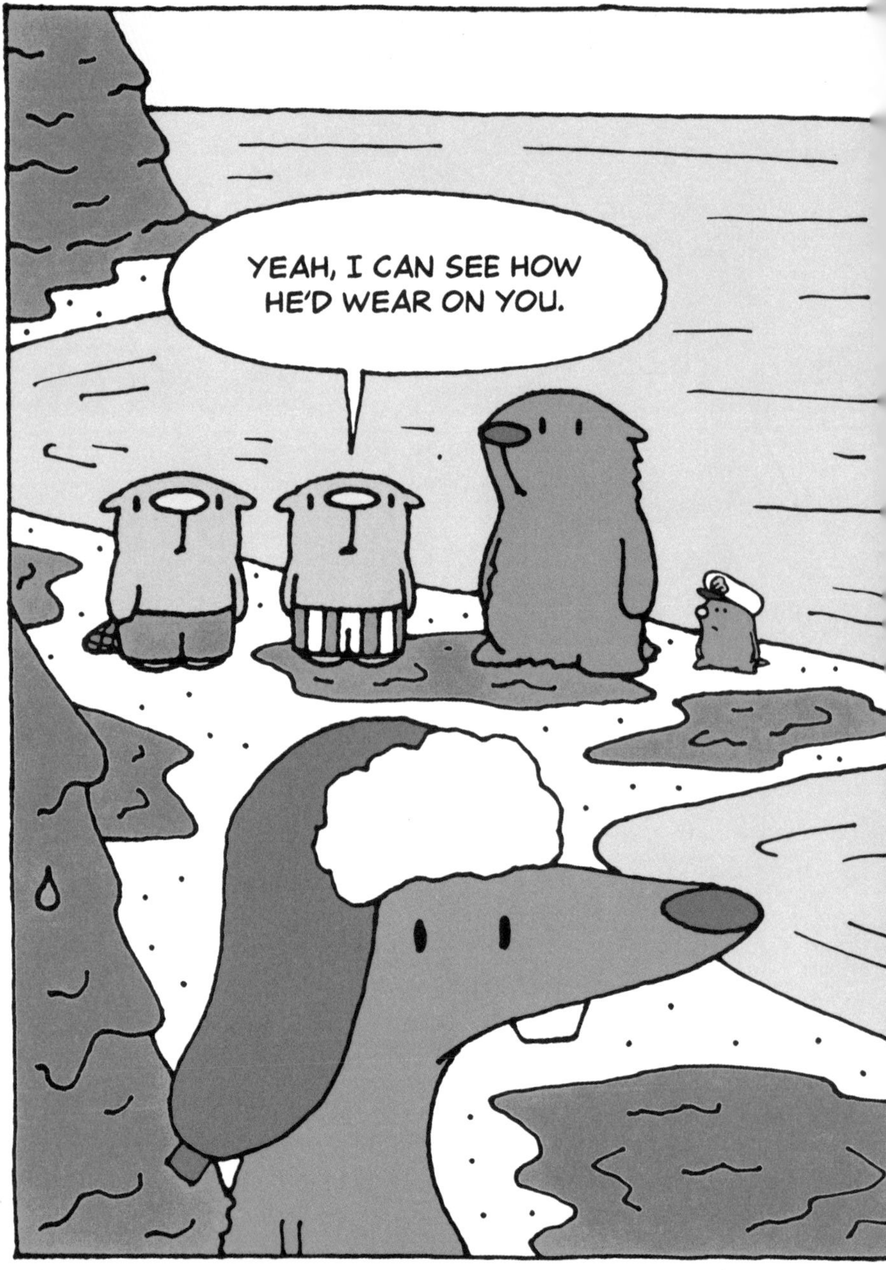
YEAH, I CAN SEE HOW HE'D WEAR ON YOU.